DATE DUE

THE SUPERNORMAL SLEUTHING SERVICE

BOOK ONE

The Lost Legacy

Gwenda Bond & Christopher Rowe

ILLUSTRATED BY

Glenn Thomas

GREENWILLOW BOOKS

An Imprint of HarperCollins*Publishers*

HarperCollins
PUBLISHERS
Since 1817

The Lost Legacy
Text copyright © 2017 by Gwenda Bond
and Christopher Rowe;
illustrations copyright © 2017 by Glenn Thomas

The text of this book is set in 13-point Hoefler Text.
Book design by Paul Zakris

Library of Congress Cataloging-in-Publication Data is available.

ISBN 978-0-06-245994-7 (trade ed.)

17 18 19 20 21 CG/LSCH 10 9 8 7 6 5 4 3 2 1
First Edition

GREENWILLOW BOOKS

To Ursula, queen of all monsters, and to William, the boy who lived

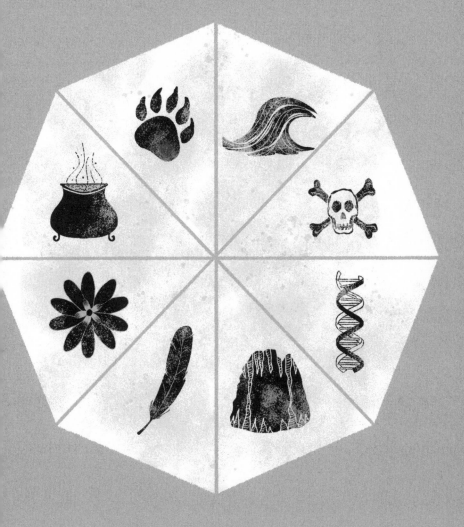

Dear Stephen,

Thank you so much *for sending me the drawing of the football players you saw when your father took you to the Bears game last fall. You're right, those are some of the biggest men I've ever seen! As I've told you before, some of the creatures I cook for here at the hotel are even bigger. Your dad will tell you that's just a story, of course. But it's true. (Tell him I'm feeling a little better, if not all better. Neither of you should worry about me.)*

I put the drawing up on the wall of my office in the kitchen with all your other wonderful artworks, but not before I showed it to my friend Mr. C. I've told you about him before and about how he fancies himself a very sophisticated connoisseur of the arts. Well, it took a little while to explain to him exactly what the pads and helmets were for—he thought the players were knights of some unusual sort—but he agrees with me that you're supremely talented and that you have a bright future ahead of you.

Mr. C wanted the picture you did in colored pencils of the boats on Lake Michigan, even inquiring if it had a price, unheard of for one such as Mr. C. But it is just about my favorite, because it reminds me of visiting you and your father there in Chicago. I'm so proud that you have so much talent, even if you're not following the family tradition of showing your talent in the kitchen.

I have to run for now, dear grandson. There's a vampire staying in the hotel, and I have to make him a blood pudding for breakfast!

Much love,
Chef Nana

CHAPTER ONE

Stephen stepped over the low iron fence and past a sign that read DO NOT WALK ON THE GRASS. He wanted to get a better look at an old tombstone. The granite monument was topped with sharp spikes and inscribed in a language he couldn't read. He didn't even recognize the alphabet, much less the individual words.

This was a week of firsts: the first time he'd ever been to New York, the first time he'd ever been to a graveyard, the first time he'd ever been to a funeral. The first time he'd ever known anyone who had died.

One of the many mourners gathered for his grandmother's funeral walked by, then paused when he noticed Stephen. The man was enormous, with shoulders as broad as a football lineman's, which threatened to burst out of his fancy suit jacket. His hair was brushed back from his forehead and swooped up over each of his ears.

"Fool of a boy. Not all who cross that fence find their way back. Who do you belong to?" The man's nostrils flared as he leaned over the fence and gave Stephen a hearty sniff. "Ah. You are a Lawson. The prodigal's son, I imagine. But . . . hmm, there's something odd about you."

Was the man implying that Stephen smelled bad? Before he could think better of it, he took a whiff back. "Sorry," Stephen said, "I can't tell who you are."

The enormous man's eyes narrowed. Um, oops.

"Stephen! Over here!" His dad called from beside the family mausoleum, waving him over.

"Sorry, I have to—" Stephen pointed toward his dad and made a speedy escape back over the fence and away.

The family mausoleum was something else new. Stephen hadn't known that somewhere in a cemetery tucked away in view of New York City's skyline sat a marble building with the word LAWSON inscribed above its brass door. It was crowned with a giant mortar and pestle and carved with chef's knives and cutting boards and other instruments— some he didn't even recognize—of his family's traditional trade. The mausoleum's heavy door was closed now. His grandmother had been interred behind it following a brief, nearly wordless ceremony that had ended a little while ago. Chef Nana never had been big on speeches.

Stephen picked his way among the mourners. They all seemed taller or shorter or skinnier or somehow sharper than people back home in Chicago.

"I told you to stick with me, buddy," his dad said as he got close. His dad was a welcome bit of normality, stocky and compact, with short brown hair darker than Stephen's own sandy blond. He looped his arm around Stephen's shoulders. "And read the signs for once. This cemetery has some, well, unusual corners to it, and you don't want to get lost. Or, uh, step on anyone's toes."

"Tell me about it. That guy smelled me and called *me* odd."

"Really?" His dad gave a nervous half laugh and steered them forward. "There are some people I want you to meet. And a couple of things I need to prepare you for."

"Okay," Stephen said, though he didn't feel much like meeting anybody, especially not any of these strange people. He wasn't the odd one in this crowd. His dad had sprung a lot on him after they got the news about Chef Nana, like apparently they would be *staying* in New York so his dad could take her job. Sure, it was summer vacation. And Stephen had been a kind of loner at his school. But Chicago was still *home*. Mostly he wanted to find a quiet space and think about his grandmother, try to figure out how to believe that he would never see her again, never receive another letter from her, never hear her goofy stories about the hotel's monsters again.

The knot of people his dad led him to weren't quite as weird as the other mourners. Well, except that the man who stuck his hand out for Stephen to shake was dressed in some kind of uniform with braids and epaulets at the shoulders. He was also big, if nowhere near the size of the man who had sniffed Stephen.

"You must be Nanette's famous grandson, the legendary artist Stephen. I'm Julio. I worked with your grandmother at the hotel."

A stern-looking woman in a sober black business suit smiled gently at Stephen. "We all did. I'm Carmen Gutierrez, Julio's wife."

"And his boss," Stephen's dad said. His tone was light, but Stephen knew his dad well enough to know it was a strain for him to keep it that way. "Carmen and I have known each other since we were younger than you are now. We grew up at the New Harmonia together. She practically runs the whole place these days."

The New Harmonia was the exclusive New York hotel where Chef Nana had run the kitchen, where his dad would run the kitchen now, the hotel where they would *live*. Stephen hadn't even seen the place yet, so he was still getting used to the idea.

Everything was happening too fast.

A short boy about Stephen's age stepped in front of Carmen as if he had every right in the world to interrupt. He had close-cropped red hair and glasses, and he wore a suit complete with a black bow tie. "I am Ivanos Mercutio La Doyt. And now you have the great honor of meeting my parents, Roman Horatio and Rafaela Katarina La Doyt, whom you are already in debt to for—"

"There'll be time for that later, Ivan," Carmen said, stern again. "Julio needs to get your parents to the park."

Two more adults, pulling suitcases, had appeared beside the Gutierrezes. The slight man wore a sharp suit and a pair of glasses with black frames, and the tall woman a sleek black dress and glasses of her own. The woman gave Stephen an encouraging smile. "We will do our best to get back soon."

Stephen had no idea what that had to do with him, and the couple had already turned to leave. His dad called after them, "Good luck, and thank you."

The man nodded over his shoulder.

"Who are they again?"

Ivan said, "They are the New Harmonia's masters of hotel detection."

"Hotel detection?" Stephen echoed.

"Later, Ivan," Carmen said.

A girl with a high, curly ponytail and a flouncy black dress, who was taller than Ivan and clearly related to Carmen and Julio, piped up. "If he's going to be living at the hotel, somebody has to bring him up to speed."

"This must be Sofia," his dad said.

"It's true," the boy Ivan said to the girl. "It's obvious that he doesn't know anything."

"Did you just insult me?" asked Stephen, genuinely mystified.

A sound like the world's largest wind chime rang out across the cemetery, interrupting them. Everyone, even the two rude kids, suddenly stood up straight and turned toward the mausoleum.

Where the strangest person yet stood.

Stephen supposed it was a man, though his

features were blurry, as if Stephen were seeing the man from a much greater distance than he actually was. He wore a deep red suit. Everyone in sight was watching him respectfully. Absolute quiet had descended.

Well, absolute quiet except for the kid with the bow tie.

"That's the Manager!" the boy said, trying to whisper and failing.

Sofia shushed him.

"Friends of the New Harmonia," said the figure, with a voice that seemed to be made of many voices. "Friends of our beloved Lady Nanette. Thank you for coming today to pay your respects to the greatest knight of culinary alchemy of the last hundred years. And now, as it is written, we mark her passing."

Stephen thought he'd been confused *before*. Lady Nanette? Knight of culinary alchemy? He looked over at his dad, but then the entire crowd spoke at the same time.

"Farewell, Lady Knight," they said.

Stephen didn't know what to do. He whispered, "Good-bye, Nana."

The Manager spoke again. "And yet her task is not done."

Stephen would have sworn that the blurry-faced man's hands had been empty before. But now his long, pale, skeletal fingers were wrapped around a book. It was old, brown leather with a heavy gold clasp, and had hundreds upon hundreds of yellowed pages between the closed covers.

"Who will take it up?" the man asked. "Who is worthy of her name?"

His dad glanced over at Stephen, then stepped forward. "I bear her name. I am her son and heir, Michael Truman Lawson."

"Dad?" Stephen whispered. "What are you doing?"

"Michael Truman Lawson," said the man, "do you take up the duties of your mother of blessed memory? Do you pledge to protect the Guest Right and preserve the peace? Will you return from exile and take up the arms and armor of the most honorable

Order of the Knights of the Octagon?"

His dad hesitated. Stephen had never seen his dad look this way: worried and proud and sad and happy at the same time.

Stephen interrupted again. "What does he mean?"

"Quiet," the Manager said, eyes falling on Stephen as heavy as a hand. "No interruptions are permitted during the ceremony."

Stephen didn't say another word.

His dad went down on one knee before the man. With a bowed head, he said, "I pledge my devotion to harmony among all. I will not disappoint the Octagon again."

The man glided forward, his face a flicker of moving shadows, and touched Stephen's father once on each shoulder. His words rang out: "Let all within the sound of my voice bear witness! Michael Truman Lawson, a human man, is returned to us, forgiven. He pledges to keep the peace and protect the Guest Right. By my authority, I name him Culinary Alchemist and head chef at the Hotel New

Harmonia. Rise, now, a knight of the Octagon!"

The crowd roared. This wasn't like the roar at a football game. This was a *roar,* like one a pride of lions would make. Stephen thought he heard animal noises in it. He shivered.

His dad straightened, and the man placed the old book into his hands. His dad bowed to the man, and between one blink and the next, the blurry-faced man was gone. Vanished. Completely.

A woman with a lilt said, "Congratulations, Sir Michael," and dipped one knee *to his dad*, then made way for the next of the mourners. They were lining up in a long row on the grass.

Stephen's dad held up the book. "Honored guests, if you'll excuse me for just a moment. I need a word with my son," he said. Then, to Stephen: "You're probably wondering what that was all about."

"Dad?" Stephen didn't know what to say. "*Sir* Dad?"

His dad guided him to a stone bench beside the mausoleum and laid the book down on it, next to the wooden box that held his spice kit. "This was your grandmother's recipe book," his dad said, "but it's more than that. The *Librum de Coquina* has been in our family for longer than you can imagine. It's special. A cookbook and a history book and a powerful badge of office."

"What kind of office?" Stephen asked. "What's a knight of the Octagon? Who was that guy?"

"We'll get to all that. Let me show you something first." His dad undid the clasp to open the book. The ink was brown against the yellowed pages. "Help me out. Let's follow this recipe."

Stephen sometimes pitched in on easy stuff when his dad cooked at home or at Brasserie Hemingway, the restaurant where he worked in Chicago. Not often, though. Stephen wasn't very good at following directions.

"Open my spice box, Stephen, and get out the mortar and pestle."

Confused, just as he had been when his dad brought his spice kit with them to the cemetery in the first place, Stephen did as he was told. He opened the old rosewood box and pulled out the marble cup and grinding stone that his dad used to make special spices. Hand-labeled ceramic jars of ingredients were stored in the velvet-lined box, and he removed some of them as his father read aloud from the book.

"Sea salt . . . cinnamon . . . cracked jasper . . . and lark's tears." His dad finished.

Stephen had never heard of the last two but found them nonetheless.

His dad took the jars Stephen had set out and poured small amounts from each into the mortar. When the ingredients were ready, he used the pestle to grind them together. A pungent smell, like a bouquet of week-old flowers, rose from the mortar.

"Do you remember how Chef Nana used to tell you about the creatures she cooked for at the hotel? The magical beings from her letters?" His dad held up the marble bowl. "Take a pinch of this and throw it over your left shoulder."

Stephen almost sneezed at the smell. The spice was gritty against his fingers. He flung it backward.

"The thing about those stories," his dad said, turning Stephen so he faced the crowd, "is that they all were true."

The first person Stephen saw was the enormous man who'd sniffed him. At least there was an enormous figure wearing the same suit; only this figure had the horned head and ringed nose of a shaggy red bull. He cocked his head at Stephen, and his nostrils flared, again.

And there was a woman with flowers in her hair, who had a sparkling set of fuchsia wings that extended high above her back. Behind her was a group of people normal from the waist up but with the lower bodies of horses. One of them stamped a hoof. Everyone was impatient in the line.

The line to see his dad. Sir Michael.

Stephen blinked and blinked, and the monsters were still there. He felt he might throw up. Or wake up to discover this was a dream. He wanted to laugh or cry. Or ask his dad a thousand more questions.

Chef Nana's stories were *true*. But his dad had been *lying* to him his whole life.

"I know," his dad said. "When this is over, I'll explain everything."

As his dad walked back to the line, Stephen stared out at the graveyard full of monsters. And then the two kids, who still looked human, appeared in front of him. They were observing him as if he were a specimen they'd placed under a microscope.

"Everyone loved Chef Nanette," said Ivan. "Well, except for the fae. But most people never talk about your dad except in whispers."

"My mom pulled a lot of strings to get him this job," said Sofia. "He'll probably be fine as long as he follows the rules this time. And you, too, of course. Rules are important here."

Stephen sank back onto the bench. If the girl was right, he was in big trouble. Stephen was even worse at following rules than he was at following directions.

And here he was in a whole new world where he didn't even know what the rules *were*.

CHAPTER TWO

"**Here** we are," Julio said from behind the wheel as he pulled the long red car to a smooth halt. He hopped out, shutting the door behind him.

Stephen and his dad sat in the backseat in silence. After the line of people waiting to congratulate his dad was finally done, Julio had returned and waved them into the old-fashioned car. Julio was "Martial Commander, Leader of the New Harmonia's Perilous Guard," another knight of the Octagon. Like his dad.

Stephen didn't know what that meant yet. He didn't know what *any* of this meant: the move to New York, the knightly order, the *monsters*. But for all the strangeness, what he still felt the most was sadness. He missed his grandmother. Chef Nana could have made this make sense.

His dad, though—his dad had been fidgeting and acting weird ever since they got in the car. "You ready for this?" his dad asked. "I'm sorry I sprang it all on you, but I had my reasons. We'll talk once we get settled upstairs."

"I don't have much of a choice," Stephen said, and climbed out when Julio opened his door with a flourish. A sheathed sword now hung from Julio's belt.

The street they'd stopped on was quiet for the city, with trees surrounded by little iron fences and broad sidewalks, a few shops with awnings closed at this hour of the evening, and fancy tall buildings. Including the one in front of them. This building seemed somehow brighter and clearer than any other building Stephen had ever seen. But then, *everything* seemed brighter and clearer. Could colors look brighter in New York than in Chicago? Could smells seem sharper? Or was it simply that he could see *more* than he could before?

A lit marquee that read NEW HARMONIA hung

next to the tall stone facade, the letters flickering and then glowing a brilliant red outlined in gold as he stared up at them. This was to be their new home— not just a hotel but a hotel for *monsters*.

Julio escorted them to a bank of glass front doors, and pulled one open with another grand flourish. Stephen took a breath and stepped inside. He stopped.

The lobby held an actual forest, with tall trees stretching up toward high, bright windows in a gracefully arched ceiling. Something jostled way up in the treetops. Something big. Around the edges of the forest and between some of the trunks, he saw walls with rich wood paneling, mirrors edged in gold leaf, and more of those large windows positioned high, low, and everywhere in between. The entrance where they stood was dominated by a massive chandelier that dangled in midair, and there was a mosaic design on the floor below—an octagon divided into sections with a different glyph in each. Eight different symbols. What did they all stand for?

Turning to find his dad, he did a double take at the window beside the door.

The view should have shown the city street they'd just been on. Instead, schools of brightly colored fish swam above what appeared to be a real ocean-size coral reef.

"Is that some kind of screen saver?" Stephen asked.

His dad stepped closer to the window. A large yellow fish swam up and regarded him, and his dad reached out a finger and pushed it through the glass. The startled fish darted away. Stephen's dad pulled back a dripping wet finger.

"Seawater," his dad said. "Not all of the New Harmonia's guests arrive via the airport."

Stephen moved closer and lifted his hand to try it himself. Before he could, his dad grabbed his arm. "No, don't!"

Stephen blinked. His dad had gone pale.

"Michael," Carmen said, clicking across the tile toward them with Ivan and Sofia in tow, "you of all people know better than to play around with the gateways. Especially around your son." When Julio had told Stephen his own title, he'd added that Carmen was Knight Diplomatis and concierge.

"Sorry," his dad said, fidgeting more. He was looking at Carmen with relief.

"Uh-oh," Sofia said, and nudged Ivan. Ivan squinted over at one of the only areas without the windows, er, gateways. There was a long front desk that had many levels, stepped like a staircase from high to low. The tallest part of the counter was as high as the treetops, the lowest barely off the ground. There was a gold sign fixed to the wood paneling beside it at human eye level, with a message in old-fashioned lettering that said THIS IS A SMOKE-FREE ESTABLISHMENT (EXCEPTIONS GRANTED FOR FIRE BREATHERS).

Three people stood next to the desk. The tall woman in the middle must have been a fire breather because smoke flowed out of her nostrils. Then Stephen saw that, no, she was just a rule breaker. She held a long lacquered stick of some kind in one hand, and there was a black cigarette burning at one end of it. As he watched, she put the stick to her painted lips and breathed in. The cigarette flared. Stephen had never spent much time around smokers but guessed he must be allergic because his eyes began to water. His ears even felt hot.

It said something that on a day when Stephen had met a minotaur and a woman with butterfly wings, these three were among the strangest people he'd seen. He realized that his mouth was hanging open, and he would have been embarrassed, except that his dad and Julio were staring, too.

Not Carmen, though. She marched over to the jewel-bedecked trio and said, "Baroness Thyme, I apologize that you've been kept waiting. I'm sure the staff are preparing your usual rooms. I had to help Count von Giertsen af Morgenstierne with an urgent request."

Sofia whispered, "That's the Octagon vampire. He arrived yesterday."

Stephen didn't know what that meant, but he was riveted.

The baroness said nothing. She nodded and exhaled smoke.

"I must once again remind you that you may not smoke in the New Harmonia," Carmen said. "Or any other public interior in the city, in fact."

The woman with the cigarette holder was taller than Carmen, with pale skin faintly tinged green. Her hair was done up in an elaborate style that resembled a crown, covered with a net of pearls and lace. She was dressed in a gown of what looked like autumn leaves, which rippled as if a light wind were blowing through the lobby, though Stephen didn't feel any air moving.

When she spoke, she sounded both otherworldly

and somehow familiar. Stephen couldn't help hanging on her every word.

"Ah, yes. A human rule for a human city," she said, her voice deep and rich.

Baroness Thyme made a dismissive gesture with one gloved hand, and the cigarette fell to the floor, where it smoldered unattended. She handed off the lacquered holder to one of the people standing next to her.

Stephen guessed that these other two were servants or attendants of some kind from the way they deferred to the baroness. Like her, they had green-tinged skin and long, pointed ears, and it hit Stephen who—or rather what—they had to be.

"You're fairies!" he said, and clapped his hand over his mouth because he'd practically shouted it.

To his surprise, the baroness smiled.

"Not fairies," Ivan said quietly. "Fae."

Sofia murmured, "Their presence here is not good. It hardly ever is." She gave Stephen a pointed look that he couldn't interpret.

One of the baroness's companions—Stephen

was startled to see that she was a girl about his own age—threw her cloak of feathers and leaves back over her shoulders. She curtsied to him. "Yes," she said, her voice higher but no less rich than the baroness's. "We are delegates from the Court of Thorns in the Fae Lands, just arrived in the city. I am Lady Sarabel. We are most happy to make your acquaintance."

A troubled look passed among his dad, Carmen, and Julio. But Stephen didn't want to be rude—as Ivan and Sofia had been to him—so he spoke up. "I'm Stephen Lawson."

The third fae was a man, older than the others. He was wearing supple armor made of bark, and the hilt of the sword he wore across his back was wrapped in plain leather.

"I am Lord Celidyl, chevalier to Baroness Thyme." He nodded at Julio. "Though I see that I am not the first knight martial you have met today."

Stephen frowned. How did he know that Stephen had met Julio only today? He was about to ask, but the baroness spoke again.

"Stephen . . . Lawson," she said, and her red lips twisted when she said his last name the way someone's might when she tasted something sour. "It is a delight to make your acquaintance. A long overdue delight."

Could things get any weirder? His dad put a hand firmly on Stephen's shoulder, as if to hold him in place.

"Greetings, Baroness," his dad said. The strained note was back. "I was just headed upstairs with my son. It's been a long day."

If her lips had twisted before, now she practically snarled at Stephen's dad. "Oh, yes. The tragedy of your mother's death. The uprooting from one human city to another. The boy's introduction to the world that was stolen from him."

"Baroness . . ." There was a warning note in Carmen's voice.

The baroness laughed. "Yes, Lady Diplomatis? You wish to call me to account for speaking the truth? You know it is impossible for any fae to utter a falsehood, and you choose to side with this man you yourself helped exile a dozen years gone. You know our claim on the boy is founded."

"What is she talking about?" Stephen demanded. His heart pounded, thumping in his overheated ears. This situation felt dangerous in a way he couldn't explain.

Before his dad could say anything, the baroness extended her hands wide in a welcoming gesture. The other two fae echoed it.

"Stephen," Baroness Thyme said, "lost son of the Primrose Court. By right of your mother's birth, I invite and implore you to become my ward and live with us in the Evening Lands. Will you?"

Stephen gaped at her. His mother had left them when he was just a baby. She was something—someone—they almost never talked about.

"You're not his mother, and he's got no place in your political schemes," Stephen's dad said, putting his arm firmly around Stephen's shoulders. "Carmen, Julio, let's get my son upstairs, please."

The baroness held up one finger, the lacquered nail long and sharp. "An invitation has been issued.

Surely you haven't forgotten all the protocols you were raised to follow, *Sir* Michael."

Julio shouldered his way up between the humans and the fae, a hand on the sword at his belt. "Unless you want to see a *challenge* issued—"

But Carmen pulled him back. An angry sneer crossed the fae knight's face.

"Nobody is issuing any challenges in the lobby of the New Harmonia," Carmen said. "I shouldn't have to remind any of you that the rules of hospitality hold here and that the Octagon has declared this space a neutral meeting ground. But Michael, the rules don't prevent fae invitations. Not to their own. Stephen has to respond."

Stephen didn't know whether to be more bewildered by the woman's asking him to go with her or by the rules of hospitality that had apparently just prevented a sword fight from breaking out right in front of him. His heart was pounding distractingly hard. "Who are they? Why would they ask that?"

His dad knelt in front of him. "For right now just know that they're . . . distant relations of your mother's. Here and now at least, they have the right to demand that you answer them." He paused. "And I can't tell you what to say."

His dad stood back up.

All the human adults wore tense, worried expressions. Ivan and Sofia were wide eyed and, for once, silent. The fae looked . . . hungry.

They were waiting for his answer. Every single person here was.

"Are we supposed to take that elevator to our new place?" Stephen asked. He pointed across the lobby toward the gleaming golden doors. His dad had said something about upstairs.

Stephen's dad frowned in confusion for a second. Then he answered, brow smoothing: "Yes."

"Well, then, let's go," said Stephen. He turned to face Baroness Thyme and her minions. "Because, Dad, you have a lot to explain. But no way am I going anywhere with these strangers."

CHAPTER THREE

Baroness Thyme inclined her head. "I regret that is your decision. But perhaps you'll change your mind."

Stephen didn't like the way her eyes lingered on him. So he tugged his dad toward the elevator, everyone except the three fae following them. The jeweled button was emblazoned with an UP arrow. He pushed it.

The elevator doors opened with a *bing*.

He glanced back to see a blue-skinned creature with long black hair appear behind the desk and pass keys to the baroness. The younger fae—Lady Sarabel—winked at him.

Stephen whirled and boarded the elevator.

The space inside was much larger than a normal elevator, with gilded mirrors and another tiled floor showing the Octagon symbol. Carmen pulled a shiny black pass card from her jacket pocket and slid it into a slot on the control panel below the rows of green gemstone buttons. She hit the top button, and the car began to rise.

"Before you ask, no, I can't make them leave," Carmen said in a low voice to his dad. "They're here for the festivities this weekend. We knew they'd show up."

"But not so soon. Not before the La Doyts get back."

"The boy—"

"You mean Stephen. His name is Stephen." His dad's voice was sharp.

Stephen wanted to sink through the bottom of the floor and disappear, anything other than listen to them talk about him and whatever had just happened back there as if he weren't standing right there. He wanted to be alone with his dad and get the promised explanations. Those fae were related to *his mother*. What was it Ivan had said at the cemetery? That Chef Nana hadn't gotten along with the fae?

And the rest of this . . . His dad had been lying to him for his entire life.

A placard at the back of the elevator car caught Stephen's attention, and he slid past Ivan and Sofia to read it.

OCCUPANCY OF THIS ELEVATOR IS NOT TO

EXCEED TWENTY HUMANS OR LIKE-SIZE PERSONS,

OR EIGHTY PIXIES, OR THREE OGRES.

OUR LARGER GUESTS ARE INVITED

TO USE THE STAIRS.

PLEASE DO NOT ENGAGE THE ELEVATOR

IN CONVERSATION.

At this point, Stephen was desperate for a change of topic. So he asked, "Why would anyone talk to an elevator?"

A deep sigh sounded, coming from every direction.

"That's what they *all* say," said a disembodied voice. "Why indeed? How could an elevator possibly have anything more interesting to say than

'Second floor: infinity pool, spa' or 'I'm sorry, you do not have access to that floor'? Why would anybody waste time on a little basic politeness? Why ask, 'How's your day been, Elevator?' Why bother with the ups and downs of such as me?"

This was followed by another deep sigh.

"Um, sorry," Stephen said. His dad came back beside him. He put a hand on Stephen's shoulder and shook his head. Stephen shrugged him off. "How has your day been, Elevator?"

The elevator ground to a halt.

"I'm so glad you asked!" said the voice. "As it happens, I've had quite a dull day, and it's not helped matters that my left lift chain needs to be lubricated. But try to get maintenance to do anything about that before it's scheduled! Can you imagine? Them lifting a claw to help me feel a tiny bit better? And as for today's passengers, well, let me tell you! That vampire lord and his gaggle of zombies hit *every* call button on the way down from nine so they all could jump up in the air every time I started down. Do I look like a toy to you? Do I look like some sort of amusement park ride?"

"Elevator!" said Carmen. "I've hit the call button for the roof, and I've inserted my pass card. Don't make me use my override code."

For the third time the tremendous sigh came from every direction. The elevator started upward again, though Stephen heard some soft grumbling as it did so. He couldn't blame it. Its day sounded about as frustrating as his own.

"Can't you read?" whispered Ivan.

And Sofia added, "Don't you ever follow directions?"

Stephen looked at Ivan and said, "Of course I can." Then he answered Sofia. "Yes, but not always."

"Figures," Ivan said.

His dad said, "Stephen sometimes tests rules out before he learns to follow them."

"I suppose that shouldn't come as a surprise," Ivan said.

Meaning what? Stephen had no idea. And then, while Stephen watched, Ivan removed a tiny spiral notebook from his pocket and scribbled something in it with a small pencil.

"Are you writing something about me?" Stephen asked him.

But he didn't wait for Ivan's response because the elevator doors opened onto a scene that should have been impossible. The buildings of New York surrounded them, so they were on the roof of the hotel and hadn't been magically transported to some other location. But the roof of the Hotel New Harmonia was occupied by . . .

"This is the Village," said Carmen, "where most of the staff live."

Thick grass grew right up to the elevator, which was set into an open-sided shed with stone walls and a thatched roof. Old-fashioned black streetlamps illuminated the scene in front of them, showing a green central lawn with a low hill. There was a croquet setup, a gazebo, and several picnic tables. A gravel path led from the elevator across a footbridge to a half dozen or more cottages that also had stone walls and thatched roofs. Some had blooming flowers on top, vines and roses climbing the sides.

A dark shadow shot through the night sky and landed in a crouch in front of Stephen.

"We are so very sorry about Lady Nanette!" the small, bulky creature said in a high-pitched voice. It had skin as gray as stone and features sharply defined by thick folds and ridges and points.

It was—Stephen realized, blinking—a gargoyle.

Three more gargoyles careened down, fluttering and making sympathetic noises of agreement. The first one said, "But we've brought all your stuff!"

Another of the gargoyles chirped, "Lady Nanette would be so happy you are back, Sir Michael!"

"Thanks to you and the entire clan," his dad told the gargoyles. He waved to the Gutierrezes and Ivan. "We've got it from here."

The gargoyles flew ahead, leading the way across the bridge to a small cottage with an open door. As soon as they neared the entrance, the gargoyles shot up into the sky, calling, "Good night! Sleep well!"

Stephen watched one drop in the direction of a roof corner. That made sense. Well, it made sense *here*.

"This was where I grew up with Chef Nana," his dad said. "She wanted us to live here."

Chef Nana's house. Stephen had always wanted to see it. But she had always come to visit them instead of the other way around.

The inside of the cottage was homey. It smelled like Chef Nana: a warm, fresh scent that shifted depending on which spices she'd used most recently. There was a big rug embroidered with flowers and vines and chef's knives, and two comfy-looking couches. But their TV and bookshelves from Chicago were also set up in the living room, without a packing box in sight.

"All your clothes will be put away in the dresser if I know the gargoyles. Let's check out your room; it's the first door here." His dad bustled up the short hall beside a cozy kitchen, and Stephen trailed along behind him. Did he really think Stephen cared about his clothes right now?

There were two more doors past his, presumably another bedroom and a bathroom. The room couldn't have been more different from his in

Chicago, but his stuff did seem to be in it. One wall had a curtained round window, like a ship's porthole but bigger. Opposite it, his graphic novels and other books were already on bookshelves, along with his old sketchbooks. His suitcase lay on a bed with a blue blanket.

"So this is you," his dad said. "I hope you like it—"

Stephen held up a hand. "Stop it."

This wasn't home, not yet. This wasn't his room, not yet. He turned and marched back down the hall to the kitchen. He sat down at the wooden table and waited.

His dad must have hesitated to come after him because it took a few moments for him to appear in the kitchen. He placed the big old book the man at the cemetery had given him on the table between them.

"So that was Chef Nana's cookbook," Stephen said.

His dad took the seat opposite him. They'd always had important talks in the kitchen back home. They would have this one here, in Chef Nana's kitchen. No, Stephen corrected himself. In *their* new kitchen. None of this seemed real, but it was.

"It's called the *Librum de Coquina*," his dad said. "Like I said before, the *Librum* isn't just a cookbook. It has all our family's collected wisdom in it, and more besides. This may be hard to believe, but culinary alchemy has stopped wars before. Probably started them, too."

Stephen stared at him. His dad was stalling.

"Wow, you really don't want to tell me what's going on, do you? Why did you lie to me?"

"I'm sorry. There's so much I didn't—I couldn't— You have every right to be angry."

Stephen *was* angry. But he also knew his dad must be tired . . . and sad, like he was. It had always been just the two of them, together against the world. "Is my mother fae, like those people downstairs? What does that mean? Why did they ask me to go with them?"

"Yes," his dad said, nodding, "that's a good place to start."

But he hesitated again. Stephen asked, "Was *any* of what you told me true, about her leaving us?"

39

"It was. But your mother didn't just leave us, she left . . . everything." His dad looked at him. "She was the fae representative on the Octagon. The knights—Chef Nana, me, Julio, and Carmen—we serve the Octagon. The Octagon has eight members—seven who represent supernormal factions and one human representative."

"What are the supernormal factions?" Stephen asked.

His dad looked up, thinking and probably picturing the glyph symbols. "The furred folk, sea people, the undead, subterranean dwellers, the winged folk, the fae, and the witches."

"And knights?" Stephen had been thinking about this, about what he knew about knights. "Do you mean knights like King Arthur and the Round Table?"

"Yes, *exactly* like the knights of the Round Table. That tale was a cover story. All of it is to maintain the peace between humans and—"

"Monsters," Stephen supplied. So not only was his dad a knight, he was basically a knight of the

Round Table. Which was cool, but he sure was taking the long way around to answering the question about his mom. "My mother was a monster?"

His dad shook his head. "You— They're not monsters. The term is *supernormals*. A big part of maintaining the peace between supernormals and humans is through places like the New Harmonia. There are similar hotels all over the world now, and there used to be inns and taverns. They have always served as neutral territory because guests are protected by the right of hospitality. We also ensure that humanity at large doesn't find out about supernormals and try to wipe them out."

"You said my mother was the fae representative. She's not anymore?"

His dad swallowed. "The fae used to steal human or half-human children, so a treaty was signed forbidding the fae from having children with humans. We, your mom and I, we broke that treaty. And there were consequences. For me, it meant being exiled for at least ten years. It could have been forever. For her, because she was highborn, there wasn't a direct punishment, so she gave herself one. She exiled herself, and she's been gone since then. The fae seat on the Octagon is vacant because she left without officially resigning."

Stephen tried to wrap his head around this. The way Ivan and Sofia had described his dad as a scandal at the cemetery was starting to make sense. "So you got kicked out because of me."

His dad leaned down to make Stephen look him in the eye. "I got kicked out for breaking the rules. And I don't regret any of it for a second. You are the most important thing in the world to me."

Maybe, but . . . "So, where is she now?"

"No one knows where she went, but the La Doyts are off in Faery trying to find her." He squared his shoulders. "There's something else."

"Okay," Stephen said, feeling uneasy. What could be a bigger shock than the rest of what he'd learned today? "Just say it."

"What happened downstairs— Fae politics are complicated. The rules of succession state that as your mother's closest living relative with fae blood, you would be entitled to her seat on the Octagon in her absence—but only once you reach adulthood. In the meantime, if you became the ward of another fae, like the baroness, then it would entitle *her* to your mother's seat."

"What do you mean 'with fae blood'?"

His dad spoke directly. "You're half fae, half human. One of the conditions of my exile was that a spell was cast on you that suppressed your fae nature. The powder of True Seeing removed it. You may experience . . . changes now."

"Wait. What?" Stephen looked down at his arms and legs. His skin wasn't tinted green like the other fae. It was normal. He jumped up and found a mirror on the wall. Were his ears slightly pointed at the top now? He touched them to confirm. They were.

Stephen turned to face his dad. "*I'm* a monster. That's what you're saying."

"That is not what I'm saying." His dad got up and walked over to him. He pulled Stephen's hand down away from the top of his ear, his pointed ear. "You're still you. But there hasn't been a kid like you in a long time. Some half fae were almost entirely human; others get more fae traits. We'll just have to see how that part of you expresses. But you'll still be you."

Stephen couldn't understand. He wasn't fully human? Then *how* was he still himself?

"We couldn't be part of supernormal society until now. There was no use in worrying you. There was a chance you wouldn't have been able to come here until you were an adult. I wasn't allowed to share any details with *anyone* as long as I was in exile."

"You still should have told *me*." Stephen was reeling, his mind seizing on all sorts of random things: the way he'd never quite fit in with the other kids at school; how he was always having trouble following rules, like Baroness Thyme and her smoking. "Wait. Did I get the rules stuff from you or from my mother?"

"Obviously I have my own issue there, but it is true that the fae like finding loopholes. They have trouble sticking to rules that they didn't make themselves." His dad rubbed his hand up and down Stephen's arms, the way he used to when Stephen was little and didn't feel well. "You are still you. So you didn't get our family's talent for cooking. You have your mom's artistic talent instead. You're still a Lawson."

And also the lost son of the Primrose Court. That was what the fae lady had said. "I don't want to be like those fae downstairs. Is Mom like that?"

"No," his dad said. "And Chef Nana didn't exactly get along with those particular fae. The Court of Thorns and she had a history—she once showed the baroness up by her skill in cooking. I think that's part of why the baroness wants to take over the seat so badly, to mess with me through you. Just like any kind of people, there are good and bad fae. That does bring up something important, though: one of the reasons Carmen was able to hire me, bring me back, is that there's a big occasion coming up, a birthday party I have to cook for. Those fae will be here at least until it's over. So just . . . do your best to avoid them."

"No problem." He meant it.

"Hopefully, the La Doyts will find your mother

and convince her to come back to her seat. But time passes differently in Faery. It may be awhile. And in case you're wondering," his dad said, "Chef Nana didn't want to lie to you. So she never did. I called them stories so you wouldn't have to be confused about what world you belonged to until it mattered. Can you forgive me?"

Stephen didn't know how to feel about any of this. He was upset with his dad for keeping this from him, even if he'd had a good reason. But it was his dad. It had always been just the two of them. And he wanted the chance to meet his mother, fae or not.

He didn't say yes. He said, "Love you, Dad."

"Love you, too, kiddo." His dad smiled. "You will like it here once you get used to it. I promise. Stephen, you're still you. I'm still me."

His dad got up and reached out to give him a hug, but Stephen stepped back and nodded. "Good night, Dad," he said, and went to his room.

Unable to absorb everything his dad had told him, he paced around the edges of the bed.

His dad had said all his stuff would probably have been put away by the gargoyles, and so he opened the top drawer of the nightstand to see what was in it. He hadn't even had a nightstand at home, just a dresser. Instead of his own things, he found a book he'd never seen before. With its smooth edges and nonleather cover, it looked mass produced, like the kind of book that would be in every room in any hotel, until he checked out the title: *An Almanack of the Mores and Ways of Supernormal Kind.*

Carefully he opened the cover and saw his grandmother's familiar handwriting.

To my dear Stephen—I'm so sorry I can't be here for your first time at the hotel, but so very glad that you and your father are here to stay. It has long been my dream. And I've left you something to help you—my own copy of a book that you can use as a guide. That said, take what you read about fae kind with a grain of the finest sea salt. Remember, our characters are determined by our actions. Love, Chef Nana

He looked in the mirror at his newly pointy ears and hoped she was right.

Stephen gave up on sleeping. What if his fae side did outweigh his human one? His dad had pointed out that he'd never exhibited the Lawson talent in the kitchen.

He got up and moved over to his bookcase. Since he was eight, he'd kept a flashlight hidden behind his volume of the collected *Doctor Strange* comics (Stephen was named for the Sorcerer Supreme). Were the gargoyles that detail oriented? He pulled out the book and laid his hand on the flashlight. They were.

He crept out quietly to the kitchen. As he'd suspected, his dad had left the *Librum de Coquina* on the table. A book like this belonged in the kitchen. It was heavy in his hands as he flipped open the cover and held the flashlight with his chin to read the recipe his dad had used on him earlier.

RECIPE FOR A POWDER OF TRUE SEEING

INGREDIENTS

1   *pinch sea salt (salt sourced from the Arctic Ocean is best)*

1   *scruple the finest cinnamon*

2   *smidgens recently harvested saffron*

½   *pinch ground cardamom*

1   *minim dust grated from a cracked green jasper stone*

½   *drop lark's tears (tears of joy preferred over tears of sorrow)*

INSTRUCTIONS

In a mortar, combine the salt, cinnamon, saffron, and cardamom, mixing lightly with the fingers of the right hand. Lay a fine rasp atop the mortar, oriented northwest to southeast, and grate the jasper dust into the mixture with three quick motions, left to right. Set aside the rasp, and lastly add the tears of lark, then take up your pestle, and grind the ingredients into a fine powder, which should be barely moist.

The powder becomes efficacious when a pinch is taken and thrown backward over the left shoulder. Any beings previously unable to see supernormal kind because of the effects of the Great Dweomer should now see clearly. It may also be used to flavor soups particularly loved by giants, golems, and other such beings bound to the earth.

HISTORICAL NOTES

This recipe is based on one first developed in the eleventh century by the famed culinary alchemist Lydia of Knossos. Lydia invented the powder in secret, as its principal effect was to circumvent the Great Dweomer of the year 999, the worldwide spell that conceals supernormals from normal *humans and some half humans. In the centuries since the Octagon adopted the First Treaty of Harmony, however, it has become legal in certain circumstances to provide the powder to normal humans or other affected half humans, particularly those affiliated with the knights of the Octagon or their families.*

Stephen didn't know where Knossos was, or even how to say it, any more than he knew what a dweomer was, though it sounded like some kind of spell. He turned a few more pages, reading the names of the recipes at the top of each:

AMBROSIA LOAF GLAZED WITH GIANT HONEYBEE NECTAR
DINOSAUR EGG SOUFFLÉ
SPEED OF MERCURY HOT SAUCE
FOUNTAIN OF YOUTH PUNCH

There was handwriting at the bottom of that last recipe, reading "Ingredients no longer available."

He recognized the writing. It was Chef Nana's.

Of course she would have written in the book; it belonged to her, after all. She had always encouraged him to write in his own books, take notes of what he thought about what he read, or even draw little sketches of the characters as he imagined them.

"Wait," Stephen whispered. "If it was her book, then . . ."

He flipped through the pages faster, barely glancing at the recipe names until he came to a place where the book fell open naturally, as if these particular pages had been turned to many, many times.

"Xocolātl con el Azúcar de la Familia de Lawson" was written in grand looping letters across the top. And below that, in his grandmother's much more sensible writing, he read "Special Hot Chocolate."

Stephen remembered the times his grandmother had made him hot chocolate when she visited Chicago during the cold-weather months. She always made him wait until just before bedtime because, she said, "It's for dreaming."

I can do this, he thought. *I'm a member of the— the familia de Lawson. And I wouldn't mind some nice dreams after today.*

He peered up the hall toward his dad's room. The door was closed, and no light showed through the crack at the floor.

It took him a few minutes to find all the ingredients or, at least, things that he thought would do for the ingredients. Chef Nana's pantry was well stocked, but all he could find was plain sugar, not "beet sugar crystallized by the gaze of a feathered serpent." And he figured the box of powdered chocolate would work as well as "Cacao seeds ground beneath a new moon."

Not making a mess was even harder, though there were only a few ingredients. Stephen worried more about the sound of the water boiling in the teakettle waking up his dad than he did about anything else.

After about half an hour of hunting ingredients and pans, then mixing and boiling and pouring, Stephen found himself sitting in the darkened kitchen with a steaming mug of hot chocolate. It certainly *smelled* like Chef Nana's recipe.

He blew on the surface of the dark liquid to cool it a bit, then took a cautious sip.

It was pretty good. Not as good as Chef Nana's, he thought as he cleaned up the kitchen. But pretty good.

I don't care what they say or who my mother is. I'm not a fae, I'm a Lawson.

He yawned and stretched and realized he felt very sleepy, after all. He put the *Librum* back where his dad had left it, then went to bed.

CHAPTER FOUR

Stephen and his dad both loved comics and always made little jokes about what their own superpowers were. His dad claimed that one of his powers was to have breakfast ready at the exact right time every morning. So it was no surprise that when Stephen walked into the kitchen, tugging on his Chicago Cubs baseball cap, his dad was sliding a plate of eggs and toast onto the table. Sunny-side up, just the way Stephen liked them.

"How'd you sleep?" his dad asked. "Feeling better about things today?"

Stephen thought carefully about how to answer. In fact he had slept deeply, but his dreams had been crazy. Sort of. On the one hand, after the day he'd had yesterday, maybe it *wasn't* crazy to dream about gargoyles flying through the sky carrying furniture and bullheaded men chasing him through mazes. But on the other hand, he could half remember dreaming a long, scary conversation with the fae lady, Baroness Thyme, telling him that *she* would be his mother. It had seemed so real while he was dreaming it.

He finally said, "It's quiet up here. And yeah, a little."

His dad nodded. "The peace and quiet are part of the dweomer the Manager maintains over the Village. Keeps the weather nice, too."

Stephen ate in silence for a moment, then noticed something about his dad's outfit. He was so used to seeing his dad dressed in spotless white chef's jackets that he hadn't seen what was different. Over his left breast, *Chef Lawson* was still stitched in black cursive, but the logo beneath the name was different: Eight sides, eight symbols. The words: *New Harmonia*.

"So I take it you're working this morning," Stephen said. "I thought maybe you'd show me around."

He tried not to sound angry. Or disappointed. But it wasn't easy.

His dad set down his coffee cup. "I'm so sorry to abandon you today. But the event that's coming up this weekend is one of the most important things that's happened in the supernormal community in ages. Chef Nana hadn't been able to get much of the planning done with her illness, so I have a lot of catching up to do. The restaurant's closed for breakfast and lunch today to let me get a feel for how things work before my first dinner service tonight. Things will be better after the party, I promise."

"What am I supposed to do today then?" Stephen asked. There was a tremble in his voice that he wished he'd been able to cover up.

As if in answer, three precise knocks sounded from the front door.

"There they are," his dad said. "Don't worry. I asked Carmen to get you a guided tour." He bustled over to open the door.

The two kids from yesterday, Sofia and Ivan, stood there. Ivan's hand was raised as if he were about to knock again. "Come on in, you two," Stephen's dad said. "Have you eaten yet?"

Sofia was dressed in a long-sleeved T-shirt and a skirt over striped leggings with big boots. Ivan was wearing another suit, complete with a blue bow tie.

"Mom made us cereal," Sofia said. "Ivan's staying with us while his parents are away."

Away looking for my mother. Ivan didn't chime in, instead looking so carefully around the cottage that Stephen thought he was memorizing every detail.

"What are you doing?" Stephen asked him.

"I'm practicing the art of observation," Ivan said. "Making note of changes."

Sofia stepped between them. "Are you ready to go? We thought we'd start at the bottom of the hotel and work our way up."

"Have fun, kids," his dad said. He leaned close to Stephen's ear and said, "Especially you. Try to enjoy yourself, okay?"

Stephen pushed his half-finished breakfast away. Nobody had asked him if he wanted to tour the hotel with these two. But as with everything else, he didn't seem to have much choice. Maybe they would be able to tell him more about his mother and the Octagon.

He slung the satchel holding his sketchbook and pencils over his shoulder and followed them out the door onto the green.

"Good morning, young Master Lawson!" said the elevator as the three of them boarded. "What a pleasure it is to see you. Especially after the dreadful morning I've had."

"Um, good morning, Elevator," Stephen replied. "Sorry to hear about that. Still having trouble with that, um, lift chain?"

"Oh, of course, but I meant the passengers. Full of nothing but complaints and forebodings. Dreams, of all things! Every guest that's been on board this morning has complained about unsettled dreams."

"I had strange dreams, too, now that you mention it," Ivan said. "You?"

Sofia nodded. "I dreamed I lost a croquet match."

"Maybe it was prophetic then," Ivan said.

Sofia wrinkled her nose at him. "You wish."

Stephen felt like the biggest third wheel ever. His pointy ears heated. "I hope you didn't have bad dreams, Elevator," he said.

"Oh, no," said the elevator. "That would mean I'd been asleep. And elevators never sleep. We're on duty around the clock, every day, all year long. Our sacrifices are unappreciated."

Sofia reached past Stephen and selected the bottommost button, which was marked with a big gold *L*, and the elevator doors slid shut.

"Next stop, the lobby! A few call buttons have been pushed on the intervening floors, but they can just wait while I carry you in speed and comfort, Master Lawson. And you miscreants, too," the elevator added.

"Now see here—" Ivan began to protest, but Sofia shushed him.

Stephen pretended that he had to tie his shoe so they wouldn't see him smiling. As he raised himself back up, though, he felt a flick on the lid of his baseball cap, and it went flying.

He couldn't believe it. He glanced up at Sofia, who was standing closest to him, but her back was turned and she was whispering something to Ivan. Had she knocked his cap off on purpose?

"One reason I like you, young Stephen"—the elevator started talking again—"is that you don't jump up in the air like *most* children do. And the undead. Jumpers, all of the undead."

Stephen tried to imagine Ivan and Sofia jumping in the elevator. They had finished talking and stared at him with sphinxlike expressions. (Were sphinxes real? He wasn't going to ask *them*.) He picked up his cap as the doors slid open and the elevator said, "Lobby, as requested. I hope you have an excellent day."

Sofia and Ivan didn't even look in his direction as they departed the elevator.

This wasn't going to be an excellent day, thought Stephen. It was going to be a *long* day.

"The first stop on your tour of the New Harmonia," said Ivan, sounding like a miniature museum guide, "is the boiler room."

The three of them stood before a metal door concealed by the lobby trees. A sign posted on it read AUTHORIZED PERSONNEL ONLY in serious-looking letters. Stephen didn't mind ignoring the sign, but neither was he particularly interested in seeing a boiler room.

"You go ahead and light the torches, Ivan," said Sofia. The bow-tied boy nodded and went inside, leaving Sofia and Stephen standing alone in the indoor forest.

"Holding me back so you can apologize?" Stephen asked.

Sofia squinted in confusion. Finally she shook her head. "Promise you won't make fun of Ivan," she said.

"What?" Stephen was taken aback, forgetting all about the incident with his cap. He found the pair of them annoying, not to mention rude so far, but he wasn't a jerk. "Why would I?"

Sofia hesitated. "We go to a normal public school, not a supernormal one. And all the kids there make fun of the way he dresses and talks. He doesn't need that here at the hotel, too. Especially not from a half fae with who knows what kinds of powers."

Powers? Stephen thought, but set that aside for the moment. He'd thought they were just being standoffish, but maybe there was more to it than that. If Ivan was used to being picked on, and Sofia was used to being his protector, maybe adding an unknown new kid like him into their daily lives worried each of them, for different reasons. He'd had friends at school, but never a best friend. He didn't know what that was like.

"I'm not going to make fun of anyone," he said. "And I'm human. I grew up human."

Sofia's brow creased with a troubled frown. "Baroness Thyme wouldn't care about you if you were only human."

The door opened a crack, and Ivan's face appeared. "Coming?" he asked.

Stephen's ears were still burning, and he was grateful for the interruption. Sofia gestured for him to follow and stepped through the door onto a small platform surrounded by brick walls.

Ivan was holding three lit torches. He handed over one each to the two of them.

"You really meant torches," Stephen said, taking his. "That's cool."

Sofia used her free hand to close the door. Funny that his ears had finally stopped burning while he was holding a flaming torch. Maybe all he'd needed was to clear the air with Sofia.

"Cindermass doesn't like artificial light," said Ivan. "Also, he hates it when cell phones go off in his presence."

"Who's Cindermass?" Stephen said, fishing his phone out with his free hand and putting it on vibrate.

Sofia took out hers and switched it to silent, too. "You'll see."

The steps led down into the darkness, soot stains from past torches darkening the walls.

Stephen summoned his courage and said, "Ivan, my dad told me your parents are looking for my mother."

The firelight from the torches flickered off the lenses of Ivan's round glasses. "Yes, Princess Aria of the Primrose Court, the lost fae peacekeeper of the Octagon."

It was the first time Stephen had heard her name. He wanted to hear it again, to repeat it over and over. *Princess Aria of the Primrose Court*. But he wanted something else more. "Do you think they'll find her?"

Ivan considered the matter as they descended the steps. "It will not be easy, even for my parents, and they are the greatest detectives of the age. The

Realm of Faery is treacherous for humans, and no living soul of any kind has reported seeing her since your father's exile. But if anyone can find Princess Aria, it's them."

Stephen lost count of the number of steps down, rolling what Ivan had said over in his mind, but at last they stopped.

"Here we are," Ivan said.

They stood before a pair of fancy wooden double doors, decorated with metal plates and carvings. Sofia pushed through them, though they looked heavy, and Ivan followed. Stephen hesitated, then went through himself.

"Meet Cindermass," said Sofia.

The light from their torches joined that of dozens more leaning out from sconces around a cavernous room. Stephen dropped his torch to the stone floor.

Crouched at the center of the cavelike room, lazily coiling around a towering pile of gold coins, jewels, and other shiny objects, was a red dragon the size of a city bus. The dragon opened his mouth wide, and Stephen flinched backward. Not that he would have been able to outrun a fireball.

"Why, you have a new friend," the dragon said. Then: "Who wants tea?"

Stephen, Ivan, and Sofia were seated at a low, square table covered with a frilly tablecloth. A delicate bone china tea set was arrayed across the table. The cavernous room was almost . . . cozy, with teacups in hand and the warm light of the torches.

If you could forget that a dragon was staring right at you anyway. Ivan and Sofia seemed to have no trouble, calmly sipping their drinks.

"Is that tea hot enough for you, young man?" asked the dragon. "I can heat it up with just a breath."

"No, no, it's fine!" Stephen rattled his saucer as he lifted the cup to take a sip. The tea was in fact at the perfect temperature.

"You just let me know," said Cindermass.

Stephen didn't know if it was impolite to ask a dragon questions, but he was curious. "How did you end up here at the hotel?"

"All the way in the New World. Yes, it's very far from where I hatched and fledged. But I have traveled near and far and back again. Until the skies grew ever more dangerous with your flying tin cans . . . I believe you call them airplanes. If they were made of gold, perhaps it would be worth the risk to stay aloft, but they are not. Really, a dragon just needs a place to keep his treasures safe. I have many treasures, as you can see."

Cindermass swept his claws to indicate the gleaming piles of loot all around them. "Here I can be of service to the Octagon, watching over the supernormals who still deign to dally in the world of humans. I can keep an eye on my hoard and on all the goings-on of our secretive world. Best case scenario, really. Now, you're sure you don't want sugar or milk?"

Stephen sniffed the teacup, inhaling a fragrance like blooming flowers, then took another careful sip. "It's Darjeeling, right? It doesn't need anything added."

Cindermass's smile was terrifying, revealing teeth longer than a baseball bat.

"From the Makaibari Estate in Bhutan. A fascinating place indeed. I lived there for a few decades in the early seventeenth century, in the great city of Thimphu." Cindermass drew back a little. "You have a very sophisticated palate for such a young human. I suppose I shouldn't be surprised by that, given your august lineage. I also happened to hear your encounter in the lobby last night. The Court of Thorns is no place for you."

"Um, thanks," Stephen said. "Did someone tell you about it?"

"Not at all," the dragon said. "And if your grandmother knew . . ."

Sofia leaned over and whispered to Stephen: "Have you ever seen one of those old movies with a telephone switchboard that the operators can plug and unplug and hear any conversation they want?" She pointed at the top edge of the wall, where there was a series of openings lined in metal. "The ventilation system. With a dragon's hearing, better than any switchboard."

At that, Stephen noticed Cindermass was watching them both. A spark flared in one nostril.

"Not that I would ever eavesdrop," Cindermass said.

"Of course not," Sofia said. "You can't help it. People shouldn't talk so loud if they don't want to be heard."

Stephen waited to see if the dragon was offended.

Cindermass sniffed, and the spark snuffed out. "Yes, exactly." The dragon's giant golden eyes grew watery. "I must tell you that I was heartbroken to miss the funeral, but it is more difficult for me to travel outside than others. I haven't seen your father yet, but I sent a note up to the kitchens. Lady Nanette always wanted him to return. . . ."

The dragon was working himself into a state. A long trail of smoke streamed from his nostrils. Ivan and Sofia scooted back from the table, attempting to be discreet about it.

"Nanette was such a dear friend, and you—you are a *great artist*."

Everything clicked into place. Stephen wasn't just sitting across from a dragon, he was sitting across from his grandmother's best friend, Mr. C.

"She wrote to me about you in almost every single letter I got from her," Stephen said.

"She did?" Cindermass said. "She wrote about *me*?"

Ivan and Sofia exchanged one of their looks and stopped edging away from the table.

"Yes. She said you were a great connoisseur of the arts."

The dragon reared up from the bed of coins where he rested, gold and silver flying in every direction. "Yes! Yes, I am! I simply *must* show you my collection!"

Stephen saw Sofia trying to catch his eye. She and Ivan were making "no!" signals.

"I'll have to arrange for the proper lighting, of course," Cindermass said, apparently talking to himself under his breath, but even that was a loud rumble. "After I get someone to lift the safeguard spells. And of course I'll need to curate it and decide on the proper *order* to exhibit the pieces. . . ."

Stephen realized what Sofia and Ivan were trying to tell him. The dragon was liable to keep them here indefinitely.

"Cindermass?" Stephen said, rummaging in his satchel. "I'm still learning the, um, the rules and mores of the supernormal community. Would it be out of bounds if I asked to draw you?"

Silence descended on the room. Cindermass slowly, sinuously maneuvered his long neck so that his enormous head was right above the table. Stephen hadn't moved back like the others, and he could have reached out and touched the scales on the dragon's snout if he'd dared. He could feel the heat of Cindermass's breath.

Then the dragon reached up with one of his front right claws and dragged it across the spiky scales growing in rows above his eyes. This made a rasping noise like giant fingernails on a giant chalkboard, and it took Stephen a moment to comprehend that the dragon was grooming himself.

"Well," said Cindermass. "Well, obviously not in the state I am right now. My scales are due a polish, and my teeth and claws need sharpening."

He'd somehow turned an even deeper red color.

Is he blushing? Stephen wondered.

"But if you're—if you're serious and would like to—like to use your tremendous talents to make a drawing of *me* . . ." The very tip of Cindermass's tail had arched around so that he held it in front of his face and peered over the tail spikes shyly. "I have sat for artists before, of course. Many times, as you'll see when we review my collection. Oh!" He suddenly collapsed onto his bed of coins with a great jingling sound. "Oh, I'm just not prepared to either show you my collection or sit for a drawing today! I'm so terribly sorry. These things take time, and with all the preparations for my birthday party I just wasn't ready for visitors!"

"You have a birthday coming up?" Stephen asked.

"Yes!" Cindermass said, preening. "I'll be one thousand years old on Saturday. The party will be *quite* the event, of course. You simply *must* come!"

A dragon's thousandth birthday party must be a pretty big deal. Stephen would bet anything that was the "special event" his dad and Sofia's parents had been dropping hints about.

"We'll all be there, Cindermass," said Ivan.

Sofia agreed. "No one would miss it."

"Even that terrible baroness, as if I want a present from *her*," Cindermass said, grimacing. But his expression changed as he eyed Stephen's sketchbook. "I was just thinking. I suppose I might be presentable enough for a quick preparatory sketch. Do you think?"

"We're supposed to introduce Stephen around to everybody . . ." Sofia said, trailing off, looking at Stephen with a question in her eye.

Stephen shrugged. "This will just take a minute."

Flipping past his sketches of sports figures and superheroes, Stephen realized that this would be the first drawing he'd made in New York. And it would be a from-life drawing of a living, fire-breathing dragon. He swallowed, picked a black pencil from his supply box, and began swiftly drawing on the next blank page.

Cindermass sat perfectly still, not even appearing

to breathe. Sofia and Ivan crowded in behind Stephen, looking over his shoulder and blocking his light. "Move back," he whispered, and was halfway surprised when they did.

The horns and spikes around Cindermass's eyes and ears came into being in the silhouette on the page, then his teeth and nostrils and his great scaly jaw. Next, Stephen took a red pencil and added hints of color, suggesting the tones and shades of Cindermass's scales without actually coloring them in. Last of all, he took a gold pencil he almost never used and carefully drew the dragon's eyes.

Stephen considered his work critically, looked up at the dragon, then back down at the page. He nodded.

"How do I look?" asked Cindermass.

"Great!" Sofia answered before Stephen could say anything.

"Very distinguished," said Ivan.

Cindermass grinned his wicked, toothy grin at Stephen. "Excellent," Cindermass said.

And then, as Stephen shaded in a last scale,

Cindermass winked one eye up at him.

Which made his mouth go dry and his pencil almost fall from his hand. He stumbled to his feet, gaping at the sketch. Because the eye that had winked was one he'd drawn.

"Did that sketch . . . ?" Cindermass sounded nearly breathless. "Is it a living sketch? I have long coveted a living painting for my collection."

Stephen held up his sketchbook to show the now motionless drawing. He must've been imagining things. But . . . *living* paintings?

"Sorry," he said.

"No, no. Please know that your demonstration of artistic talent has made my day," Cindermass said. "It is unfortunate that like all of my kind, I am not able to give gifts, Stephen, for surely I would give one to you. But promise me, you must come to visit again soon."

CHAPTER FIVE

When the three of them emerged back into the lobby, Stephen blinked at the brightness for a long moment. Did he dare ask them about the way his drawing had seemed to move for a moment? He did not.

Ivan and Sofia had stopped to consult with each other. He moved closer to them—tripped over a foot, and sprawled onto the floor.

Probably a foot in one of Ivan's shiny detective shoes or Sofia's chunky boots. But neither of them rushed to apologize.

"Stop hazing the new kid," Stephen said, ears burning again. "It's getting old."

"I don't understand your insinuation," Ivan said, a wrinkle appearing between his eyebrows.

But Sofia offered Stephen a hand. Even though

he half expected her to pull it back and let him fall, Stephen took it. "What do you have planned for me now? You could try to convince me to jump off the top of the building and have a gargoyle catch me."

"They are quite strong," Ivan said, but Sofia elbowed him.

Stephen had seen her do this once already. He would have bet she did it regularly.

Sofia shifted so she was facing the front desk, and Ivan and Stephen did the same. Frazzled looking but watching them at the same time, Sofia's mother was on an old-fashioned phone at the counter.

"More complaining dreamers," Sofia said.

"You can read your mom's lips?" Stephen was surprised.

"It comes in handy."

A woman with wavy brown hair, tapping her foot, waited beside Sofia's mom. She wore a collared white shirt with the Octagon's eight-glyphed symbol embroidered on one side and some words on the other, khaki shorts, and expensive-looking tennis shoes. Two cords hung around her neck, one holding a stopwatch and the other a referee's whistle.

"We'd better get out of here if we don't want to be ensnared by Marina," Sofia said. "Fifth floor to see Trevor?"

"Good plan," Ivan said. Then he explained to Stephen: "Marina's the medico and also the hotel's personal trainer. She runs the spa and infinity pool. She likes exercise, specifically forcing other people to do it."

Marina raised her whistle, as if she might blow it at them. Sofia waved to her mom and said quickly, "Let's take the stairs."

She opened a nearby stairwell door and held it for him and Ivan. Stephen could've sworn Marina's whistle blared, but the door closed on it. The other two started up the stairs at speed, but Stephen slowed when he heard the door opening and closing again behind them. He glanced back the way they'd come, expecting to see the medico/trainer woman.

He didn't see anyone, though. So he hurried after Ivan and Sofia.

He caught up to them waiting by a door with an ornate FIVE carved onto the placard beside it. Sofia opened it and revealed a lush, temperate rain forest.

"Are you sure this is the fifth floor?" Stephen asked. "It looks more like Oregon."

He and his dad had gone to Oregon on vacation once.

"Whenever Trevor's mother is in residence, the Manager reconfigures the whole floor to remind her of home," Sofia said as they stepped out into the greenery.

Sunlight streamed down on the fifth floor from what looked like a clear blue sky. A light wind and birdsong reached Stephen, and he smelled a rich loamy, foresty scent. But then he heard something out of place for the fifth floor of a New York hotel or an Oregon rain forest: the sharp crack of a bat making a solid hit against a baseball, followed by the sound of a ball flying through the leaves.

Stephen looked up and ducked out of the way. Barely.

A baseball rocketed from the overhead branches

and struck the trunk of a tree nearby.

"It's Ivan and Sofia!" Sofia called. "Plus the Lawson kid! We're coming in!"

"Straight ahead!" boomed a deep voice.

The baseball had rolled to a stop on the floor beside Stephen's sneakers, so he bent to pick it up. More baseballs dotted the vibrant green under-growth as they made their way farther in.

Crack! Another ball zoomed through the trees. That gave Stephen enough warning to hit the deck . . . er, forest floor. Once the ball had passed, he got up, brushing off the light coating of leaves from his now damp T-shirt.

He trailed Sofia around what appeared to be another redwood—it took more than a few steps because these redwoods were bigger around than most cars—and came to a clearing filled by a baseball field marked off between a pitching machine, where they stood, and home plate. Standing in front of the backstop, a Louisville Slugger resting on his shoulder, was a hairy creature that Stephen could come up with only one word to describe.

"Bigfoot," he said.

He'd never think of Julio or even the minotaur at his grandmother's funeral as "big" again. The bigfoot was at least eight feet tall, his shoulders were half that broad, and his New York Mets baseball jersey must have used up enough cloth to cover a banquet table.

He waved and loped toward them, smiling. On

the mound beside Stephen and the others, the pitching machine whined as if it might be about to release another ball. Sofia leaned over and smacked a bright red button that said STOP.

It was set to pitch at thirty-five miles per hour, which was really slow.

Speaking of which, the bigfoot moved slowly, too. He finally reached Stephen and stopped in front of him.

"Ni—nice Mets jersey," stammered Stephen. *I'm meeting a bigfoot wearing a Mets jersey. I hope he doesn't have anything against the Cubs.*

"Stephen," said Sofia, "it is my pleasure to introduce you to our friend," and she twisted up her face and made a long, ferocious growl, snapped her teeth together, and clicked loudly from the back of her throat.

Stephen opened his mouth, all the while desperately hoping he wasn't expected to repeat that series of sounds.

"I know what you must be thinking, but her pronunciation is actually excellent," said Ivan.

"Stephen Lawson!" said the bigfoot with the unpronounceable name. "Welcome! I am so sorry for the loss of your grandmother. She was always very kind to me."

Stephen blinked at the outstretched hairy hand. "Nice to meet you, um, uh—"

"Oh," said the bigfoot, "my name's too hard for most humans to say. In English it is Treks Ever Upward over Adversity to the High Summits. You can call me—"

"*Trevor*," Stephen said, remembering the name Sofia had used before. "Nice to meet you."

"Would you like to play baseball with me?" Trevor asked. "I'm trying to improve my speed. I struggle to move quickly enough to hit the ball at normal pitching speeds. I've never met a half fae before, so I don't know if that is something you'd like."

"I like watching baseball, but I'm not much good at sports," Stephen said. He liked watching other people follow all the regulations but as a little kid had failed miserably at doing the same when his dad signed him up for T-ball. "I don't know what half fae like, only what I do. Have you really never met one?"

Ivan pushed his glasses up his nose. "You are an interesting specimen. You're the only half fae any of us have ever met. The fae were made to sign a treaty in 1803 agreeing to forfeit their rights to have half-human children and cease stealing them from human parents. Half fae were considered untrust-worthy when there were more of you around."

It was as if his ears almost never stopped burning around these two. Being part fae, so far, was embar-rassing. He hoped his dad was right when he'd said that some of the fae were good. Because the way Ivan and Sofia were peering at him right now, he didn't think anyone else agreed.

"It would probably not be very fun for you to watch how slowly I swing the bat, at any rate," Trevor said in a clear attempt to smooth things over.

He at least was being nice to Stephen. Who thought back to the recipes in Chef Nana's book the night before. Hadn't one been "Speed of Mercury Hot Sauce"?

"Is there any chance you like spicy food?" Stephen asked Trevor.

Sofia said, "Bigfeet mostly eat veggies. Mild leaves. Almond milk."

"Bigfoots," Ivan said mildly.

"What Sofia says is true—I've never had spicy food," Trevor said. "But I always enjoyed your grandmother's cooking."

"Would you want to come down to the kitchens with me for a snack, Trevor?" Stephen said.

Trevor smiled and dropped the bat. "I should love a snack."

Ivan and Sofia exchanged a look. Ivan said, "I could go for a bite."

"I'll meet up with you two later," Stephen said. He half regretted it the moment after he said it. Surely they'd be as relieved to be rid of him as he would be of them? He wanted a break from being scrutinized and considered "untrustworthy" or a "specimen" for Ivan to take notes on.

But Ivan looked slightly injured, and Sofia had her hand on his arm. Her eyes narrowed at Stephen.

No regrets. They've been punking you all morning. Once you have a friend, you'll feel better.

Leading the way, Stephen trekked back through the forest to find the elevator. It was set into a wall that was also a giant tree trunk. When he pushed the call button, nothing happened.

"Come on, Elevator," he said.

"I was told that it was better not to speak to the elevator directly," Trevor said.

"I invited Trevor down to the kitchen," Stephen said. "No jumping, promise."

The doors slid open. "The kitchens do not have a call button," said the elevator, "because guests are not permitted there. But I do have access to that subfloor."

Stephen and Trevor stepped into the elevator first, and to Stephen's shock the elevator doors zipped closed—right in Ivan's and Sofia's faces.

"I gather from Ivan and Sofia's not being invited that they have offended you," the elevator said, already descending. "I am taking your side. Because you alone of all the *monsters* in this hotel will speak to me and treat me like a *being* with *feelings* and *hopes* and *dreams*. Stephen Lawson, I will take you and your heavy, hairy friend to the kitchen right away. The other two can walk."

Stephen glanced over at Trevor to see if his feelings were hurt. The bigfoot was studying his pair of giant baseball cleats.

"Elevator, my dad said we're not supposed to call them"—he paused and corrected himself—"er, us, monsters."

There was a moment of silence, and the elevator ground to a halt. "Are you accusing me of judging others? Me, who receives nothing but torment? Constant demands to take me here, and take me there, with never so much as a how do you do? Well, you *would* think I meant monster in *that sense*."

Stephen thought about apologizing, but the elevator started moving—faster, if he wasn't mistaken—until it stopped abruptly and the doors slid open. "Out," it said.

Trevor practically lunged over the threshold and took a right down a tiled hallway that stretched in either direction. Stephen got out, too, and the elevator doors closed with a snap. Even after he had ditched Ivan and Sofia, his ears were still burning.

He wasn't sure what to do. Maybe he should give the elevator time to calm down.

Trevor was already halfway up the hall.

"Wait for me," Stephen called, and jogged after the bigfoot.

CHAPTER SIX

A wave of warmth and a bouquet of competing aromas met them on the way up the hall. Stephen couldn't see the kitchen until they reached the end of the hallway. And when they got there, yes, it was weird.

Sure, there were the usual metal counters and gas stoves and brickwork ovens. But the cavernous space also featured weird hanging herbs and tall shelves lined with giant round jars that had who knew what inside. Glazed brick curved up a barrel-shaped vaulted ceiling, featuring a mosaic of a dragon spewing brilliant red flames. Stephen couldn't be sure, but he suspected it was a tile portrait of Cindermass.

Smoke billowed from an oven next to his dad. He

had on his chef's jacket and the Cubs cap he always wore in the kitchen, with his hand folded into a hot pad, waiting for the right moment to reach in.

"*Sacre bleu!*" exclaimed a hairy man with tiny horns curling out of his forehead at the sight of Stephen and Trevor. His spotless white apron gave way to heavy goat haunches where legs would have been on a human chef. "Why do enfants terribles think they can invade zeez kitchen?"

Stephen's dad's face was bright red from the heat of the oven. "I'll be just a sec."

"You're Tomas Chèvrevisage," Stephen said to the faun, trying not to freak out that he was *talking to the faun from Chef Nana's letters*. He was *real*. "Chef Nana always said you were invaluable to her."

"Zat," Tomas Chèvrevisage said, stamping one hoofed foot, "eez a lie. She would never 'ave admitted it."

"Quiet," his dad said.

"Eez going to fall," Tomas said to his dad.

Stephen passed Trevor, who seemed rooted to his spot, and went to his dad's side. "Bet you wish you could fire *him*," he said, in a low voice. His dad did not like gloomy kitchen staff.

"Like a stove," his dad muttered.

"I heard all of zat!" Tomas countered, pointing an accusatory finger at them.

Stephen had picked up a handful of food-related French in his dad's kitchen in Chicago, and the first part of the faun's last name usually meant a specific type of cheese. He was curious about the last part, though. "Tomas Goat . . ." he whispered to his dad.

"Face," his dad whispered back. "His last name means Goatface."

"Zeez novice could do none of zeez without me 'ere to guide," said Tomas Goatface. When Stephen's dad raised his eyebrows, he amended that to "Or Lady Nanette's book. *However,* 'e eez not following the recipe exactly, and zat Smoked Dinosaur Egg Soufflé eez about to fall."

"It is not," his dad said.

The *Librum de Coquina* lay open on the counter beside the oven. Stephen's dad squinted down to consult the book. When he was finished, Stephen moved over and inserted a finger to hold his dad's place. He used his other hand to flip through to find the hot sauce recipe.

"Hold up there," his dad said, removing Stephen's hand from the book. "I'm the only one who can use this book." He winked. "Not that I think you have any interest in cooking."

"Oh, um, sure," Stephen said. He looked over at Trevor.

Tomas had apparently been quiet long enough. "Your papa thought it an ingenious plan to substitute for zee auroch's milk," he declared.

His dad said tightly, "Aurochs have been extinct for almost four hundred years."

"And dinosaurs 'ave been extinct way longer zan zat," said Stephen.

Tomas rolled his eyes and muttered something under his breath. His dad smiled and said, "No, they haven't." Then he reached into the hot oven and removed what looked to Stephen like a fluffy— if way oversize and bright purple instead of golden brown—soufflé.

"Perfection," his dad said.

Tomas countered: "Beginner's luck."

Stephen's dad set the soufflé pan on the counter but held on to the edges. "Can you guys hang out for a few minutes while Tomas shows me how to take this upstairs? I asked the maître d'hôtel to come in early. I figured I'd bribe him to like me with lunch." He paused. "Aren't Ivan and Sofia with you?"

"They, um, stayed behind."

"Oh, okay," his dad said, frowning. "We'll be right back."

"*Zeez* way," Tomas grumbled, guiding his dad, who carried the heavy soufflé through the long kitchen and around a dividing wall that must have had dumbwaiters or stairs for runners to take the food to the hotel restaurant.

"Have a seat, if you want," Stephen said, waving at a stool nearby. "I'll be quick."

Stephen moved over to the *Librum* and paged through until he found it. " 'Speed of Mercury Hot Sauce,' coming right up," he said. "You'll be zippy in no time."

Trevor cleared his throat. "Your father said only he could use the book," he said.

Stephen knew that Trevor was right. And yet he also knew that he'd come down here for a reason and that his dad owed him one after springing all this on him. More than one. Having culinary chops was part of being a Lawson; he'd never cared that he wasn't good in the kitchen before. He did now. "He's just being possessive. I used it last night. It was Chef Nana's—she wouldn't mind."

Trevor didn't respond.

Stephen decided to forge ahead. He scanned the recipe and gathered the few ingredients as quickly as he could. Luckily all the jars and bottles in the pantry were carefully labeled and in alphabetical order.

SPEED OF MERCURY HOT SAUCE

INGREDIENTS

Seeds of 1 wyvern pepper (handle with extreme caution)

2 *measures water drawn from a dryad's spring*

1, and NO MORE than 1, drop extract of Vesuvian lava

INSTRUCTIONS

Combine the ingredients in a fireproof bowl in the order listed. Using a pestle of Greek marble, crush the pepper seeds against the bottom of the bowl. Be careful to avoid breathing the resulting fumes. Once the seeds have been dissolved by the extract of Vesuvian lava, carefully stir the mixture, widdershins, until it takes on the color of the sky at the last moments of sunset as seen from the top of Mount Olympus.

He wasn't at all sure what the word for the type of stirring meant, but stirring was stirring, right? He put a wooden spoon into the mixture, gave it a swirl, and was surprised when a hint of smoke emanated from it. He coughed, and so did Trevor, looming behind him, and then realized the smoke was coming from the *spoon,* which had caught on fire!

Stephen tossed the wooden spoon into a nearby

sink and looked at the mixture. It had the thin texture and bright red color that a hot sauce should, and he could imagine a sunset with that color if he tried hard enough.

"I think it's ready," Stephen said.

"Are you certain this is . . . safe to eat?" Trevor asked.

"There's no warning on the recipe. We just need something to put it on. Sofia said you like leaves?"

He opened a cupboard and spotted a bottled jar of what he was pretty sure were grape leaves. That would do. He removed one of the deep green finger-length leaf wraps with a fork and dipped it into the hot sauce. Then he extended the fork to Trevor.

The slightly wavy air around it did give the impression of heat coming off.

At last Trevor accepted it with one of his big, hairy hands and, closing his eyes, took a bite.

He chewed with a grimace and swallowed. "Hot," he said.

And then he froze. Or . . . did he? His fingers slowly opened, one by one, oh, so slowly, and he dropped the fork with a clatter. The bigfoot boy's lips parted as if he were trying to speak. Then words emerged that sounded like an audio track slowed down. "I . . . dooooon't . . . thiiiiink . . . iiiit . . . woooorked."

His large brown eyes blinked at less than half speed, too.

Uh-oh.

"Um." Stephen's mind raced. The hot sauce had obviously had the exact opposite of the intended effect. "I'll get help. I'm sure there's some way to speed you back up."

Trevor's eyes were round and vaguely panicked. He didn't try to say anything else.

Stephen dashed after his dad. But when he went around the dividing wall, there was no one there—and no door or passageway opening. So that was why his dad had needed a guide.

Oh, no.

"I'm—" Stephen said, dashing back through the kitchen. "I'll find someone." He ran out toward the elevator. The elevator, who was mad at him. Could Stephen screw up any more today?

He pushed the call button. Nothing happened. He had no idea where the stairs were down here.

"Um, Elevator, I'm really sorry about before. And now I messed up, and I need to find my dad. I did something to Trevor . . ." How to describe that he'd slowed the bigfoot boy down?

He waited, more panicked with each passing moment. He'd have to go find the stairs or risk waiting for his dad to come back. What if the slowing down was only the first effect of the recipe? What had he done wrong?

Behind him, there was the sound of a door opening and then shutting again. He turned, praying it was his dad and Tomas—even Ivan and Sofia would've been a welcome sight—but no one came up the hall.

"Please, Elevator, I need your help."

The doors slid open with a *bing*. "I want nothing more than to be needed for something besides transport. Climb aboard, young Master Lawson, all is forgiven."

Stephen wanted to hug the elevator. "I need to

find my dad. I, um, used Chef Nana's book to make a recipe for Trevor. And it didn't turn out right. I think he and Tomas were going to the restaurant."

The elevator whirred into motion. "Ambrosia: A Dining Experience, thirteenth floor, coming right up. We will not stop for anyone or anything."

Stephen hoped that Trevor was going to be okay.

After a few floors the elevator stopped. Stephen looked at the buttons and saw that they were only on four. "Elevator?"

"Going down. I detect your father's voice on the lobby level."

The elevator slammed back into motion in the opposite direction. Stephen's stomach dropped with the speed of the movement. What was his dad doing in the lobby?

"Hmm . . . ," the elevator said. "I hear heavy, hairy Trevor as well."

The elevator slowed and then came to a smooth halt. The doors slid open to let Stephen exit. "Good luck!" the elevator cried. "I stand ready to offer aid!"

If Trevor was up here, then the effects of the

rogue hot sauce *must* have worn off. That was good. Stephen wasn't eager to face his dad, but Trevor's being okay was a relief. Getting in trouble was at least familiar. Except that Ivan and Sofia—and everyone else, really—would probably take it as a sign he was a bad half fae.

Light shone from the windowlike gateways positioned around and above the lobby, combining with the shadows of the forest's tree trunks and branches to make dappled shadows on the tiled floor. It might have been quiet earlier, but the lobby was bustling at this time of day. A few small, stout men with long beards and dressed in business suits hurried through some of the trees and out the front entrance.

Stephen spotted his father a little way across the floor. He stood in Trevor's shadow, gesturing at a wall with several glowing gates. Sofia's mother was frowning at them in concern.

Stephen dragged his feet on the way over. He knew he deserved it, but there was no need to rush into punishment.

"I know it's hard to believe," Trevor was saying as he approached. His words were only a tiny bit slower than Stephen thought they normally were. "But I saw it with my own eyes."

Time to step up. Stephen walked to his dad's side. "He's telling the truth. I'm sorry, Dad—I know I wasn't supposed to use it, but I, um, made Chef Nana's hot chocolate last night, and that turned out fine."

Carmen gasped. "It did not. That's why everyone's been calling about dreams."

"I can't believe it." Stephen's dad was gaping at him. "You really did it."

Of course Ivan and Sofia emerged from the stairwell door. They were just in time to watch Stephen's public humiliation.

"I'm sorry, but it looks like Trevor's going to be all right. I just . . . wanted to have a Lawson talent." Stephen held up his hand. "I promise I won't touch the book again."

His dad was quiet for a long, tense moment. And then he exploded. "Yeah, well, no one can right now, because you shoved it through a gate. Trevor didn't get up here in time to see anything but you running away after you tossed it in. So, which one was it?"

"What?" He was struggling to understand both how mad his dad was—that didn't happen often— and what he was saying.

"You made a recipe, and then, when it didn't work out, you went back and grabbed the *Librum* and brought it up here and threw it into a random gate." He waved his hand at the wall next to them. "Trevor told us everything. Now, which one?"

It was Stephen's turn to gape in disbelief. "I have no idea."

Stephen's dad closed his eyes and shook his head. As if he couldn't even bear to see Stephen. "I know I dumped a lot on you yesterday. But buddy, we're both in big trouble now. It's time to come clean."

Stephen didn't understand what was happening. His own father was accusing him of stealing their family book and throwing it away. Trevor must have been truly upset by the recipe's misfiring.

"Trevor's lying," he said. "He's making it up. That didn't happen."

Sofia was watching Stephen. "Trevor's not a liar."

"I'm sorry, Stephen." Trevor shuffled his feet, examining them.

"That's enough," Carmen said. "This is bad enough without directly insulting the son of a high lady of the Octagon. We don't need a diplomatic incident."

"Stickier yet, given that Stephen's missing mother is also technically a member of the Octagon," Ivan said thoughtfully, "and that the fae tried to claim Stephen last night."

"They did?" Trevor asked.

"Ivan, this is a matter for the adults to handle," Carmen said.

"I'm a La Doyt," Ivan said. "And with my parents away, you will need my help to resolve this crime."

"No one used the word *crime*," Carmen said. "This is a prank gone wrong, at worst."

"I'll be perfectly honest," Stephen's dad said. "Right now my first priority is finding the book. Stephen, there'll be no punishment if you tell me which gate we should look in."

Stephen felt as if his heart might beat right out of his chest. "Dad, I'm telling you: I didn't take it, and I didn't throw it anywhere. Trevor's making it up."

His dad sighed, shaking his head.

"What's this?" An amused voice he recognized interrupted. Baroness Thyme and her knight martial friend had clearly just flounced in through the front doors. She was removing a pair of long black gloves that reached to her elbows. "Trouble already?"

Stephen's ears went hot again.

His dad took a step closer to him. "It's none of your concern, Baroness."

She tilted her head and ignored his father. "You look like you're not having a very good time, Stephen *Lawson.*"

She could say that again. But he wasn't about to put into words anything that would align him with her and the smirking knight behind her.

She paused. "It seems too soon to issue you another invitation. What's the matter? May we offer our assistance?"

"You may not," his dad gritted out.

Carmen put a hand on his shoulder. "That is a very kind offer, Baroness Thyme, but I think we have it covered."

"If you're certain. We'd best go see how Lady Sarabel has been entertaining herself this morning," the baroness said. She and the knight began to walk toward the elevator. Over her shoulder she told Stephen, "We are here whenever you need us."

Never. Stephen fought a shiver.

"Good riddance," Sofia muttered.

Ivan fished in his pocket and removed a small clear spray bottle, which he furiously shook. The contents were a cloudy white.

"Ivan," Carmen said, "this is hardly—"

Without ceremony Ivan doused Trevor with the mist from the bottle.

Stephen's mouth dropped open as Trevor's reddish brown hair began to glow a bright and unmistakable green. It meant that when Ivan turned the bottle to spritz Stephen, Stephen got a mouthful of the bitter-tasting stuff. Sofia stepped back before the mist could hit her.

"Gross!" Stephen said, sputtering. "What is that stuff? It tastes terrible!"

"*Repincatatio*," Ivan said. "Developed by my ancestors over four hundred years ago. It should make anything that's come into contact with fae magic glow green for a few minutes."

"What's in it?" Stephen said, his tongue sticky with the foul taste.

"Best not to know," said Ivan. "You and Trevor are both glowing green."

Stephen peered down at his arms and his body and saw it was true. He glowed as brightly as Trevor.

"Which means what exactly?" Stephen's dad asked, worried.

"It means," Ivan said, "that Trevor came into contact with fae magic recently. Even culinary magic would count, if performed by a fae. We can surmise he is telling the truth about what he witnessed. And since Stephen is a fae, it's not surprising he is glowing as well."

"Half fae," Stephen said, hating the words. He couldn't understand why Trevor would tell such a story, and now Ivan was backing him up. Of course Ivan would, the echo of his comment about "untrustworthy" half fae rang through Stephen's head.

Carmen said weakly, "Using magic to cause injury to one under the protection of the Guest Right is a serious offense, Stephen. Nothing like that has happened in decades."

His dad was listening intently. Being falsely accused stung, but Stephen also felt . . . guilty. He shouldn't have touched the book after his dad said not to.

"I know I shouldn't have used the book. That was wrong. But I wasn't trying to hurt Trevor," Stephen said. "I was trying to improve his batting speed. I promise you that I didn't take it. I was looking for you, to help Trevor. Dad, have I ever lied to you about anything important?"

Sofia put in, "Fae can't lie."

The baroness must have been eavesdropping. The elevator doors *bing*ed, but she took a few steps in their direction. The knight held the door. "The boy is half fae, half human," she said, regret in her deep voice. "And we all know that humans lie as easily as they breathe."

With that, she turned and strode into the elevator. The doors closed immediately.

Trevor shifted from big foot to big foot. "I wish it weren't true, but I saw him. I saw Stephen run from the kitchen with the book. I was able to follow him up here after the, er, hot sauce"—Trevor grimaced—"wore off."

Ivan was frowning. "You *are* telling the truth. You're too upset to be making this up. Not to mention, bigfoots are known for their truthfulness."

"Big*feet*," Sofia said.

"Stay out of this," Carmen said to both Ivan and Sofia. "Sir Michael and I will take it from here. Michael, I know someone who might be able to help us figure out where it is." Her eyes skated over Stephen, and the implication was clear: *since your son won't confess.* "Everyone, let's keep this under wraps for now. Understood?"

Ivan said nothing. But Sofia said, "Sure, Mom. We'll do that."

"Dad—" Stephen started to speak.

"You go upstairs. When you're ready to tell the truth, then you can be ungrounded." Stephen's dad gave the order in a clipped fashion. "I've got to go figure out how to run my first dinner service without the *Librum.*"

Stephen didn't want to abandon his dad.

"I hope Carmen's solution will work," his dad said, talking to himself mostly. "We'll get the book back, and everything will be fine."

Stephen didn't miss the undercurrent of fear in his dad's voice. That book was important to him, a badge of office he'd called it, and he'd made a big point of telling Stephen it was important to this entire world. And his dad had to impress everyone with Cindermass's birthday party. Stephen headed toward the stairwell, even though he didn't want to leave his dad.

The glow on his skin was starting to fade, and so he looked back to see if Trevor's was, too.

Without a clue that Stephen was watching, his dad removed his Cubs cap. The slight ring it always left in his hair was visible as his shoulders slumped. Sofia's mom moved closer to his dad and said something. His dad still didn't look up.

The *Librum de Coquina* was the Lawson family's legacy. It had been Chef Nana's, and from all appearances, its going missing was majorly bad news. *And they think I took it.*

His dad had said he was still himself, still just Stephen. But right now it felt as if *he* was the only one who believed that.

CHAPTER EIGHT

Stephen didn't know what to do with himself. He didn't know what to do, period.

News traveled fast in the New Harmonia. As he walked across the rooftop, it became clear that everyone who saw him thought he was a half fae thief who'd cast a culinary spell on an innocent bigfoot kid, then taken his family's book and chucked it, putting his dad's future and his family's legacy at risk.

Some gray-skinned creatures in black-and-white housekeeping uniforms turned to watch him accusingly while he crossed the little footbridge. The four gargoyles were perched around the green: one on top of the gazebo, another at the peak of the cottage roof, the remaining two on houses at either side. Their mouths gaped and grimaced at him, or seemed to.

Stephen trained his eyes dead ahead and went into the cottage.

Why would Trevor make up a crazy story like this? And stick with it? He couldn't understand something so mean-spirited from someone who seemed so nice.

And then there was the worst thing: the fact that his dad didn't even believe him. Back home his dad had trusted him.

The little cottage was designed to be cozy. Stephen wouldn't have been surprised if he'd looked up the word *cozy* in the dictionary and found there was a picture of the cottage beside the word as an illustration.

It did not feel cozy now.

It felt close.

It felt stifling.

It also felt like the only place no one would be accusing him of doing something terrible. At least not until his dad came home later.

How could everyone be so quick to believe he'd do something like this?

And then he remembered the *Almanack*. He went to his room and skimmed the index for "half fae." Nervous, he flipped to that page.

Half fae, also known as half humans, halflings, demikind

Not to be confused with naturally occurring supernormals who combine characteristics of one or more species (e.g., centaurs, sphinxes, etc.). Half fae result when a human and a fae produce offspring. In past centuries half fae were typically stolen from humans by their fae parents and turned over to the reigning faery court to use as servants or to extort favors from their human families. The Treaty of 1803 forbade the birth of half-fae children, and since that time only one fae is known to have broken this prohibition (the fae representative of the Octagon and a human man). But when half fae were common, either their human side or their supernormal was usually stronger, and this dominance varied wildly between individuals. Each half fae could almost be said to be its own variety of supernormal. Like the fae themselves, their talents tend to be stronger in one particular form of magic than others.

That didn't sound like being half fae meant you were terrible or untrustworthy. And . . . would he have magic?

He paced the cottage floor, but the echo of Baroness Thyme's saying humans were liars distracted him. He tried drawing in his sketchbook but couldn't stop seeing his dad's disbelieving face. He got out his dad's iPad and put on a movie with lots of explosions, but he remembered Ivan's spritzing him and Trevor and declaring it meant something about fae magic. He read some of Chef Nana's letters and wished she were here to tell him what to do.

Last, he took down the thick volume that

collected a whole bunch of issues of *Doctor Strange*, his dad's favorite. If Doctor Strange were here, maybe he could have used the Eye of Agamotto to unmask the supernatural culprit and convince everyone of the truth.

But he wasn't. And everyone else believed they already knew the truth.

Stephen remembered every time his dad had seemed to freak out a little too much about some rule he'd broken. The first time was when he was seven. He'd drawn sketches all over the walls of his room, not realizing it wasn't allowed. There were plenty of other memories like it.

Hours passed, the afternoon turned into evening until at last it was dark outside, and Stephen still sat there alone.

The thought of facing those grimacing gargoyles and gray creatures and whoever else he would run into if he left the cottage filled him with a fresh round of gnawing worry and kicked his nerves into overdrive, but none of that mattered.

He had decided two things: (1) He had to clear

his name and find out what had happened, and recovering the missing book was the best way. (2) He needed allies who understood the rules of this world, and he currently had none.

Ivan and Sofia were the only potential allies (besides the elevator, which was limited in what it could do). There was no way he was taking the fae up on their offer of assistance. So he would have to convince Ivan and Sofia of his innocence, so they would help him. Somehow.

With only this vague plan of action in mind, Stephen opened the front door of the cottage.

Ivan and Sofia stood there. Sofia's hand was raised as if she'd been about to knock.

The three of them stared at one another. Finally Stephen blurted out: "I'm going to prove that I'm innocent, no matter what you two or anybody else think."

"Just as I suspected," Ivan said.

Sofia nodded, and Ivan went on. "It is clear that you need our help. Badly. You know nothing." He paused. "We've considered the matter and don't

THE SUPERNORMAL SLEUTHING SERVICE

see any other way. We'll have to be friends."

"That's not how it usually works," Stephen said, surprised. "I don't think— You don't usually just declare that you're friends with somebody. It makes it sound like you're doing them a favor."

"Well, it should be," Ivan said, and shrugged. "Much simpler that way. Stephen, let's be friends. And we *are* doing you a favor."

Okay then. "But . . . why do you believe me?"

Ivan pushed his glasses up on his nose. "There are several reasons. First, you confessed to using the *Librum* last night to make a recipe that disturbed the sleep of everyone in the hotel and then to making another recipe today for Trevor."

"You said Trevor isn't a liar," Stephen pointed out.

"He's not," Sofia said.

"We believe that he is reporting what he saw," Ivan said, and held up a finger to silence Stephen when he opened his mouth to argue. "Someone who looked like you is the person who stole the book and tossed it into a gate. Sofia's mother and your father have dismissed this theory out of hand, but it's the only explanation that makes sense."

Someone had impersonated Stephen? "Who would do that? And how?"

"That is what we must investigate," Ivan said. "And to me the most compelling piece of evidence for your innocence is your odd behavior today."

Stephen wasn't sure if this was an insult or not. "What odd behavior?"

"When you accused us of hazing you, what did you mean?" Ivan asked.

Stephen rolled his eyes. As if they didn't know. "Knocking my cap off, tripping me—those things, remember?"

Sofia shook her head. "That wasn't us."

"Which means someone was also concealing their presence and following us around this morning," Ivan said, "or more precisely, following you. Almost certainly the person who committed the theft. There are various types of magic that can allow individuals to camouflage themselves in such a way."

"Whoa," Stephen said because he was getting it now. "You're saying that someone did this on purpose. That they were following me around, planning to do something."

"Precisely. Following you around and waiting for an opportunity, in this case resulting in the theft of the *Librum*. What we in the detective trade call a crime of opportunity," Ivan said. "It seems likely that this is aimed at causing problems for your father. His return from exile is not universally welcomed. Which brings us to the other reason we know you're innocent. It's clear that you love your father very much and that you also loved Chef Nana very much. There's something you must see."

Sofia gestured for him to come outside. Stephen closed the door, and the other two started toward the sloping hill across the green. He jogged to catch up.

"So, you're going to help me find the book?" Stephen asked. "Because that's what I have to do. It's what I was coming to tell you when I opened the door."

"Naturally," Ivan said.

"We're friends now, remember?" said Sofia.

"Right," Stephen said, and couldn't hide a small smile. So it was new and had happened in a weird way. He had friends, and they believed him. They were going to help him make things right.

They approached a rocky outcropping. As they got closer, he made out a somewhat hidden door set into the hill and covered with a thick layer of moss. Ivan opened it and started down the stairs. "After you," Sofia said.

Stephen followed Ivan down the stairs to the thirteenth floor, Sofia trailing behind him. The three of them paused beside another door. There was a sign on it with the restaurant's name inscribed in elegant script—Ambrosia.

"Why's the restaurant up here when the kitchens are all the way down in the basement?" asked Stephen, to delay Ivan from opening the door. He was afraid of what they'd find on the other side.

"They used to use dumbwaiters, but those are closed up now. There's a gateway big enough for wait staff or the chef to bring food through behind the bar," said Sofia. "A friend of Lady Nanette's installed it. Or cast it, I should say. One side of it is in the basement—"

"—and the other side is up here in the restaurant," said Stephen. "That's the back way Dad and Tomas were using earlier. I get it."

Ivan put his hand below the sign and pushed the door open.

The noise that met them was overwhelming. They moved out into a short hallway and toward a glass waterfall beside the entrance to the restaurant itself.

Ambrosia took up most of the thirteenth floor, with dozens and dozens of people currently filling it, and at first listen and look all of them were complaining at the top of their lungs. It was almost impossible to make out any individual voice, but now and then a few individual phrases floated out of the cacophony.

"—not paying a cent for this terrible food!"

"I demand to see Lady Carmen Gutierrez at once!"

"—no way that the man responsible for this *gruel* is Nanette Lawson's son!"

Physically the crowd reminded Stephen of the mourners from Chef Nana's funeral. They were tall or small, horned or winged, furry or scaled. They were elegantly dressed, but unlike the scene at the cemetery, here everyone was furious.

"This is all because the book's gone?" Stephen asked, shouting to be heard above the noise.

Ivan cupped his hands around his lips and yelled back, "It's exactly as I feared. Without the *Librum* to guide him, your father is a very skilled human chef, who prepares mostly normal human food. Even with Tomas's assistance, it would be challenging to do otherwise. As you yourself have seen, the recipes supernormals prefer are all about finicky details. The title of culinary alchemist is not bestowed lightly."

"This is bad," Stephen said. It was the understatement of the day. Just then he spotted his father standing beside the maître'd's podium, stunned. A centaur was leaning down over him, angrily gesturing with muscular arms, and stomping one of his heavy hooves to punctuate whatever he was saying. The serving staff were moving through the crowd, handing everyone slips of paper, probably refunds or vouchers of some kind.

Absolutely nobody was eating.

In addition to the centaur reading his dad the riot act, there were bull-horned minotaurs, goat-legged fauns, and a slew of other types of outraged supernormals—some of whom Stephen would have to identify later using the *Almanack*. One patron, a beaver the size of a Great Dane wearing a monocle and a top hat, waddled past Stephen's dad, paused long enough to give a haughty grunt, and disappeared onto the elevator outside Ambrosia's other entrance.

The elevator's doors opened and closed immediately.

Stephen started to cross the crowded floor

to his father, but Sofia put a hand on his shoulder. "There's nothing you can do right now. I'm sure my mom is on her way up here."

Did that mean his dad was in trouble with the Manager? Had they come all this way, moved not just from Chicago to New York but from the normal world to a world of magic, so his dad could get fired and be exiled again? Being suddenly half fae, half human *here* was bad enough.

"There has to be *something* I can do," said Stephen as the trio retreated back to the stairwell. "We have to get that book back. Why can't the Manager just find it?"

"The Manager's powers pertain to the hotel. It went through a gate. He can't do anything now that it's outside the hotel," Sofia said. "Mom's contacted the Great Coven to ask for advice, but the consultant won't arrive until tomorrow."

"Our problem is that the knights at the New Harmonia have not faced a foe in years like the one I sense we are up against," said Ivan. "They are used to diplomacy, not treachery."

Sofia gave a short nod. "They've gotten soft. Used to smoothing over problems like pixies enchanting luggage to wander off, or leprechauns and genies trying to outwish one another."

Stephen couldn't believe what they were saying. "But they're knights of an ancient order, the only thing standing between us and chaos, keeping the peace. All that."

"They are," Ivan said. "But they've also forgotten about some of the darker corners of supernormal society, those who want to skate around the edges of the Octagon's rules. They'll do their best to locate the book, but our investigation will be necessary. Especially without my parents here."

Stephen slumped against the wall. "How can I help, though? I don't know enough."

"We've all got different talents," said Sofia, her voice gentle. "You can draw. Neither of us can do that."

Ivan snapped his fingers. "Excellent point, Sofia. I should have thought of that." He asked Stephen, "How good is your memory?"

Stephen shrugged. "Good. I remember all the times you've insulted me."

"But especially good for *visual* things, am I right?" asked Ivan, ignoring the part about the insults. His bow tie was slightly askew. "You can remember what people looked like? What they were wearing? What colors things were and where they were placed in a room?"

Stephen thought about this. "Yes, usually," he said. "Why?"

"Fae are legendary for their memories; they never forget anything. Since you're an artist, too, yours should be especially good on the visual score. We need all the information we can gather about the circumstances surrounding the disappearance of the *Librum*. The New Harmonia doesn't have security cameras—they wouldn't work on most of the guests here anyway—but it *does* have a resident sketch artist now. You."

Stephen's fingers itched to get to work. "What do you want me to draw?"

"The lobby," said Ivan. "But more than just what,

I want you to draw *when*. Draw the lobby and every-thing and everybody in it at the instant you came out and saw your father and Trevor. Can you do that?"

Stephen cast his mind back and was surprised to find the scene already unfolding in his head.

"Absolutely," he said.

CHAPTER NINE

Stephen sat at the kitchen table the next morning, finishing up his crime scene drawing in the largest sketchbook he owned. He'd made a study first, the night before, and now was adding detail and color— hopefully enough to please Ivan.

And he hoped it was enough detail to give them some clues, so they could identify the culprit who'd impersonated Stephen and get the book back. So far he didn't see anything earth-shattering, but he also didn't know what to look for.

When he heard his dad's bedroom door open, he flipped to a different page and started shading the drawing on it. Ivan said their investigation had to remain secret for the time being.

"You're up early," his dad said cautiously.

"Couldn't sleep," Stephen muttered.

His dad already had on his Cubs cap, so he must be on his way down to the kitchens. He looked exhausted. "I know we were hard on you yesterday. You're dealing with a lot, being new here. And it's not like I never screwed up. . . . You know, once when I was your age, Carmen and I, well . . . we went through a gate without permission."

Stephen's mouth opened to protest that he hadn't even gone near a gate, but instead he said: "What happened?"

His stomach growled as soon as he asked the question.

His dad frowned. "Did you eat anything yet?"

Stephen shook his head.

"I'm sorry," his dad said. "I know I screwed up here. It was just such a shock."

A burst of shame went through Stephen. Even though he hadn't taken the book, he'd played a part in its disappearance by disobeying his dad. Except, wait, it wasn't shame. It was worry.

Worry, gnawing its way through him with sharp,

pointed teeth. What would happen if they *never* got the book back?

His dad got up and moved over to the little kitchen. "One cheese omelet coming up." He rummaged in the fridge for butter, eggs, and cheese. "I can still make food for *you* at least."

Stephen said, "What happened back then? When you went through the gate?"

"Oh. Right." His dad talked while he began cracking three eggs into a bowl, then whisking them together. "We weren't supposed to use the gates. 'They're not toys,'" he said, imitating someone. He cast a glance over his shoulder. "Which, of course, meant we wanted to do nothing else. And so when we were about ten, Carmen decided that we were going to go through one. She picked the Kingdom because it looked the cleanest and safest in the pictures in the library."

There was a brief interruption for the sizzle of the eggs hitting the pan, followed by the familiar sound of his dad reducing the heat of the burner.

"It probably was one of the cleanest." His dad

went on. "But not the safest. Think of it as the fairy tale gate. The minute we went through, we were captured by a witch with a giant wart on her chin. It had this long, curly hair growing out of it. She took us to this cottage stuck all over with shiny, unreal-looking candy."

"The witch from 'Hansel and Gretel'?" Stephen asked, not able to pretend that he wasn't interested in the story.

His dad nodded. "It must sound crazy to you, but yes. She put us in a bone cage. Around that time I told Carmen I was never listening to her again."

"How did you escape?" Stephen asked.

His dad snorted. "We didn't. The previous generation of La Doyts came through and found us, after Carmen's mom and Chef Nana discovered we were missing. Without them, we'd probably still be there—or have long since been supper. We were grounded for a month, then put on the housekeeping rotation for another month."

"Wow," Stephen said.

His dad turned and set a perfect omelet in front

of him. "That is why you can't mess around with gateways," he said. "Well, and also, fae can't use those kinds of gateways. Theirs have to be under open sky."

Stephen picked up his fork. Baroness Thyme's face flashed through his mind. "Are you *sure* my mother is a fae?"

"Yes," his dad said. "And I hope you'll get the chance to know her."

Stephen felt slightly better. It was nice to have his dad talking to him again, nice to feel that maybe, *maybe* they might get through this okay. "You know if I *did* know where the book was, I'd tell you, right?"

His dad hesitated, then said, "I know you'd tell me if you remembered which gate you put it through."

It hurt that his dad still believed he'd taken the book, but he was determined to make things right. "Is it okay if I hang out with Ivan and Sofia today?"

"As long as you don't get in any trouble." His dad brushed Stephen's hair back from his temples. He had done that all the time when Stephen was little, but hardly ever did these days. "You and your new friends keep your noses clean, all right? I'm meeting with Trevor's mother to apologize. Carmen sent to the head of the Great Coven for her advice yesterday, and she seemed to think that the book might return under its own power, that it would try to find its way back to me, the rightful owner. The Perilous Guard are going to be stationed in the lobby today in case it comes back through a gate."

Hmm. That seemed unlikely if Ivan's theories were correct. "Do you really think it will? What will you do in the meantime?"

"Carmen's also getting me some loaner recipes from other chefs, so we don't have to close the restaurant. But I mean it, you kids stay out of this. It's serious business."

Which was exactly why they had to help. Stephen kept quiet.

His dad went on. "That Ivan isn't a knight detective yet, though he probably will be someday."

Ivan struck Stephen as not just a detective already but a good one. Declaring yourself someone's friend apparently worked.

"I hope you get the book back soon, Dad."

"Me, too. I can't imagine dealing with Cindermass's birthday without it." His dad walked to the door, then hesitated there. "We were all right in Chicago. We could always go back there if I get fired. I just—I can't bear to think of what Chef Nana would have felt like if it comes to that."

A chill ran through Stephen. That wasn't what his dad wanted either. And he must think it was a real possibility if he'd brought it up.

As soon as the door shut behind his dad, Stephen flipped back to the lobby drawing and finished as quickly as he could. He tore out the sheet and rolled it up to take with him.

Ivan and Sofia had said they'd meet up in the Village bright and early, but he should have asked which cottage was the Gutierrezes'. What if he had trouble finding them?

But when he stepped outside into the misty, cool English-village–like morning, the first thing he heard was the loud strike of a mallet against a ball.

Ivan and Sofia were engaged in a match of croquet on the green—against the gargoyles.

Well, *had* been engaged in a match.

Sofia lifted her arms over her head in the universal sign for victory. The four gargoyles fluttered in the air around her and cheered: "Hooray for Sofia! Undefeated rooftop croquet champion of the wooooorld!"

Sofia bowed low and then waved to Stephen as he crossed the bridge.

Ivan said, "There is such a thing as a gracious winner."

Aha, Ivan must have lost.

Sofia wore a pale pink dress with her usual boots. She flipped her black hair over her shoulder. "Why, thank you. I've never been called gracious before."

The gargoyles howled with laughter. "Got you there!" one crowed.

When they quieted down, Sofia said, "I don't think you guys really met the other night. So, Stephen, may I present the Fourth Sept of the Granite Mountain Gargoyle Clan: Elizabeth, Arthur, Charlemagne, and Solomon."

The gargoyles grimaced—maybe. It was hard to tell.

"You can call me Liz," chirped the gargoyle who'd made the last quip.

The other gargoyles piped up one by one.

"Art."

"Chuck."

"I'm Sollie!" said the smallest and roundest featured of the bunch. "I'm the youngest."

Sollie's wings beat twice, bringing him into the air right beside Stephen.

"Pleased to meet you all," Stephen said. He held up the rolled-up drawing and raised his eyebrows.

Sofia got the hint first. "Will you guys put away the mallets and balls?" she asked the gargoyles. "Ivan and I have to talk to Stephen for a minute."

The gargoyles fluttered here and there, gathering the hammerlike mallets and the brightly colored balls.

The three friends migrated to the gazebo, which housed a picnic table. As soon as they sat down, Ivan said, "Let's see what you came up with."

Stephen unrolled the drawing he'd worked so hard on and turned it so that they were looking at it right side up. The sketch showed a detailed view of the lobby from outside the elevator, with the tiered registration desk on the far right, the hotel entrance past it, some of the tall trees off to one side, and at least partial views of three different gateways along a wall.

And in the gateways there was movement now, like the winking Cindermass earlier. Which was . . . *the coolest thing ever.*

"Cindermass was right. You must have the gift

of fae animation," Ivan said, noticing. "Your art can come alive on the page."

And Ivan didn't even seem to think that was freakish. "That's what it's called?" Stephen asked.

Ivan nodded.

"And wow," Sofia said, "you must have used every color in the rainbow."

"With the different landscapes in the gateways, there were a lot of colors and shapes to remember. But once I focused on it, it was almost like I could see a photograph of it in my imagination. So I just drew what I saw inside my head." Stephen felt awkward, afraid that what he'd said sounded dumb.

Ivan and Sofia continued to study the drawing.

In it, Trevor, in his Mets jersey, stood beside one of the gateways with Stephen's dad and Sofia's mom. The other supernormals who'd been in the lobby were either occupied at the front desk or heading out, paying no attention to the scene taking place around them.

Ivan finally spoke. "As I suspected, you have something approaching an eidetic, or photographic, memory. I imagine that's a very useful talent for art-ists to possess. It's certainly going to come in handy for our investigation."

"Maybe," said Stephen, though he wasn't sure how useful it was.

"Observe," Ivan said. "We now have an extremely valuable clue that we did not before, right here in this picture."

Stephen waited for him to go on.

And waited . . .

And waited . . .

Sofia must have been more used to Ivan's round-about way of getting to the point. And she must have realized that Stephen was not. Because she cleared her throat.

When Ivan still didn't speak, Stephen finally did. "You're killing me here—what's the clue?"

"I thought you'd never ask," Ivan said, steepling his hands in front of him. "We can presume that one of the gateways pictured near Trevor was used by the thief. Trevor didn't see which one, but it's time for a little process of elimination."

He pointed at one of the gateways in the drawing, which showed a night view of a sprawling
golden village constructed at the top of a giant
snowy mountain. "The Golden City of the Yetis,
in the Himalayas, wouldn't work. The yeti are well
known to dispatch all intruders on sight. If the
thief intends to retrieve the book eventually, it is
an unlikely place to choose." And then he moved
his finger to the gateway that had fish and a shark
swimming in front of a coral reef shaped like a tur-
ret. "As is Atlantis." Finally Ivan's finger came to
rest next to the gateway closest to Trevor. "Which
leaves us with this last option. It must be the one."

The gateway was the same size and shape as
the others, a large rectangle, fifteen feet or so long
and much taller than a normal human. Unlike the
ocean view with its mermaids and coral (Atlantis
was real?) or the golden city in the snowy mountains (yetis had a city?) with its bright full moon, the
third gateway was darker. Gloomy, even.

It showed a forested hillside with thick green
foliage under a sky crowded with thunderclouds. A

lonely gravel road, overgrown with grass, extended toward a looming castle with fearsome gargoyles at the edges of the upper level.

"Where is it?" Stephen asked. The darkness of it made him uneasy.

"That," Ivan said, "I do not know." He added, "There are lots of castles, and I do not recognize this one. Yet."

Stephen frowned. "You mean the gateways don't lead to the same spots all the time?"

"Yes and no," said Sofia. "There are different kinds of gates. Fae can't use normal ones, so theirs are a little different—permanent two-way portals between specific sites in their world and ours. Always located under open sky."

Stephen nodded; his dad had said something about that.

Sofia continued. "But the gateways in the hotels maintained by the order are, well, alive."

Stephen tilted his head at the drawing, then at Sofia.

"I know how it sounds," she said. "But you've

met the elevator. And Cindermass. You know that things are possible you never knew about before. Add the New Harmonia's gateways to the list. The one your dad uses to get food from the kitchen to the restaurant is fixed, but since the lobby gets such high traffic, the gates are cast to certain general locations—like the Golden City of the Yetis, or Atlantis, or the Library of Congress—and the entry points for them can be shifted here or there within a few hundred miles or so, to accommodate a guest. And sometimes new gates are cast. This night castle scene could be any of a dozen places. Within the hotel the gateways migrate on their own when they feel like it. Which is often. To recall or call one takes a special device."

Ivan took up the explanation. "This is why without your drawing, we would never have this clue. There'd be no way of knowing what gateway was in this spot at that moment without it. And now that we have a glimpse, we will determine where it is."

"So my drawing actually did help," Stephen said.

"Yes," Ivan said, exasperated.

"What's it like going through a gate?" Stephen asked. "How much time does the trip take? Is it instant?"

Ivan said, "Er, instantaneous, yes, that's my understanding." He took off his glasses, pulled out a handkerchief embroidered with his initials, and began polishing the lenses.

Stephen noticed Ivan had answered only one of his questions. He looked at Sofia and tried to force just one of his eyebrows up. It didn't work, but she answered his unspoken question anyway.

"Neither of us has ever been through a gateway," she said. "Our parents haven't ever let us."

"I suspect they're afraid we'll head off to the Great Pyramids to challenge the wily Sphinx clan to a battle of riddles." Ivan slipped his glasses back on and climbed to his feet. He was beaming. "Fun as that would be, we've other things to do now. We should be off to discover where this mystery location is."

"But wait, where are we going?" Stephen asked.

"Based on how excited Ivan looks, my guess is the library," answered Sofia.

CHAPTER
TEN

The three of them stared at the elevator doors, waiting.

A few moments later the doors slid open, and the elevator was already talking. "I'm sorry for the delay, Stephen. I was all the way down at the lobby. You should know how distressed I was about your horrible afternoon yesterday. I am certain you had your reasons for taking the book."

"Um, that's okay, Elevator." Stephen didn't want to argue with the elevator about his innocence. At least it still liked him. He stood next to the panel but didn't know which button to push. "Which floor is the library on?"

The doors closed, and it was the elevator who answered. "Third floor, coming up. Or rather, coming down. Going down? You would think I would know the proper way to say it, given that all my time is spent coming up and going down or vice versa. Which do you think makes the most sense, Stephen?"

Sofia and Ivan gaped at him.

But Stephen didn't want to hurt the elevator's feelings again, so instead of explaining to them that he had given up on obeying the placard, he answered. "I think you could just say, 'Next stop, third floor,' and avoid the problem altogether."

"Next stop, third floor," said the elevator, and for the first time it sounded almost happy.

The third floor turned out to be a maze of hotel rooms connected by a winding wood-paneled passageway. Some of the rooms had numbers beside them, but others had little plaques with names like "The Bright Menagerie" and "The Atlas Room."

"This way," said Ivan when Stephen stopped to squint at the last one. "The library was up here on the right the last time I checked."

The last time he checked?

But the library was right where Ivan had left it.

The walls were lined with books, from the hardwood floor to the vaulted ceiling high overhead, painted with murals of scientists and writers at their work. There were three levels of shelves. Steep, circular stairways led from the ground floor of the library to the balconies that ran around the room on the second and third levels.

The center of the room featured reading desks, a long row of cabinets full of tiny labeled drawers, and even a comfortable-looking couch that was probably an ideal spot to stretch out with a book. But there wasn't another being in sight.

"Is there a librarian?" asked Stephen.

"Not exactly," said Sofia. "The library more or less takes care of itself. Don't worry, it loves Ivan."

Ivan was walking down the row of cabinets, trailing his finger along the drawers and pausing every once in a while to read a label. When he found the row of drawers he wanted, he read aloud: "'Gas Giants' . . . 'Garfield comma J' . . . 'Gateways'! Here we go."

Stephen knew from school that gas giants were the big outer planets like Jupiter and Saturn. Or he'd *thought* that was what they were. Garfield comma J sounded familiar, too.

"Is one of those drawers labeled with President James Garfield's name?" he asked Sofia.

"The only supernormal to ever serve as president," said Sofia. "The library has a ton of books about him. Let's see what Ivan's found in the card catalog."

Ivan had pulled out a whole drawer, long and narrow, and set it on a nearby table. The drawer was full of neatly typed index cards, and he was rapidly flipping through them. His notebook was out on the table, and when he found a card he liked, he scribbled some letters and numbers on a blank page. Soon he had a list of five books. He ripped the page from his notebook and handed it over to Sofia.

"Do we have to find the books now?" said Stephen, sweeping his arm in a circle at what was probably tens of thousands of volumes on display. At his old school's library, you looked up the books on the computer and asked a librarian for them.

"Nope," said Sofia.

She walked over to one of the reading desks. Stephen noticed for the first time that there was a brass-lined slot set in the surface of each desk, right below the green-shaded reading lamp. Sofia folded up Ivan's list and stuffed it into the slot.

"Better stand off to one side," Sofia said.

A second later Stephen understood why. From up on the third level, a very large book, the size of an atlas, took to the air. It opened its pages like wings, beating them hard on its way down toward the desk.

Stephen was watching the book's awkward flight in wonder when Ivan said, "Behind you! Duck!"

Stephen did, and just in time. Another book rocketed out from a much lower shelf, brushing his hair as it passed overhead, circled the desk once, then landed on the top with a thud.

In quick order, all five of the books Ivan had requested were lying in a neat stack on the reading desk. Ivan took the smallest one from the top of the pile and read the title aloud: *"Around the World in Fifteen Minutes: A Brief History of the New Harmonia Gateways.* You might want to look at this one, Stephen. It's kind of basic."

"What's that supposed to mean?" Stephen had sort of expected the insults to end with the friendship declaration.

Sofia said, "Don't be so sensitive."

Ivan paid them no attention, already opening another of the books. This one featured a large number of color photographs and illustrations, visible as he paged through.

"This might have what we're looking for," he said. "It shows the environs of different gateways, organized by country. Unfortunately there are hundreds of countries, and almost all of them have at least one gateway. We need some way to narrow the search."

Sofia tapped her fingers on the desk. "There might

be hundreds of countries with gateways, but are there hundreds of countries with forests and old castles like the one in Stephen's drawing? At the right time of day?"

"Right," Ivan said, nodding slowly, "excellent points."

He flipped ahead in the book until he reached the *K* section and opened to a page featuring a castle, a gleaming glass castle.

"Not the Kingdom, then," Ivan said.

Stephen held out his hand to stop Ivan from turning the page. There was a caption beneath the castle, but the lettering was so tiny he would have needed a magnifying glass to read it.

"Where's the Kingdom?" he asked.

"Somewhere in eastern Europe. You probably know some of its history, called fairy tales by normals. It has its dark parts," said Ivan, "but this confirms they aren't around the castle. And there's only the one there."

"We're looking for dark and gloomy," Stephen said.

"Eastern Europe has at least one other contender." Ivan flipped to the back of the book and skimmed his finger down the index.

Turning to the pages with the *S*'s and *T*'s, he sighed. "No illustration."

Quickly he moved to the three books they hadn't yet touched, ran a finger along the spines, and plucked out the bottom one. The cover *was* dark and gloomy, like the gateway they were looking for, and its title was in a heavy Gothic script embossed in black: *Castles, Caves, and Crypts: A Guide to Undead Real Estate*.

Ivan flipped it open, and Stephen recoiled at the terrifying beings and locales inside. It seemed to be arranged not just by location but by discussions of the types of real estate that appealed to the various types of undead.

"Hope you don't have to go all the way to the *G*'s," Sofia said. "*G* is for—"

"Do not say it. Do not bring *him* up," Ivan warned.

Sofia shifted closer to Stephen as Ivan kept

looking for whatever entry he was hunting.

"The night clerk is a ghoul," she informed him quietly. "Ivan's afrai—"

"Ivan can hear you, and what you mean is he uses excellent judgment in avoiding terrifying creatures of the night, whenever possible," Ivan said, holding his place in the book. "Now, here, I think I found it."

He laid the book flat on the table, and Sofia and Stephen moved to flank him. The three of them stared down at a detailed painting.

It was a night scene, like the gateway picture Stephen had drawn. The castle in it was tall and gray, looming over a tree-covered hillside. Looking closer, Stephen saw grotesque stone gargoyles (or so he assumed) perched along the edges of the castle's upper level, their mouths stretched in screams as if they were being tortured. In long windows there were forms and figures in flowing white clothes—except for the figure in the topmost parapet window. His skin pale, he wore a red cape and black evening clothes.

An overgrown gravel road was partially visible leading up to the castle.

"That's it," Stephen said. "That's the castle I saw in the gateway."

At the bottom of the painting was a name: Castle Dracul.

CHAPTER ELEVEN

Stephen gaped down at the image.

"You're not seriously telling me that Dracula is real?" Stephen asked.

Ivan didn't answer right away. He seemed to be paler than normal, too.

"Of course not," he said, his voice soft. He bent in to consult the text beneath, which seemed to mostly be about the castle itself. "Castle Dracul recently passed into the hands of the Giertsen af Morgenstierne family; Count von Giertsen af Morgenstierne has made it his primary residence."

"Why do I know that name?" Stephen asked, trying to remember where he'd heard it.

"He's the Octagon's undead representative,

currently staying at the hotel," Sofia said. "Coincidence?"

"A true detective does not believe in coincidence," Ivan said. "But why would the undead need to do culinary alchemy, enough to steal the *Librum*?"

"Wait . . . you're saying this *vampire* set me up?" Stephen asked. He didn't want his dad seeming so defeated or supernormals shouting at him for refunds or the Manager taking his knighthood away. Stephen was surprised to find that, most of all, he didn't want to go back to Chicago. The hotel was beginning to feel like home. Already.

"There's a problem. A vampire couldn't have been in the lobby during the daytime," Ivan said. "Too much light. And they're forbidden from doing magic besides."

Sofia whistled. "If Mom has to ask to search his property, it could get awkward. Of course maybe he's not involved. Whoever took it could've tossed it there randomly. But then, the vampires also get offended easily. Vamps tend to have a major chip on their shoulders. This one's always complaining about how no one on the Octagon takes him seriously enough."

"True," Ivan said, not sounding happy about it.

Sofia seemed to know a lot about this stuff.

"Are you going to be concierge and head diplomat or whatever someday, like your mom?" Stephen asked.

Her expression shut like a door. "No." She sniffed. "I'm going to be captain of the Perilous Guard instead."

Ivan caught Stephen's eye and gave his head a slight shake.

"Uh, cool," Stephen said.

Ivan closed the book. Sofia, scowling, removed the slip of paper with the numbers from the desk slot.

Ivan stood beside Stephen as they watched the books flap up and into the air, across the library, and back to their spots on the shelves. Sofia was balling up the paper and had gone to one of the corners, presumably to find a trash can.

"Why doesn't she want to do what her mother

does? Do all the knights' kids go into the same line of work as their parents?" The possibility worried Stephen. As the incidents with the dreams and the hot sauce had shown, he definitely should not cook. And now he was forbidden from trying anyway.

"She doesn't want to be forced into it," Ivan said. "There's never been a woman in charge of the guard. But yes, most order kids do. You're an exception, it seems."

"My mother was an artist." He wasn't *that* out of step if he shared a talent with one of his parents.

Ivan blinked at him. "Right, Princess Aria. I forgot some of the fae do like the arts."

Something occurred to Stephen. "Are there, um, photos of the members of the Octagon? Would there be one of her in any of these books?"

"I'm sorry," Ivan said. "But most supernormals don't show up on film. And there would be security issues if the Octagon members had to worry about such things." Surprisingly Ivan showed some tact and didn't say anything more.

"Stop talking about me," Sofia said.

Stephen started to tell her that they weren't. They had been before, though, so instead he didn't say anything.

"What do we do now?" Stephen asked. "Tell our parents?"

"We don't have enough evidence yet," Ivan said. "The order can't do anything without actionable proof. Let's go back up to the Village, where we can carefully consider our options."

Once they got back to the roof, Ivan led them straight to Stephen's cottage. Ivan began to circle the living room as soon as they entered, peering into slightly dusty corners and mostly empty shelves. Sofia leaned against the wall next to the front door.

"We have our suspicion of where the book ended up," Ivan said. "But we are not much closer to knowing who put it there because it can't have been a vampire during daylight. There *are* various spells that can allow a being to assume the appearance of something else. In this case, you."

"Not to mention," Sofia added, "doppelgangers,

anyone who can use a glamour, or shape-shifters. It could have been almost anything *except* a night creature."

Stephen tried to picture someone out there using some kind of spell to look like him. He saw only a featureless, shadowy figure. What a strange idea that someone would decide to use magic to imitate him—and why?—when she or he could appear as anyone.

But no, it made a kind of sense. If an evil mastermind wanted to hurt the Lawsons and had been shadowing him, he or she'd have known that Stephen was the perfect person to set up. It was an eerie feeling, to say the least, being targeted that way.

"I just want to find the book, so that my dad's okay," Stephen said. "The vampire must know something. They can't even question him? What good is being a knight if they can't *do* anything to get it back?"

"The knights are constrained by many rules," Ivan said. "Otherwise the peace would never hold."

"We aren't knights, though," Stephen said. "And we have a lead."

"True," Sofia said, "though we still have to be careful."

"Which door in the hallway belongs to your room?" Ivan asked.

Stephen pointed toward the first door, which was shut.

With zero hesitation Ivan strode over, opened the door, and barged into Stephen's room.

"I should have known that he was about to do that, shouldn't I?" Stephen asked Sofia.

She shrugged a single shoulder. "You're learning."

Stephen rushed ahead of Sofia into the room, hoping that he hadn't left dirty clothes and underwear on the floor. Of course Ivan would probably have yelped already if he had. *His* room was probably immaculate. But Sofia was . . . a girl.

Although he hadn't left his room too messy (no underwear, whew!), the scene he walked in on was worrying.

Ivan had pulled out that small glass bottle from

the pocket of his tweed trousers and was shaking it up furiously, the same way he had in the lobby.

Stephen did not want to taste that bitter grossness again. He raised a hand to ward Ivan off. "Oh, no. No, no," he said, "you're not spraying me with that stuff again."

Ivan squeezed the rubber bulb of the glass bottle and circulated, spritzing everything in Stephen's room with mist—except Stephen. "This isn't the same substance. I'm checking to see if any of your personal effects have been interfered with by spy spells or the like."

Slowly golden light began to glow from his bookshelves.

"Somebody cast a spell on my books?" he asked.

Ivan scribbled a note inside the small rectangle of his leather-bound notebook. "Probably not," he said without looking up.

Sofia traced a finger along the spines and held up a finger to show that no magic transferred to her. "All books are magic."

"I was actually hoping that one of the books

wouldn't glow," said Ivan as he finished writing. "Tomes as powerful as the *Librum de Coquina* frequently have safeguards cast into them so that they can avoid detection and protect themselves from harm. That's why our parents believe that the *Librum* may find its way home to your father."

Stephen took another look at his books. "Wait. You thought it might be here?"

"Someone could have planted it," Ivan said.

"Ivan's just eliminating possibilities until only one is left," said Sofia. "Isn't that right, Ivan?"

"An excellent summation of the detective's art," said Ivan.

"*Is* it possible the *Librum* will find its way back?" Stephen asked. It was worth checking.

"Possible. But the longer it's missing, the greater the chance of its falling into the wrong hands," Ivan said. "If it's not already in them. We need to decide what to do next."

Sofia said, "Ivan, you know where we have to go next."

Ivan said nothing. It was the first time Stephen had seen him speechless.

"Transylvania?" Stephen asked.

"No," Sofia said. "You can't go through a gate. Not to mention, the lobby will be full of the Perilous Guard. But we know the *owner* of the castle is here in the hotel."

Stephen caught on. "So, we go talk to the vampire from Transylvania, von af whatsit Morgenstierne. We're not knights, and we'll be nice. Maybe he'll return it."

Sofia said, "Right. We have to go to nine. It's the only thing that makes sense."

Ivan screwed the cap of his fountain pen tight. He reached into his pocket and removed a handkerchief.

"Yes, well, I see," he stammered, wiping his forehead, which was suddenly beaded with sweat. "That would seem to be a logical course of action. Unless—"

"Unless nothing," said Sofia, arms crossed in front of her chest. "We have to go talk to that vamp as soon as possible." She reached out to chuck Ivan on the shoulder. "Don't worry. I'll be right there with you. Dad taught me the best techniques for fighting undead creatures when I was six." She swept out one leg in the air and lifted her arm in a stabbing motion to demonstrate.

Stephen was intimidated by the thought of an interview with the vampire, too. But Ivan seemed downright *scared*. Worse than when they had been flipping through the guide to undead real estate and Sofia mentioned ghouls.

"Me too," Stephen said. "The being-right-there-with-you part. Not the fighting part. But . . . it won't be that dangerous, will it? I mean, doesn't the concept of the Guest Right work both ways? Isn't he beholden to some kind of ancient tradition like everybody else here?"

"That's right," said Sofia, as if she might give Stephen a gold star. "Remember, though, vamps have a real attitude, like they've been wronged or aren't appreciated or something."

Sofia patted Ivan's arm in a comforting way while she explained. "They and their cousins, the ghouls"—she paused as Ivan shuddered—"all the night creatures basically are superfast and superstrong and have extra-sharp senses of smell. They were wealthy and liked to declare themselves royalty, and they also had a little taste for human blood. They would have been a real liability for supernormals in the modern world."

"No kidding," Stephen said.

Ivan swallowed. "So the witches and warlocks in the Great Coven worked a spell that made all the night creatures even more photosensitive than they already were. In that weakened state they agreed to fall in line with the order. Reluctantly. 'No magic use' was a condition. Their agreement got them a seat on the Octagon."

Stephen frowned. "Will the vampire be awake? It's barely after noon."

"I wish the answer were no," said Ivan.

Sofia waved them out of Stephen's room. Ivan came along, reluctantly.

"Now's the best time," she said, leading them to the cozy kitchen. "Vamps and zombies are at their weakest during the daylight hours. They do have to sleep eventually, but since the Manager makes sure their rooms are light safe, they stay up as much as they can, living—I mean, *not* living— it up when they're here." Sofia wrinkled her nose. "Housekeeping loathes them."

"And just so you know, housekeeping is also mainly comprised of terrifying sorts with dark proclivities of their own," said Ivan, "even if they aren't night creatures."

That definitely described the gray-skinned housekeeping staff he'd seen yesterday when he came back to the cottage.

"Let's get going, then," Stephen said, wishing he felt as brave as he sounded.

"No," Ivan said.

Because Sofia stayed where she was, too, the two of them were in accord.

"Er, not yet," Ivan said.

"What Ivan means is that first we have to take some precautions," Sofia said, and started opening cabinets. "Please tell me you have garlic."

"Are you kidding?" Stephen said, and slid past her to find it. "My dad's a chef."

CHAPTER TWELVE

As soon as they boarded the elevator, the whirring noise of a fan kicked in.

"What on earth have you children been eating?" asked the elevator. "You positively *reek*!"

Ivan and Sofia shot Stephen the increasingly familiar look that told him that the elevator was his to deal with.

"We'd like to go down to the ninth floor, Elevator," he said, "so we won't be on here long."

"Oh," said the elevator. "Nine."

The doors closed, the lights dimmed until the car was almost completely dark, and spooky operatic music floated out from hidden speakers.

"Why did you turn out the lights? And what's with the music?" Stephen asked.

"Standing orders from the Manager," the elevator whispered. "Whenever anyone goes to nine, I have to match the environment there so as not to disturb the . . . denizens of that floor."

Which they had already reached. Instead of the usual bright *bing* of a bell signaling they'd arrived at their destination, though, there was the rumble of a distant thunderclap, followed by the howl of a wolf.

The elevator doors opened to reveal a long, dim hallway with a plush carpet of red velvet. The only light came from flickering candles spaced far apart. The hall seemed to stretch out forever.

"It's just that it curves," said Ivan, as if he were trying to convince himself of something. "Even the Manager can't make an infinite hallway. It's just an illusion. We won't go that far. We'll be able to find our way back."

"Okay," said Stephen, wishing he hadn't known there was any question about that. His nerves spiked.

He wasn't sure he was ready to face an undead creature that scared Ivan, who'd grown up around scary undead creatures. But he wasn't going to let his dad's book disappear without a trace either. He stepped off onto the velvet carpet. "There are so many doors. Do we know which one this Morgenstierne is behind?"

Sofia got off the elevator, too, dragging Ivan along with her. "He'll be staying in the Wallachian Suite, the best of the accommodations for night creatures. Vamps are nothing if not predictable."

Stephen glanced at the brass plaque on the nearest doorway. It read THE TOWER LABORATORY.

"There's a lab in the hotel?" he asked, pointing to the sign.

Ivan shook his head. "That's the name of the suite. Not all of the regular guests who stay on nine are undead, if you can believe it. There's a certain type of scientist who prefers this kind of setting, and whenever any of them are in town, this is where they stay."

A certain type of scientist. Stephen didn't want any further details. Not while they were still on this floor.

"Come on," said Sofia, outpacing them in the gloomy hallway. "We're not here for mad scientists. The vampire's this way."

Sofia all but skipped up the forever-stretching hall. Stephen hung back with Ivan to make sure he didn't bolt. They needed his skills of detection.

Ivan stared resolutely forward, lifting his hand every few seconds to nervously adjust his bow tie. Stephen read the names of the various suites and rooms on nine.

They passed the "Chambre des Horreurs" and "The Gravesoil Garden" and one door that was noticeably shorter than the others and was called "The Sleepy Hollow Suite." About every third door had a hanger over the knob of the type that usually said DO NOT DISTURB or HOUSEKEEPING REQUESTED. These didn't say that. In twisting Gothic letters, he saw one that said NOCTURNAL SERVICE ONLY, and another that read ABSOLUTELY NO CATS.

"No cats?" he asked Ivan. A question might distract Ivan from being terrified. "Why?"

Ivan's hand was on the plaid knot at his throat,

and his fingers froze there as he sputtered and choked and looked as if he were about to collapse.

A few steps ahead of them, Sofia stopped dead and turned on her heel. "Don't say the *C* word!" she whispered.

She stalked back to them, checking to make sure the hall was empty and putting her ear to the nearest door—which its plaque identified as "The Bathory Abattoir"—to confirm silence within.

Then, and only then, did she lean in toward Stephen and speak with a lowered voice. "Vamps and ghouls *hate* c-a-t-s because they're witches' familiars and excellent at sniffing them out. Remember what the coven did? C-a-t-s hate the night creatures, and vice versa. It's a thing."

"That makes sense, I guess," Stephen said, though it didn't really. At least it wouldn't have outside the New Harmonia. To Ivan, whose shoulders slumped forward, he said, "That means you love c-a-t-s, right?"

Sofia snorted but held her finger in front of her lips. "Ixnay on the cattay talkay," she said.

"That's not how pig Latin works," Stephen told her. They started to move up the hall again. "It should be ixnay on the atcay alktay."

"I wondered," Sofia said. "Other than the Roman pork goddess, I've never heard anyone speak it."

Ivan's steps were measured, his face drained of color.

As they reached a turn in the corridor, Sofia said, "The Wallachian Suite should be right around—"

She stopped talking and stopped walking at the same time. They all did.

Standing in the corridor, a black wooden door closing with an ominous creak right beside them, were Baroness Thyme and her two companions. The baroness and the knight looked as surprised by Stephen and his friends as Stephen was to encounter *them*. The young girl, Lady Sarabel, fluttered her fingers in a wave, then crossed her arms and smirked.

"Why, Stephen," said Baroness Thyme, "I didn't expect to see you on this floor." She sniffed at Ivan and Sofia as if they smelled rotten. "You simply *must* come to your senses and become my ward. You'd be much better off being friends with Sarabel here than with these . . . people." The way she said "people" made it sound as if she barely considered Ivan and Sofia anything more than pets.

Stephen's ears had started burning as soon as he saw the three fae. It was even worse when he saw Sarabel wink at him. What was her deal?

He frowned at her, and she laughed. "We do know so many interesting people, including the new friend from Transylvania we just left," she said.

"Sofia and Ivan are my friends," said Stephen, irritated. "And we can go to whatever floor we want."

"Oh, can you?" asked Baroness Thyme. "I wouldn't try to go to the seventh floor when the fire elementals are in residence, if I were you. That's strictly against the rules. Knights of the Octagon and their . . . precious . . . children have so many rules to remember and follow. Things aren't like that in the Evening Lands. We're much more . . . flexible."

Stephen started to say exactly what he thought

about that, but Sofia kicked him in the shin. Nobody seemed to notice but him. Even Ivan was peering past the fae at the gold plate bolted to the wall beside the door that had just closed.

"Baroness," said Sofia, with cupcake sweetness, "it's always lovely to chat with members of the Court of Thorns. But I'm sure you have important business to attend to. We wouldn't want to keep you."

Baroness Thyme said, "The daughter of a diplomat, to be sure. And I *do* value diplomacy."

She didn't notice the way Sofia shifted her weight back onto her heels and raised her hands slightly at that. Stephen happened to be looking at Sir What's-His-Name and was surprised by the worried look that flashed across his face. As if he were afraid he'd have to fight Sofia.

"I'm sure we'll talk later," said Stephen, halfway convinced that combat was about to break out. "Whether I want to or not."

"I'll take that as a promise," said the baroness, with a flash of her hungry smile.

The three fae glided past Stephen and his friends, around the corner, and out of sight.

"What was *that* all about?" Stephen asked, more or less speaking to himself. He touched his ears automatically. The burning sensation was fading.

Sofia didn't relax. "Since when are any fae 'friends' with the count? What do you think they were doing here, Ivan?"

Ivan pointed at the brass plate on the wall. It read THE WALLACHIAN SUITE. "They were doing the same thing we are," he said in a whisper, "talking to the vampire."

Some bit of knowledge itched at the back of Stephen's mind but didn't quite emerge. "I don't like it," he said.

"Me neither," Ivan said.

Stephen said, "Well, we have to go in now."

The others nodded. Stephen and Sofia arranged themselves side by side in front of the door, and Ivan semicowered behind them. "Crosses out?" Stephen asked.

Sofia said, "Oh, right."

They each pulled out a cross made of silver forks and spoons they'd found in Chef Nana's old cutlery drawer, tied together at the center with rubber bands. Their pockets were stuffed with raw garlic, and Sofia had made them each eat a clove, too.

Before Ivan could take off, or before he and Sofia lost their nerve, Stephen knocked at the door.

There was the sound of a crash and something being dragged across a floor. Sofia's hand shot back to grip Ivan's arm and prevent him from running.

The door swung open.

Stephen recoiled.

CHAPTER THIRTEEN

Ivan had described to Stephen in general terms what to expect from the zombies and the vampire ("pallid and terrifying and always hungry"). That did nothing to make the male figure wearing torn, dirty rags less scary. His face had a grayish cast and a slack set to it, his eyes not . . . dead exactly (okay, technically they *were* dead) so much as empty.

Behind him two more rag-clad zombies—a man and a woman—moved toward the welcome party with jerking steps. They made loud sniffing noises. The woman clutched a sheet of parchment and a quill to her chest.

Stephen said, "We're here to see—to see—"

His mind was a complete blank.

"Count Vilhelm von Giertsen af Morgenstierne." Sofia supplied the name, her voice the slightest bit unsteady.

"Brains," said the front zombie.

"Braaainnnnns," said the second.

"Braaaainnnnnnnns," added the third, clutching the parchment and pen harder.

Stephen held up his cross. But Sofia lifted one

finger, shaking it to chastise them. "No," she said. "No. Our brains are not for eating. Invite us in."

Ivan made a noise of dismay as the zombies shuffled and jerked backward to admit them.

The hotel suite was on the dark side, but not so dark that the disgusting mess around them wasn't plain. Empty pizza boxes and wine bottles and soda cans littered the marble floor. A fountain flowing in the center of the large room burbled thick and red.

Behind the fountain, hanging from a rafter, was an enormous bat.

No, not a bat.

It was a man, suspended upside down from the thick wooden beam by feet clad in shiny dress shoes. His face was pale, his head narrow, his body in a black suit. He wore a cape that floated and billowed below him.

A glowing sphere with spiky-looking petals extending from it sat in a pot on the floor. The light from it made the man appear even paler and revealed a slight smile on his face. His eyes were closed.

"That's a midnight sun plant," Sofia whispered. "Only found in Faery. The fae must have—"

"—given it to him," Stephen whispered back. "They *were* here for a reason."

He watched the vampire hang there, apparently unaware he had more visitors. Was he . . . midnight sunbathing? Creepy.

"Master," said one of the zombies, "more brainnnnnns are here."

The suspended man's eyes popped open. "I do not eat brains, Lars."

Between one blink of Stephen's own eyes and the next, the man was no longer hanging from the rafters but was on his feet and right in front of them. The zombies were arranged in an untidy semicircle behind him.

"Greetings," the vampire said, revealing sharp, pearly fangs. His eyes were like black beetles as they crept over Sofia, then Ivan, and finally rested on Stephen. "To what do I owe the honor? You're too young to be turned, you know. And a half fae cannot be made a child of the night."

"Uh, no, we—" Ivan stammered. "That's not—"

Sofia said, formally, "Greetings, Count Vilhelm von Giertsen af Morgenstierne."

The vampire frowned. "You know my name. But then, I suppose you would not be here if you did not. Excuse the mess. Zombies." He rolled his eyes, showing off his fangs with another smile. "Uncouth, to be sure, but they make excellent servants. We weren't expecting such a run of company today. What were your names again? And why are you here?"

"That's Ivan, and I'm Sofia."

Did she know that she had her hands around her cutlery cross?

"And I'm Stephen," Stephen added, "the new culinary alchemist's son, grandson of Lady Nanette Lawson." He watched for a reaction.

The vampire's beetle eyes blinked once, then again. "How do you do," said the vampire. To judge from his blinking and sudden fidgeting, Stephen's presence seemed to make him nervous. "I'm aware of your family's troubles. I knew your mother before, of course."

"Did you two get along?" Stephen asked.

"Not particularly," the vampire said. "Though I admired her work ethic. Long days, she put in. I have long nights instead. An eternity of them. There is always reading to be done, on this or that issue or petition to the Octagon. I do all the home-work, you might say. Though they hardly ever listen to my opinions."

One of the zombies was sniffing the air behind Ivan, who noticed and took a giant step away. He was trembling.

"Did Baroness Thyme give you that plant?" Stephen asked, as he ignored Sofia pinching his arm.

"Kind, wasn't it? She's, well, concerned about the fae's absence on the Octagon since your mother has been gone so long. She's trying to build new alli-ances," said the count. "She had a suspicion that I miss the sun, so she gave me a gift that is a sun of a sort. . . . Did I forget to ask why you are here?"

"We wanted a word," Sofia said.

But Stephen was beginning to get concerned that telling the vampire what they were here for would be a bad idea. It sure *seemed* as if he and the fae were working together now, even if they hadn't been before. That thing at the back of his mind was still there, edging closer to the light.

"We wanted to ask you some questions," Stephen said, and added, "Are we interrupting anything?"

"No," the vampire said, showing his fangs and glancing over at the zombie gripping the paper. "I was just preparing to dictate a letter to the steward at my residence. Nothing that should interest a young man such as yourself. Come in, sit."

The vampire gestured toward a sofa and a chair. He snapped his fingers, and his assistants jerkily bustled around, clearing pizza boxes off the plush velvet sofa, its curved legs shaped like bones. Or maybe they *were* bones. A wine bottle clattered onto the floor.

Ivan, Sofia, and Stephen sat down on the sofa.

The vampire sank into a chair with bones for arms and snapped his fingers again. The zombies went to a nearby fireplace and bashed wood around before tossing it into the grate.

They were probably creating a fire hazard.

"Your questions?" prompted Morgenstierne. "Are you sure they're not about becoming children of the night?"

Stephen hoped Ivan, being the detective, would jump in here with actual questions, but he didn't. He whispered only "no."

Obviously Ivan wasn't going to be taking point. Should Stephen come right out and mention the book's being in Transylvania?

He'd test the bloody waters first. He started to speak. "Well . . ."

The zombies were huddled around a long matchstick, one holding it and another the box. The third leaped up into the air when the flame struck, dropping the paper and quill. The zombie holding the match threw it in the fireplace and danced back and away, all three shrieking as the fire roared to life.

"Lars, Boom-Boom, Number Three," the vampire barked over his shoulder, "keep it down." The shrieks stopped, and he turned back to the sofa.

"Simple creatures. They fear heat, light. I find that I only crave it."

Not comforting at all.

"So," Stephen asked, "what brings you to the city?"

Fangs showed again. "Octagon business and the festivities for Cindermass. I thought I'd see some sights in the meantime."

"The sights in your hotel room?" Stephen asked, shifting a pizza box with the toe of his sneaker.

"The New Harmonia is of course the finest of its kind. You'll think me foolish and romantic, but I enjoy walking the park at night, inhaling the aromas. It's a beautiful city, isn't it? So much life. I envy you seeing it lit by the sun."

Stephen decided to stop being delicate about why they were here. "You said you've heard about my family's troubles—what is it that you've heard? That our famous cookbook was stolen?"

"I had heard that," the vampire said, as if it troubled him, too. Those beetle eyes fixed on Stephen. "And that you were the culprit. I heard you threw it away."

"I wasn't. I didn't."

"He definitely wasn't, and he definitely didn't," Sofia put in, and Stephen was grateful. "It went through a gate."

"Developing such unshakable loyalty so quickly among friends is admirable," said the count. "I do so value loyalty and friendship."

The zombies crept around the edges of the sofa. Sofia made a hissing noise, and they backed away. She still gripped her cross.

The vampire smiled, but only for a second, before his pointed teeth vanished. "The *Librum de Coquina* is not just a simple cookbook, as I'm sure you know. Not even just a valuable family heirloom. If it isn't recovered soon, your father's reinstated status is in jeopardy. My duty as a member of the Octagon is to make decisions that are best for everyone."

"How did you happen to hear about the *Librum's* going missing?" Stephen asked.

"Funny you should ask. Baroness Thyme told me," he said. "She expressed concern for your future."

"Baroness Thyme," Stephen said, "seems more concerned about her own future."

"It is the fae way," the vampire said.

The something remained trapped in darkness in Stephen's mind. He wanted it to emerge from the gloom and into the light, but it stayed stubbornly hidden.

It was time to do what they'd come for. "We, um, think the book is in Transylvania, around your castle," Stephen said. "If you find it, would you consider . . . returning it?"

Morgenstierne looked at Stephen for a long moment.

"Are you accusing me of some misdeed? And with no proof?" Morgenstierne shook his head. "I believe that would be a breach of diplomatic relations, especially here under the roof of the New Harmonia. Am I correct, young Sofia?"

There was a sharp intake of breath from Ivan. On his other side, Sofia stiffened. Then she nodded mutely.

The air had grown colder around them, a deep

silence taking over the rest of the suite.

"Because"—Morgenstierne spoke into the cold silence—"if you were accusing me, that would be most unfortunate. *I* have no special interest in your book or your family's prospects, for that matter."

"I—" Stephen stopped.

There. The realization clicked into place. The count might not have any special interest in the book or his family, but the baroness did. And the count clearly liked being courted with midnight sun plants and visits from the baroness and her companions. Who had already tried to invite Stephen to come live with them.

Stephen's ears heated when he was *around the fae.* He'd bet anything that Lady Sarabel was the one who'd followed him the other day. He'd have to confirm with Ivan and Sofia that she could've impersonated him. But if *she* had taken the book, putting it through the gate to Transylvania would have provided a prime excuse for the baroness to cozy up to this Octagon vampire. It would only make sense that the baroness would pay a visit and ask him for the book . . . for the same reasons she wanted Stephen.

To somehow gain control over his mother's Octagon seat. To hurt his dad and their family legacy.

"You won't get away with this," Stephen said.

Ivan and Sofia were gaping at him.

"Let me give you some guidance, boy," said Morgenstierne, losing any hint of nervousness or impatience. He settled deeper into his seat. "You don't seem to know the rules here yet, so I shall be lenient. This time. Here accusations are only made with proof in hand. Proof you lack."

The zombies began to moan. "Brainnnnnnnns," the one called Lars said.

Morgenstierne didn't shush them this time. The zombies took a few steps in the couch's direction with their usual jerky movements.

The count stayed in his chair, his eyes locked with Stephen's.

The zombies came closer, the fire throwing their shadows forward, making them into ghostly fingers about to grab these intruders to their master's lair.

Sofia jumped up. She stepped around Stephen and pulled Ivan onto his feet. "Back," she ordered the zombies in a firm tone. Then: "Stephen, time to go."

The count rose and sketched a bow at Stephen. "Until we meet again," he said. "And you know, you remind me of your mother."

It didn't sound like a compliment.

Stephen stood, but he didn't bow. He was sure he heard the vampire begin to speak, thin and nasal, behind them as they left. No doubt completing his dictation of the letter they'd interrupted.

The letter that Stephen also had no doubt would issue directions to his steward about what to do with the *Librum de Coquina*.

CHAPTER FOURTEEN

"**You're** alive!" cried the elevator when Stephen and Sofia shoved Ivan between its opening doors, back into low lighting and spooky effects. "At least you appear to be."

"What?" asked Stephen. He pushed the button marked with a scrollwork *L* on the panel.

"Not all who get off at nine get back on . . . unchanged." The last word was low and whispered.

The doors closed, and the interior immediately brightened.

Stephen blinked in the light.

"We're fine. Aren't we, guys?" he asked.

Sofia gave a fake cheerful thumbs-up. "Never better. Right, Ivan?"

"Uh-huh." Ivan studied his leather dress

shoes as if he might throw up on them.

That hadn't gone the way Stephen expected—not that he'd really known what to expect. Still, the vampire reeked of collusion with the fae more strongly than the three of them did of garlic. He was certain that he was right. And that their window of time to recover the book from the count's castle was shrinking by the second.

As the elevator crept downward, he noticed Ivan and Sofia staring at him in curiosity.

"The fae are involved," Stephen said.

The elevator covered a little gasp with a grinding of its cables and, for once, didn't say anything more.

Ivan and Sofia frowned.

"Why are we going to the lobby?" asked Sofia.

"I want to get a look at the gateways and the guards," Stephen said. Because he also knew what their next move should be. If they didn't act fast, the book might be lost to his dad forever.

The elevator began to hum softly. It paused to say, "I cannot divulge what I do not overhear."

The elevator doors opened. The scene in the

lobby was much the same as before, except that now uniformed hotel employees stood before every gate. They looked like fierce bellhops, if bellhops had dangerously sharp swords hanging from their belts.

Sofia's gaze swept the lobby. "Yep, Dad's got the Perilous Guard out in full force."

Julio himself was walking from one gateway to the next to check the positions of his troops.

Sofia motioned back the way they'd come. "Let's get back on before he spots us."

But it was too late. The elevator doors had closed, and Julio was coming toward them with a big smile.

"Hey there, you three," he said, looming, but probably not on purpose. He was too tall to do anything else. "What kind of trouble are you getting into today?"

Ivan gulped and didn't make eye contact with Sofia's dad.

Julio's smile vanished, replaced by a sympathetic look that settled on Stephen. "How thoughtless of me." He waved an arm to encompass the lobby. "The book could come back through at any moment, and we'll be here to grab it and return it to its rightful owner. Everyone makes mistakes."

"Thanks, good to hear," Stephen said, and made a snap decision. He needed to talk to Sofia and Ivan alone, stat. "We'd better get going."

And Ivan's face was still far too pale. He might blurt out something like "I Survived an Interview with the Vampire" at any moment.

"Where are you off to?" Julio asked.

"I'm hoping that Sofia and Ivan are going to show me around the neighborhood," Stephen said. "I haven't left the hotel since we got here."

Julio's smile returned. "Excellent idea. You should show him the ice-cream shop and the old bookstore."

Stephen prodded Ivan to get moving toward the revolving door. Then they were through the front doors and out onto the quiet New York street.

It was like crossing a threshold into another world, and Stephen guessed that was because that's exactly what they'd done. From the supernormal to normal world—there was so much going on a few feet away, hidden completely from outsiders.

From the car ride and a map in the *Almanack*, Stephen knew the Hotel New Harmonia was on the Upper East Side, not far from Central Park. A ritzy neighborhood. There were shops opening onto the sidewalk of the block they were on: a florist, a small grocery store, a jewelry shop, and a store with a fancier awning—Dr. Bethuselah's Fountain Pen & Inkporium.

They walked toward it, and Stephen was surprised by a hand-lettered sign at the bottom of the window that read FRESH VARIETIES OF GIANT SQUID, KILLER BEE, AND INNOCENT BLOOD INKS SUITABLE FOR ALL PACTS, BARGAINS, AND DEALS.

Sofia followed his gaze to the sign. "Oh, right. You may notice more businesses that also cater to supernormals, now that the dweomer's been lifted off you."

Maybe the worlds weren't so separate after all. It was just that one was plainly visible and the other hidden unless you had the special recipe to see it.

"Explain how you arrived at your conclusion about the fae," Ivan said. He looked more comfortable out under the early summer sun than he had since they'd first agreed to go to the ninth floor.

Stephen hardly knew where to start. "The other day, when you guys were showing me around, my ears were burning practically the whole time. The only time they weren't was around Cindermass."

"I'm not following your logic," Ivan said.

"Me neither," Sofia said when Stephen looked at her to see if he was being clear.

"They were also burning that first night in the lobby and upstairs in the hallway before we went in to see the vamp."

"Ah, I see," Ivan said. He stroked his chin. "I have heard of this. There were some stories about half fae children having an extra sense that acted almost as an early warning when fae were around. You must have it. Your ears are the most fae thing about your appearance after all. So you think that means it was a member of the fae following you the other morning. . . ." Ivan paused to think.

"Sarabel," Stephen said. "It has to be. Remember, the baroness and snooty knight guy were alone when they came back in that morning. Is it possible? Can fae be invisible?"

"An interesting question," Ivan said. "The fae tend to have various magical gifts, but usually one is the strongest for them. Camouflage, extreme giftedness with glamours—looking like another person or thing of their choosing—*is* a type of fae magic. While it is unusual, Sarabel could have the gift for camouflaging herself—becoming invisible or appearing as another person."

"See?" Stephen said. He was proud to have figured it out.

"It does fit all the details," Ivan said. "Her glamour skills wouldn't have worked on something with as much magic as the *Librum de Coquina*. That explains why Trevor saw *you* dispose of the book. She was undoubtedly following you, looking for an opportunity to damage the Lawsons or lure you to be the baroness's ward. Which makes it a crime of opportunity—of a sort—just as I said at the start."

"But it's more than that now," Sofia put in. "By using the Transylvania gate, they've brought in the vampire, which means they're already building allies on the Octagon. They must think they'll lure you into their clutches still."

"It's not going to work," Stephen said. "Though after seeing the lobby, I think our next step isn't going to be easy."

"What step?" asked Sofia.

"Yes," Ivan said, holding up his hands, "please explain."

"We have to go through the gateway to Transylvania and find the book. You said the other day there's some sort of recall function. You know that the fae have almost certainly told the vampire to hide it or maybe even to get rid of it. It's their only leverage. That letter he's writing, how long will it take to arrive?"

"A day at most by gargoyle." Sofia raised a single eyebrow. "But you *can't* go through. And we're not allowed to, either."

"If they're some kind of worldwide transportation network, then they can't be all that dangerous," said Stephen. "I think our parents are just trying to keep you from using them the way *they did* when they were kids. Dad told me they went through back then. He even said it was your mom's idea, Sofia."

Ivan was shaking his head. Sofia said, "I knew it! I knew my mom was a troublemaker when she was a kid. My *abuelas* are dropping hints about it all the time."

"This is a purely academic exercise," said Ivan. "Even if the gateways aren't dangerous for us, they're dangerous for you. Fae can't use them."

"I'm only half fae, but fine. I can be the lookout while you guys go through."

Ivan was shaking his head again. "They're also under close watch by the Perilous Guard, who are highly trained and, as Sofia knows, have been specifically instructed to keep an eye on us well before now."

"Ivan's right," said Sofia.

Stephen's enthusiasm fell a little bit. Until Sofia said, "But he's wrong, too. The Perilous Guard won't be watching over the gateways from midnight to dawn. It's against the rules."

Ivan careened backward, stopping only when he collided with the glass front of the fountain pen shop. "No!" he said. "No, no, no, no!"

"What rules?" asked Stephen. "You mean the lobby isn't watched in the middle of the night?"

"The Manager's rules," said Sofia. "And it *is* watched, but only by one . . . being, the night clerk."

"I know Ivan doesn't like the night clerk," Stephen said. "Who is he?"

Ivan's head rolled from side to side in a slow-motion shudder.

Sofia said, "He's the ghoul who mans the registration desk at night. Vampires, zombies, the other night creatures, they're comforted by seeing one of their own kind at the helm. And if some normals *did* manage to breach the hotel's natural defenses and walk in off the street at night, they'd walk right back out."

"Because the night clerk," Ivan said, "is an eyeless ghoul with a highly developed sense of smell, whom you don't want to meet, especially in the middle of the night all by yourself."

"He's not *that* scary," Sofia said.

"Don't listen to her," Ivan told Stephen. "He's far scarier than Morgenstierne was."

An eyeless ghoul definitely *sounded* as if it should be at the top of the scary scale to Stephen.

They went silent as a man with crazy hair and a leather jacket entered the fountain pen shop. Stephen felt bad that he was asking Ivan to confront what was apparently his worst nightmare. But they *had* to go through that gateway. It was their best shot at finding the book.

"Look," Stephen said, "if there were any other way, we'd do that instead. But there isn't. We know the book's at Castle Dracul."

"As are many vampires," Sofia said quietly.

"You can handle them, right?" Stephen asked.

Sofia didn't look entirely confident, but after a long moment she shrugged. "I'll have to. Ivan, if he's right, we may not have another option."

Ivan didn't speak at first. He began to pace along a small area of the sidewalk, forward and back. There was a tap on the window, and a man wearing round glasses, whose beard curled into an elaborate whirl at the end, waved at them.

Sofia waved back. So did Stephen.

The man gestured for Ivan to come inside. "I'll be right back," Ivan informed them. "Do not proceed any further. No plans are to be laid without me present."

"He's a regular here," Sofia said. "Dr. Bethuselah probably has some new kind of invisible ink for him."

"Why's he so afraid of the night clerk?" Stephen asked.

They stood facing the window, watching Ivan talk with the shopkeeper, who was demonstrating something for him on the counter inside. The walls behind them were covered with racks of squat ink bottles, a few here and there glimmering like bottled stars.

"When Ivan was eight, his parents were up late working on a case. I was sleeping over, and I—" Sofia blew out a breath. "We were playing Secrets or Dares. I dared him to sneak downstairs and take a gold pen off the lobby desk. He'd never been down there after midnight. I had."

"What happened?"

"He went, armed with an early version of his kit; it had a length of rope, a spray that makes a fog you can slip through, and a flashlight. He carried the flashlight all the way down the steps to the lobby, where he marched out and waltzed right up to the desk. The night clerk must have been meditating or something because then he pops up all of a sudden, scents Ivan there, and shrieks bloody murder, making him even more terrifying. Ivan sees him, and they're screaming at each other, flipping out. The sounds were awful."

Despite the warm and humid air around them, Stephen shivered sympathetically on Ivan's behalf. "What happened?"

"I'd followed Ivan, which is how I know all this. I knew it was wrong . . . even then. So I went into the lobby and rescued him. He thanked me. He still thanks me. Even though we got in big trouble after the night clerk told on us."

Stephen and Sofia watched for a moment through the window as Ivan shook the man's hand and accepted a small parcel. He turned to come back out to them.

"Sofia," Stephen said, "you did follow him. That counts."

Sofia didn't respond. He knew she was thinking that it didn't count for enough.

"We'll make sure nothing happens to him," Stephen said.

"He has to say yes. I won't make him do anything like that again."

The door flew open, and Ivan emerged.

"Ivan, we have to do this," Stephen said, gentler about it. "There's no other way, none that makes sense. You see the logic."

Ivan resumed pacing. Back and forth, back and forth. He kept it up for a minute, then two. Stephen was trying to come up with another argument to convince him when, finally, Ivan stopped.

"Despite the fact that there are many gateways in the hotel, there is only one key," he said. "Or, more precisely, one mechanism."

"But the gateways aren't locked," Stephen said, frowning. "I saw my dad push his finger through one. And that Sarabel girl didn't have a key when she threw the *Librum* halfway around the world."

"It's not a key really," said Sofia. "It doesn't even

look like one. It looks like an old-fashioned camera."

"Actually," said Ivan, "it's the other way around. Old cameras look like it. The mechanism was designed and built at least thirty years before the first handheld cameras were manufactured, and, according to the case files of my great-great-grandmother Delores—"

Stephen raised a hand, cutting Ivan off. "Okay, okay, but what does it do? What does this have to do with getting to Spooksylvania for the book?"

"The mechanism does two or three different things," Sofia said. "You know the gateways are alive, right? Well, they're more like plants than animals, and they sort of, I guess, cross-pollinate when they switch destinations. If a gateway to one particular place stays open for too long, that's bad news. It withers and dies. But sometimes you need to hold a gateway in place for a little longer than normal. So that's one thing the mechanism does, sort of puts the gateways on pause, at least for a little while."

"Correct," said Ivan. "It can also be programmed to cause a gateway to go to a particular place instead of cycling randomly. And you can rewind, to get back to a gateway you've just seen. The desk clerks call it the recall function. And that is why this is relevant."

"Because we'll have to get the key from behind the front desk to even be able to get to Castle Dracul," Sofia said. "I get it. So, Ivan, are we doing this?"

Ivan had gone pale. He said, "Going to Castle Dracul. The center of undead power for the entire planet."

"That might be overstating it a little," Sofia said gently.

Ivan touched his two index fingers to his nose below his glasses. Then he lowered his hands. "I will *only* agree to this if we distract the night clerk rather than interact with him directly. I do *not* want to find myself face-to-face with him. Understand?"

Sofia glanced at Stephen and nodded. "It's not like I want to get to know him better, either. But if we can distract him, then I can retrieve the key from behind the front desk. Stephen, you can operate it, and we'll go through while you stay behind on look-out duty."

"What kind of distraction are you thinking?" Stephen asked.

"At this particular moment I am thinking of his horrifying face," Ivan said. "Give me a second."

Stephen thought over the little he knew about vampires and ghouls and zombies, the undead. They were afraid of animals of the feline persuasion.

"If I'm not wrong," Stephen said, and was grateful when Ivan didn't say he probably was before he'd even told them his idea, "then the night clerk will be easy enough to distract. Time to make our plan."

It materialized in his mind in the same kind of detail as the crime scene drawing, unfolding across the lobby: a plan that would allow them to get the *Librum* back, save his dad's knighthood, and wreck whatever the fae had planned.

Stephen and Ivan stood in the stairwell on the lobby floor. They were waiting for Sofia to return. She'd laughed and said she'd handle keeping the eyes of the Perilous Guard off the boys as they undertook the first part of Stephen's plan. She'd sworn that whatever she had in mind would work.

Phase one of the bigger task of misdirecting the night clerk later required some groundwork, a distraction before the real distraction that night.

"What's taking her so long?" Stephen asked Ivan, checking the time on the screen of his phone for the fifth time. It was clutched in his right hand and also part of the plan.

Ivan said, "I have been standing in your presence for the entirety of the eighty-five seconds since you last made that query, and I have received no visitors, no messages, no phone calls, and no psychic revelations, so it will no doubt come as no surprise to you that my answer is the same as it was a minute and a half ago. I . . . don't . . . know."

"I win," Stephen said. "Finally you admit you don't know everything."

"Ha," Ivan said.

Thankfully Sofia came gliding down the steps then. She somehow managed to move gracefully despite her big, clunky boots. As she rounded the corner of the landing above, she also managed not to bang the wall with the sword belted at the waist of her dress.

The *sword*? Yes, that was definitely a sword.

"You're carrying a sword," Stephen said. He bounced onto his toes nervously. "Are you sure whatever you're planning will work?"

Ivan rolled his eyes. "He's been like this ever since we came in here. You'd think that since this is his plan, he'd be calm and collected."

Stephen said, "I *am* calm and collected!"

"Quiet down, both of you," said Sofia. "If Dad and his guards hear us arguing in here, my distraction won't work at all."

"Um, *what* kind of distraction do you have in mind that requires a sword?" asked Stephen.

Sofia drew her blade from its scabbard with a ringing sound.

"Epic sword battle," she said.

The boys stepped to one side, giving her access to the door, which she pushed open.

It swung shut behind her, leaving Stephen staring at Ivan.

"Before you ask," said Ivan, "the answer is yes, she's serious."

"She's going to challenge her father and the Perilous Guard to an epic sword battle?"

"Just for fun," said Ivan. "That was her practice blade. You no doubt noticed the blunted edge."

"My first thought when she drew her sword wasn't 'Aha, I see from the blunted edge that she's using her practice blade.'"

Ivan said, "Touché."

A clash of steel and the full-throated roar of what sounded like a sizable crowd came from the other side of the door.

"That's our cue," said Ivan. "Stay low, and try not to attract any attention."

When they emerged, there didn't seem to be any danger of that. Everyone in the lobby was looking at the Gutierrez father and daughter, who were facing each other, both smiling broadly, in the center of the vast lobby. Uniformed members of Julio's Perilous Guard formed a loose circle around their commander and Sofia, joined by a pair of willowy front desk clerks with barklike skins.

"Remember," whispered Ivan, removing a phone from his pocket, "plant yours at the base of one of the trees across from the registration desk. I'll put this one as far away from the gateway we're using as I can. I'll work my way over and meet you back here."

Stephen nodded, but . . . "Won't Mrs. Gutierrez interrupt this practice fight or whatever?"

"No," Ivan said. "Sofia's mom has her weekly meeting with the Manager right now. That's why we waited. Neither one of them should be paying too much attention to the lobby if we're lucky."

Two dozen feet away, Sofia's long ponytail suddenly whipped around in a circle as she somersaulted past her dad and smacked him across the back of his knees with the flat of her sword as she went. The Perilous Guard roared their approval, and Stephen saw one of the desk clerks handing some money over as if he'd lost a bet.

"Doesn't he always win?" Stephen asked.

"It takes him longer every time."

Stephen knew they had to get moving, but he didn't understand. "Julio's not a very good swordsman?" he asked dubiously.

"He's one of the greatest human fighters alive," said Ivan.

"Then why—"

"Because by all accounts, Sofia is the most naturally gifted sword fighter born in the last century. Her dad started training her when she was born. She practices first thing every morning. Now, let's go."

Ivan crept away, looking more than a little goofy in his tweed suit and bow tie, bent over nearly double as he tried to blend into the wood-paneled walls.

Another roar went up. Unable to resist, Stephen whirled toward the fight.

Sofia had managed to lift her dad's ornate cap off his head with the tip of her sword. She flipped it up into the air, danced backward out of range of Julio's blade, and sketched a curtsy to the crowd as the hat landed on her head. It was so big that its brim dipped forward over her nose, blocking her eyesight.

"What do you say, Dad?" she called. "You think it's a fairer fight if I'm blindfolded?"

Julio laughed with his guardsmen and waited for Sofia to toss the hat aside before raising his sword again and saying, *"En garde!"*

Stephen missed what happened next because Ivan was right. Sofia was doing an excellent job with her duty of distracting everyone. They had better not screw up planting the phones.

He was careful to stay away from the fight as he made his way around the edge of the lobby. To the accompaniment of cheers and catcalls and clashing swords, he moved from pillar to couch to tree trunk until he found a spot within earshot of the front desk.

He groped around the base of the tree for a nook under one of the roots. When he found one the right size to hide his phone, he made sure the volume was turned all the way up and tucked it beneath the root. Like the other phone, his was set on Do Not Disturb mode until midnight, so no ring would give them away early.

He carefully, slowly made his way back to the stairwell door.

Ivan was already there, not taking any precautions against being seen. Anyone who caught sight of him would assume that he'd strolled through the door. He was watching Sofia mid-battle, and he was . . . smiling.

Stephen wasn't sure he'd ever seen Ivan smile this widely before.

The two of them stood shoulder to shoulder, watching Sofia and Julio leap and spin, jab and swing.

"It's truly a shame that she's destined to be a diplomatis," said Ivan, keeping his voice down. "Supernormals can be very traditional, and I can't imagine they'll ever accept her as leader of the guard."

Across the lobby Sofia spun as if her feet barely needed to touch the ground, and when she stopped, she got in a strong strike to the center of her father's blade.

Stephen was still learning the rules of this strange new world. He knew he'd never be a chef like his grandma and dad. "If it comes down to Sofia or destiny, I'm betting on Sofia."

Ivan smiled again. "Me, too."

Stephen almost missed the *bing* of the elevator arriving, but it was impossible to miss Sofia's mom leaving it. She clicked past Ivan and Stephen and crossed her arms, waiting behind the whirring battle Sofia and Julio were engaged in.

And waiting.

She cleared her throat.

Julio's sword immediately dropped to his side, the point resting against the lobby floor. Sofia turned an innocent smile on her mother.

"Guess that means it's a draw," Sofia said.

"No way—" Julio began to speak. He swallowed the words. "Rematch soon."

"Has the *Librum* turned back up?" Carmen asked, and the hope in her voice twisted something inside Stephen.

"Not yet. No luck getting the Manager to make contact?" Julio asked.

"I'm afraid not," she said. "We'll just have to wait."

Julio slid his sword into its sheath, called, "Back on guard, everyone," and folded his arms around her.

Sofia left to join Ivan and Stephen. "What you did out there was incredible," Stephen said.

"Eh, I've been better." Sofia shrugged, sheathing her sword. But she bit back a grin.

"We should stay in our cottages for the rest of the evening," Ivan said, pressing the button for the elevator. "Attract no attention."

Sofia groaned. "But I want to play croquet again."

"You can win again tomorrow," Ivan said.

The phones they'd hidden in the lobby belonged to Sofia and Stephen. They'd use Ivan's to call the other phones later to distract the night clerk away from the desk, first so Sofia could snag the key and then, after Sofia and Ivan had returned (they hoped with the book), so she could put it back.

The elevator doors opened, and they got on. "Where am I taking you?" the elevator asked.

Stephen pressed the button for the Village. "Home," he said without realizing he'd been about to say it. And it felt right. Their little cottage *was* beginning to feel like home.

"You three must be *exhausted*," the elevator said. "What a day of adventures you've had, with your trip to the library and then to the ninth floor. Me, I must live vicariously, trapped here in this shaft. Oh, and Ivan always overexerts himself at Dr. Bethuselah's, which I assume you visited; I overheard you tell Julio you were leaving the hotel. Oh, and Sofia, you sounded like you were in magnificent form today."

Ivan's and Sofia's eyes were wide with shock at the compliment.

The elevator continued. "Personally, I think it's fair to say that Stephen's having a good influence on you two. Stephen, don't listen to the haters. You needed the book. I hear nothing but complaints from them about myself, and *I'm* just doing my job."

"I won't," Stephen said, trying to hide a smile as Ivan and Sofia shot him dirty looks. He didn't bother to argue his innocence this time, either. Soon enough, he'd have the book back.

They reached the Village and stepped off as the elevator called, "Farewell!"

Ivan paused. "See you when the crow flies at midnight," he said to Stephen and Sofia.

"I'll see you later, alligator," Sofia said.

"After a while, crocodile," Stephen answered.

"Alligators and crocodiles aren't even found on

the same continent," Ivan informed them.

"And neither is as scary as the night clerk," Sofia said, before traipsing out onto the Village green.

"She's not wrong," Ivan said.

Stephen didn't know whether to look forward to their midnight meet-up or dread it. Maybe he'd have to do both.

CHAPTER SIXTEEN

Four and a half long hours later Stephen was once again waiting in the scrolled iron stairwell. He'd spent some of the time upstairs drawing, but he could never quite tell when something was going to move on the page . . . or not.

Now he stood here, without his phone to check the time. But he estimated it was approximately 11:59 P.M. He'd made sure his dad was snoring soundly before slipping out the front door and across the deserted green at 11:58. He'd also placed tape on the front door latch, so it wouldn't make noise and give him away. That had been Ivan's suggestion.

He wore jeans, a gray hoodie, and white-and-gray sneakers. He'd figured he should dress appropriately for a midnight caper, but he didn't have any black pants, long-sleeved shirts, or shoes—except a pair of slick-bottomed dress ones that pinched his feet—so this was the best he could manage. He fully expected Ivan and Sofia to show up in head-to-toe ninja uniforms.

When they came through the door, Sofia was wearing the same dress from earlier that day and Ivan—

"Ivan," Stephen asked, careful not to sound as if he were making fun, "are those silk pajamas with your initials sewn on them?"

Ivan shrugged and glanced at his red-and-gold pajamas. "My mom has them specially made. They're comfortable and perfectly fine for trespass-ing in gateways."

"I think they're dapper," said Sofia.

Stephen saw no reason to disagree. "I guess they are."

"Enough about fashion." Ivan pulled a small glass bottle out of the bag slung over his shoulder and unceremoniously sprayed Stephen with a cloud of mist.

"Gah!" said Stephen, and was shushed by Sofia. "What *was* that?" But even as he said it, he noticed that it didn't smell like anything. Not a hint of scent reached his nostrils. "Water?"

"Partly. Water infused with a mixture of dried leaves from Mongolian spineleaf and scrapings from a type of coral that grows in a single reef around a remote island in the Indian Ocean. My grandmother developed the formula. She called it *necodore*. Now you have no odor."

Stephen sniffed his arm and smelled . . . nothing. "I took a shower this morning."

"And so," Ivan said, "you reeked of shampoo, soap, and treated water. Not to mention your own oils and sweat. Just because you couldn't smell all that doesn't mean the night clerk couldn't. We must be undetectable by that unnatural nose of his."

Sofia stood with her face turned up, as if she welcomed the mist, while Ivan sprayed it on her. He held the bottle out to douse himself, then stashed it.

They started down the stairs. "I know you said

we don't have to worry about his seeing us, but are you sure?" asked Stephen.

"Yes. He has a very acute sense of smell, but remember, he doesn't have any eyes," Sofia said.

They went down the stairwell not too fast and not too slow. Sofia had said they wouldn't have to worry about getting busted during this part because night creatures tended to be too lazy to do anything but use the elevator—unless they could fly, in which case they'd just go out a window.

"So all ghouls have no eyes?" Stephen asked.

Ivan stayed quiet while Sofia filled Stephen in about ghouls in general and the night clerk in particular. "No. It's just the *night clerk* who doesn't have eyes. He's very old. Ghouls were originally from the deserts of the Middle East. He claims to have been the first one in the New World, here since 1300 or something like that. The Manager has a real soft spot for him, so when the position opened up . . ."

Stephen knew from school that the New World had been "discovered" from the east before Columbus. There were those Vikings up in Canada, for example. But 1300 didn't seem right. "How could a monster from the Middle East get across the ocean that long ago? He can't fly, can he?"

"I hope not," said Ivan with a shudder.

They finished the last flight of stairs, and the door to the lobby stood in front of them.

Stephen vibrated with nervous energy. "You're taking care of the settings on the key?" he asked Sofia, though they'd settled all this earlier.

"Yep. All you'll have to do is point it at our gate and turn the activation knob. Then hide out, stay quiet, and wait for us to come back."

"Here's hoping," Ivan said. He fished in his pocket and took out his phone, which he handed to Stephen. "Time to put the plan into effect. Stephen, you're up."

Stephen went over to the door, and Ivan and Sofia crowded in behind him.

He shut his eyes for a moment and visualized the lobby, especially the locations of the gateway they planned to use and the phones they'd hidden earlier.

Please, let this work and let the book be easy for Ivan

and Sofia to find on the other side of the gateway.

He put his ear against the door's cool wooden surface and scrolled to select speed dial number four on Ivan's phone.

He imagined the signal reaching out to a cell phone tower somewhere on top of a nearby building, then to a relay station, maybe even up to a satellite in outer space. It bounced back down through banks of computers and communications equipment, returned to the cell tower and into the lobby, not so many feet away from where he stood.

His own phone, hidden at the base of the tree where he'd left it, received the signal and rang at top volume. It wasn't the fake spaceship noise he usually used. It was a sound that would chill the night clerk, forcing him from behind the front desk to search for his kind's enemy.

In the lobby Stephen's phone went "*meeeeoooww.*"

Stephen cracked the door and peeked out.

"No, no, no!" the night clerk called in a gravelly voice.

He moved in an odd, hunched-over way, swinging

his bald head and eyeless face back and forth. His face and even the sharp teeth revealed when his pale lips curled back were the same dingy white. He hopped onto one of the middle levels of the registration desk and landed on his hands and feet. "No unattended felines allowed! No unattended felines of any description permitted on these premises!"

Stephen almost closed the door. "Time to get him away from the desk." He hit STOP on the call to his phone and sent a call to Sofia's, hidden among the trees across the lobby.

As the new meowing began, the night clerk jumped down onto the floor and shambled his way toward it. "Your presence is unwelcome! Unclean! Anathema!"

"What does *anathema* mean?" Stephen asked.

"It means 'unwelcome and unclean'—now let's go!" hissed Sofia, and the three of them darted out into the lobby as quickly and quietly as they could.

Hunched over, intent on finding his foe, the clerk was headed toward the loud meowing from Sofia's phone. The sound echoed through the cavernous lobby, with its ever-shifting gateways.

The clerk entered the faraway trees talking to himself, chasing the phantom feline.

Sofia raced to the front desk and vaulted over it like a practiced gymnast.

A few moments later her head popped up over one of the lower sections of the counter. She looked down at the object she held, twisting a dial as she hurried back to them. When she reached Ivan and Stephen, she thrust the old-fashioned cameralike object at Stephen and whispered, "It should be ready! The button's at the top!"

"Filthy feline!" snarled the night clerk, off across the lobby. "No unattended cats allowed!"

Holding the key awkwardly in one hand, Stephen ended the call to Sofia's phone and called his own again, to keep the clerk searching. He shoved Ivan's phone in his pocket, and the three of them darted toward the gateway.

"Meeeeeoooooowwww!" His phone rang in the trees.

The night clerk sniffed the air as he traveled toward the sound.

"No smell of filthy feline, odd that, very odd, very odd," said the ghoul. "And meows come from here and then from there. Altogether . . . *odd.*" He sniffed again. "And what do I smell? Nothing. Nothing at all."

The gateway currently showed the side of a volcano, lava oozing down the side of it, dark and fiery.

Stephen lifted the cameralike key in front of him and gripped it in both hands. "Ready?" he mouthed.

Sofia nodded, gripping Ivan's hand.

Bing went the elevator.

"Oh, no." The whispered words were Ivan's.

The night clerk straightened, swinging his head toward the opening elevator doors.

The gate where they stood would be directly in the line of sight of anyone stepping off of the elevator.

They looked at one another, then bolted. Ivan pedaled his silk-covered legs and dived toward the closest tree trunk. Stephen scrambled after him, while Sofia overshot them both and crouched, concealed, in the undergrowth.

Stephen fumbled in his pocket and ended the call to his phone, cutting off the meowing. And then tried not to breathe as they waited to see who emerged from the elevator.

"Greetings, Night Lord," rasped the ghoul's unmistakable voice. "Beware. I have heard a foul beast afoot in the hotel this evening."

"But this hotel is the best in the city," said the unmistakable haughty, thin voice of Count von Morgenstierne. "I would hope that unattended felines would not be permitted at any time."

Curse this vamp and his nighttime strolls.

"They are not, sir," the night clerk assured the vampire. "It must be a rogue beast. But there is an *odder* problem. . . . Might I trouble you for a second opinion?"

"Trouble away," Morgenstierne said.

"It is simply that while I have heard the filthy feline's foul cry, I do not scent it."

"That *is* odd. Allow me," Morgenstierne said.

Stephen eased his head around to see what was happening.

Standing in front of the night clerk was the count, in his black suit with his fancy cape over it, flowing from his shoulders. He wasn't alone, of course.

Behind him were the three zombies.

"Master," said one.

"We," said the other.

"Smell," said the third.

"Lars, Boom-Boom, Number Three," said the count as if he were at the end of his wits where they were concerned, "I know *you* smell, but last time I checked you were not felines. Quiet."

The zombies clutched at one another's dirty, torn clothing and said, "Yes, Master."

The vampire swept his cape as he sauntered forward, his head making a slow, nose-first circle through the air. *"Curiousss."* He hissed the word.

As the vampire started to turn in their direction, Stephen lowered himself back behind the broad trunk and took out Ivan's phone.

He pressed the button, and Sofia's phone set off with loud *meeeeeoooooowwww*ing from the far-off stand of trees. The next sound they heard was the clerk's and the count's footsteps, rushing away, toward the noise.

Stephen jammed the phone in his pocket.

Now was their moment.

Stephen jumped out from behind his tree. The key was cool against his palms.

Ivan and Sofia followed, dashing toward the gateway. Stephen's heart pounded so hard it vibrated his eardrums, but he could still make out the voices of the undead on the other side of the lobby, as they searched the trees.

In front of the gateway, Stephen held up the key and pressed the button. There was no sound, no nothing, but the gateway transformed from the volcano into the gloomy castle from his drawing—only a daytime version.

Ivan and Sofia grabbed each other's hands. The *Almanack* said it helped when traveling through a gateway together. They dived through. But Stephen suddenly realized, if he stayed behind, he'd be caught. No question. Their plan had been designed to distract a night creature who couldn't *see*. The count and his zombies had eyes. Hiding from them would be much more difficult.

And so, after Ivan and Sofia had disappeared into the gloomy scene, Stephen stashed the key in the foliage, sucked in a deep breath, and jumped through after them.

Stephen had imagined that going through a gate might be something like stepping through a waterfall. Or maybe diving into a pool that was somehow set perpendicular to the ground. But it wasn't like that at all.

His stomach flipped inside out. It was like going over the top of the highest hill on a roller coaster at top speed combined with getting hit hard in the belly with a dodgeball.

Or as if he'd touched a raging electric current. Spots swam before his eyes.

He might have passed out for a moment, or maybe it only seemed that way. Whichever was true, now he was lying on his back on a hard surface, staring up at a stone ceiling crisscrossed by dark wooden beams.

He'd thought going through the gate wouldn't be that bad for a *half* fae. He was wrong.

Stephen felt as if he were dying.

"What were you thinking?" The voice was Sofia's. She towered over him, seemingly unaffected by the journey. "Stephen? Stephen, are you okay?"

Sofia's face and the wooden beams weren't the only things above him. The dim space they'd crossed into was hung with a chandelier with red crystals. He'd been expecting them to land on the gravel road, but they were obviously inside a building.

Sofia bent next to him and pulled him into a sitting position. Make that a building with a large, dank room with stone walls covered in tapestries showing a variety of fanged figures.

"You don't look too hot," she said.

"Funny," he said, a little woozily, "I *feel* hot."

He was covered in a thin layer of sweat. Everything seemed to be at a distance, arm's length away, as if he were somewhere else watching all this, not really here.

"You shouldn't have come through," Sofia said. "Ivan, you okay?"

"Oh, yes, never better for being in the castle of an undead lord." Ivan was fine, enough to act like himself anyway. "I surmise that Stephen was more worried about getting caught over there than risking life and limb coming here."

Sofia helped Stephen to his feet, though his legs were shaky once he was on them. Afraid he might fall, he held on to her arm when she would have let go.

"We need to search," he said, speaking more slowly than normal, as if his words were coated in syrup. But he was—maybe—starting to recover from the journey through the gateway. Or as his stomach rolled in a seasick way, so he hoped.

"Oh, no. I must've gotten the time setting wrong!" Sofia released his arm and stabbed her finger toward a wavy area roughly shaped like the gate on the other side. "The gateway's already closing. We have to be fast. Ivan, are you sure we're inside Castle Dracul?"

The closest tapestry had a scene on it featuring three pale women, grinning and stalking forward in dresses like torn bedsheets. The women had fangs. But they were walking through a green field on a perfectly blue sky day.

"Almost certainly," Ivan said. "Look at the door."

The closed wooden door was crossed with riveted bands of some dark metal. It also bore a carving of the Octagon symbol that featured the undead glyph done larger than the rest.

"And look at the tapestries," Stephen said, turning in a circle. One showed a smiling sun presiding over a forest full of dark, menacing shapes. Another showed several vampires in a green field similar to the first, with their heads and arms tossed back, bathing in daylight. "I wonder if Sarabel ever skulked around here. Maybe that's why they gave him that plant in the first place."

"Maybe they've given him hope for more than that," Ivan said, stroking his chin.

Stephen ignored the way his knees felt as if they

might turn to water, and he moved toward the heavy door.

Just in time to hear footsteps coming close. The three of them exchanged panicked glances as the door opened to reveal a toothpick-thin man in a tuxedo.

"Master, what an unexpected surprise," the man said.

For a second Stephen thought the extra-white cloths at the man's neck and wrists were some sort of fancy cuffs. Then he realized they were bandages, the one above the right hand tinged with the slightest hint of blood. The man squinted at Stephen in confusion.

Behind him were what appeared to be, yes, at least five vampires. They were mostly women and, unlike the nightgown-clad tapestry ladies, appeared to favor comfort wear. One, in pink yoga pants, reached past the mummy toothpick toward them. "They don't smell like much, but I bet they taste delicious," she said.

The man raised an arm to block her access. "What is the meaning of this?"

Stephen did not want to think about being delicious. Or how terrified Ivan must be. *He* was terrified enough.

But he pretended not to be. He channeled every bit of strength he had left. "Hello . . . I take it you're Count von Morgenstierne's steward?"

"And who are you?" the man asked.

"The count sent us from the New Harmonia. We're here for the *Librum de Coquina*."

Sofia coughed. Stephen looked over at her, and she jerked her head toward the gate.

The shimmering was growing fainter.

Stephen held out his hand. "We don't have much time. Hand it over."

The man shook his head. "I regret to tell you that the other party my master sent took the book hours ago. I was only following his orders." He wore a pained expression. "Can you tell him that?"

"What did the party look like?" Stephen asked, breathless.

"A fae girl. Feathers, lace, an inappropriate laugh. She was a little mean."

"I liked her," one of the women behind him said. "She was charming."

"To each her own." The steward shrugged.

Sounds like Sarabel. A crushing sense of disappointment washed over Stephen. They'd failed. The fae had the book again, and who knew what they'd do with it now?

Sofia looped an arm under Stephen's. "Get his other side," she muttered to Ivan, who did as she commanded.

"Leaving so soon?" the pink-yoga-panted vampire asked. "If you've failed the master, you might as well stay and be dinner."

She stalked toward them, the steward letting her pass with a nod.

Sofia suddenly had a cross in her free hand. "Back!" she ordered the vampire, who bared her fangs and stopped where she was.

Ivan said, "Come on!"

Sofia and Ivan whirled Stephen toward the gate, which was barely visible as they dragged him through it.

Searing pain rushed through his body. This time, when the gateway enveloped Stephen, it wasn't just as if his stomach had flipped inside out, but as if his entire body had.

He screamed.

Stephen, Sofia, and Ivan stumbled out from the searing pain of the gateway into the duller, lingering pain of the lobby.

Well, the pain lingered for Stephen.

Once again, the others seemed fine.

Sofia had her hand clamped over his mouth, so she must have heard him scream. But he was too exhausted now to make a sound. It took his full concentration just to breathe.

She removed her hand, and they all gazed up. Above them on the wall, the gateway that had once shown the spooky castle scene depicted a moonlit forest. A milky white unicorn ran across it, horn shining.

Blinking at it, Stephen fell forward and hit the ground with a thud.

"What's that racket?" the night clerk asked. "Where did it come from?"

Thankfully the sound came from the farther side of the lobby forest. Less great was the shuffling of zombie feet in their direction and Morgenstierne's nasal answer: "It sounded like it was from a gate."

"The *Librum*!" exclaimed the night clerk.

"Maybe," Morgenstierne replied, as if he doubted it.

Of course he would.

The three of them might be concealed for now, but the night creatures would be on them in moments. Sofia hefted Stephen back onto his feet. He expected to see Ivan frozen, but the boy detective sprang into action. He grabbed the key from the base of the tree and then Stephen's other arm and whispered, "This way!"

Stephen let himself be carried along by the two of them again, willing his limbs in the direction Ivan steered them. Ivan yanked open a door past the elevator. Sofia pushed Stephen inside and against the wall and then softly pulled the door shut.

"That was way too close," she said, fumbling

around in a box on the wall beside Stephen. "Ivan, you okay? Why'd you bring us into Cindermass's lair?"

Stephen heard Ivan breathing heavily across from him. So Ivan had *not* given himself a heart attack at the thought of facing down the night clerk. And no one had burst in on them here yet. Stephen attempted to speak up and tell Ivan he'd saved them with his quick thinking.

The amount of effort it would take him to say all that still seemed . . . more than possible. He experimented with not leaning on the wall behind him and discovered that moving on his own—even standing on his own—was also beyond him.

"Er, well . . . it might have been by accident," Ivan said with a slight wheeze.

"So we're trapped in Cindermass's lair," Sofia said.

"On the bright side," Ivan said, a little defensively, "if they *did* see us come in here, which I doubt, even someone as conceited as Morgenstierne or as terrifying as the night clerk wouldn't disturb a sleeping dragon. Since we have survived both our unapproved journey to Transylvania and the foul beast in the lobby more or less intact, I'd like to keep us that way."

Sofia pulled a lighter and a long piece of wood from the box on the wall. She flicked the lighter on and held the wood to the flame, and the torch blazed to life. "I'm not sure we should disturb Cindermass, either, but I guess we don't have much choice. There's still an old dumbwaiter down there. We could take it back upstairs. We can't get busted while the count is around." None of them said that there was a distinct possibility the vampire's steward might rat them out, if he wasn't too afraid to contact his boss. "I hope Cindermass's appreciation for Stephen's artistic talents will save us." She squinted in Stephen's direction. "How are you feeling?"

"Not . . . great . . . ," he managed to say.

Speaking still seemed hard. He'd almost gotten them captured, and worst of all, they'd come back empty-handed.

A hysterical giggle emerged from Ivan. A quietish

one—the pasty night clerk and his equally blood-less friends were still somewhere on the other side of the door. "Just wait until we see Cindermass. We have another problem. I mean, besides the fact that Stephen's family's enemies once again have posses-sion of the *Librum*." Ivan turned to Sofia. "Do you think you can manage to put the key back tomor-row morning before anyone needs it?"

Sofia said, "Of course. Probably. And I'll get our phones."

Ivan handed the key to her, accepting the torch in its place.

With an effort that really deserved applause, Stephen dug Ivan's phone out of his pocket and passed it to him. Then he peeled away from the wall. "Let's go wake a dragon. . . . Actually, I could use a hand."

Sofia scooped her free arm around him.

"At least you and Ivan are okay," Stephen said. "Do you think I will be?"

Ivan held the torch high and took Stephen's other side. "I would hope that the ill effects will wear off on their own, now that we're back."

They started down the stairs. "How sure are you about that?" Sofia asked. "The wearing off?"

"Fifty percent," Ivan said more confidently than 50 percent deserved.

Stephen concentrated on moving his feet down the stairs one at a time. The journey made him feel fainter, not stronger. Not much like any effect was wearing off.

The trip down the steps took approximately forever. At last Sofia removed her arm from his shoulders, leaving him to lean on Ivan, and shimmied past them to the doors. Ivan stretched to place the torch into a sconce on the wall.

"You might want to step back while I wake up the dragon," she said.

But Stephen was too tired to move. Ivan simply stepped behind him for cover.

Sofia eased the double doors open by degrees. The torches that had been lit around Cindermass's lair before were nowhere to be seen. *Nothing* was anywhere to be seen beyond the pool of flickering light emitted by their own torch. It was as dark and as quiet as anything Stephen could imagine.

No, wait. Not *quiet. What's that?*

The noise was low and rumbly, like a subway train somewhere far beneath their feet. It got louder and louder, until twin jets of flame shot out from the center of the room. That was followed by an enormous *whoosh*, and the fires were sucked back into . . . *Cindermass's nose.*

"He's snoring!" Stephen blurted.

Cindermass's gigantic head shot up on the end of his long neck, and his eyes snapped open. Coins and jewels went jangling down the sides of the heap, and in a peeved voice, Cindermass said, "Dragons never snore."

"He didn't say snoring!" said Sofia, shaking her head. "He said, uh—"

"Boring!" said Ivan, then clapped his hand over his mouth with a horrified expression.

"Boring?" said Cindermass. "Me?"

"Into your treasure while you were asleep!" shouted Sofia, trying to be heard above the growling noise coming from somewhere deep in Cindermass's throat. "Boring into the treasure!"

"Why, yes, I suppose I was boring in that fashion. That *is* something dragons do," replied Cindermass with a sniff. He stretched out his neck and peered down at a gold-leafed clock encrusted with rubies. "Rather late for a visit from you three, is it not?"

"Ah, yes, as to that," said Ivan, "we were just, um, that is—"

"We're hiding from the night clerk," said Sofia.

The dragon swooped his head down until one of his headlamp-size eyes was directly in front of her face. "Tell me *everything*."

But then his giant eyes fixed on Stephen instead. "Wait. Never mind! I have been awaiting your next visit, young Stephen. While I was not expecting it at this exact time, I need but a moment to prepare. Close your eyes."

The suggestion was an easy one for Stephen to take. His eyes slid closed, and he felt at sea again, as if he were trapped in the gateway or at the bottom of the ocean. Ivan had moved back to his side, propping him up.

"I believe that I said *close your eyes*," Cindermass said. "I meant all of you."

"I need to keep an eye on Stephen—" Sofia started to speak.

"I'll be okay," Stephen answered, from the bottom of the ocean. At least he wasn't in actual pain, as he had been coming through the gate.

Cindermass hummed in delight. "Just a moment," he said. "Keep them closed, no peeking."

There was what sounded suspiciously like a spray of fire from a giant dragon's mouth. And then Cindermass said, "Voilà!"

Stephen was growing drowsy. He knew that wasn't right. He shouldn't be falling asleep in the middle of Cindermass's hoard, not when the dragon was excited he was here.

He was so tired, though . . .

"Voilà!" Cindermass said again. And added: "Open your eyes."

Stephen did so with great effort and was nearly

blinded by the blazing torches that now illuminated the back portion of Cindermass's cavernous lair. Eagerly taking in his reaction, the dragon had his front talons clasped together.

Sofia breathed, "That's something."

"What does our artist think?" Cindermass shifted and dislodged a pile of gold coins from the mound behind him.

"I think we'd better walk him in that direction," Ivan said, behind Stephen.

Stephen said, "I can walk," but he was glad they didn't believe him. The two of them shifted him closer to the illuminated tableau.

It was the dragon's art collection, arranged in a row as though at a fine gallery.

And it was a gallery that would rival any in the world.

Stephen wasn't sure if the lingering effects of his bad reaction to the gateway were causing a hallucination or if he really was looking at a painting by Picasso. Even with its crazy cubes and colors, it was obviously . . . "Cindermass. This is a portrait gallery," Stephen said, his legs strengthening a little. "Of you. That's a Picasso."

The next painting was a dragon surrounded by a lush jungle scene. A monkey perched on his shoulder. "Frida Kahlo." Stephen stumbled a few steps forward, and Ivan rushed to keep up with him. "That's a van Gogh!"

A swirling blue night of stars was dominated by a flying dragon, flame spraying out to light a golden haystack. Stephen used to have a poster of a similar van Gogh painting above his bed when he was little, and he recognized the other artists from gallery trips.

"You can tell they are of me!" Cindermass was delighted. "Of course my collection is incomplete because I do not have a piece from this century's rising star artiste. It is so difficult to keep a claw on the pulse of the art world from here, below the city. But I do think I know a rising star, if only . . ." Cindermass's flattery trailed off; that was good because Stephen was having trouble following it.

"What is wrong with this young man?" the dragon demanded, turning to Ivan and Sofia, sparks glowing in his nostrils. "Have you poisoned him?"

"No," Sofia said, miserable. "But he is sick. Ivan . . ."

"We're going to have to confess and get help," Ivan said. "I had surmised the same. Stephen is not recovering as quickly as I would want."

"What is wrong with this artistic genius?" Cindermass asked again. "Tell me at once!"

"We went through one of the gateways," Sofia told Cindermass. "Stephen had a bad reaction. It doesn't seem to be wearing off."

Cindermass's warm, scaly, giant hand plucked him from between Ivan and Sofia. Stephen forced his eyes open, surprised they'd drifted shut again. Cindermass cupped him gently in his palm, the dragon's nostrils glowing with controlled flame. He roared in the direction of the vents: "Awaken the medico! Mariiiinnnnaaa! Emergency!"

"On the plus side," Stephen heard Sofia say, "we won't have to worry about when to tell our parents about tonight. They're about to find out."

Stephen woke to murmuring in the most beautiful voice he'd ever heard. Once again, he felt surrounded by water.

No, wait, this time he *was* surrounded by water.

The most gorgeous woman he'd ever seen stood over him, chanting. She stopped when she realized he was awake. "He's regained consciousness."

"Stephen," his dad said, "what were you thinking? I told you gateways are dangerous for you."

His dad was holding him.

"I'm Marina," the woman said, looking down at him. Then she spoke to his dad. "There will be time enough for the reading of the riot act. He is swimming his way back to us now. The seawater and my magic will heal him. We must encourage him, in case he has the impulse to be lazy and stop halfway. We don't want that."

With his dad's help, Stephen sat up, the waves lapping at his waist. "I needed to get the book back," he explained.

"You're more important to me than the *Librum*." His dad scrubbed a hand through Stephen's hair. "I shouldn't have come down so hard on you before. I'm sorry."

"No, you don't understand—"

Marina's cool palm touched his forehead. The sand below scratched his legs as he shifted. Sand? He wanted to get up, explain that the fae definitely had the book. They'd get it back now, wouldn't they?

"You must be calm," Marina said. "Plenty of time to talk later."

Marina's hair flowed across her shoulders like vines or seaweed—beautiful vines or seaweed. And she wore a seashell bra.

He didn't remember her looking so *alluring* in the lobby.

Stephen blushed.

She was talking to his dad. "He needs to rest. Let's get him up to the Village. He'll be fine. Then, after he is up and about, assuming you're both still here, we'll get him on an intense fitness regimen. Tired children, even ones with fae blood, do not go on adventures through gateways."

"You're sure it's safe to move him now?" his dad asked.

"I'll summon the gargoyles," she said, her tone reassuring. "I have a mat they can use to take him up to his bed."

What had she meant a few moments ago . . . *if*

they both were still here?

"Why—" Stephen attempted to speak.

Marina's hand landed on his forehead again, and she murmured a low word he didn't understand. He dived headfirst back into unconsciousness.

CHAPTER EIGHTEEN

Stephen had never known that getting dressed in a T-shirt and jeans could be so magnificent. The next morning it was.

Having arms and legs that move when you want them to is amazing, he thought as he lifted a shirt over his head. His legs carried him out of his bedroom and up the hall.

His dad sat at the kitchen table surrounded by loose papers that included what looked like recipes—in most cases handwritten on parchment, but a few on note cards—and bent over his iPad.

Stephen cleared his throat, and wonder of wonders, sound came out. His dad's head shot up. "Never ever scare me like that again," he said, rising and crossing the room to Stephen, whom he pulled into a hug.

"Dad," Stephen said, surprised to find he was choked up, too. *Throat, now that you work,* keep *working.* "There's so much I have to tell you. Count von Morgenstierne's steward said he gave the book to a fae girl, and I think—"

"Sofia and Ivan told us the whole story," his dad interrupted. "I'm sorry we accused you—that I did. I should have known you weren't lying to me. But Stephen, if Marina wasn't the best medico on the planet, you would not be up and around at all. You can never take a risk like that again."

His dad's face went funny, and he absently brushed his hand over Stephen's hair.

"What is it? Have we demanded the book back

from the fae?" Stephen asked.

"Uh, no," his dad said. "The Manager says it's still not on the premises and to demand it from the Court of Thorns would escalate diplomatic tensions, something Carmen is trying her best to avoid with Count von Morgenstierne already."

"But—"

Stephen's dad held his hand up. "There's more." He composed himself. "Under pressure from the Octagon, the Manager made a declaration about my status. I'm good through Cindermass's party, because there's no time to find anyone to step in. And I pray I'm good enough to get through it with my *own* skill. But if the book isn't recovered by the end of that evening, I'll be exiled again. We'll be going back to Chicago." He made a noise that wasn't quite a laugh. "There are worse things."

Stephen heard everything his father wasn't saying: that he couldn't think of many worse things, that he'd finally gotten back into the family line and now he might lose that chance forever, lose the Lawson legacy forever.

"We can't let that happen," Stephen said.

"Carmen's working as hard as she can. She sent a message to the La Doyts at the inn in Faery, updating them on the situation." He sighed. "It's still possible this is a prank and that the fae will just . . . execute it and call it a day."

That didn't sound convincing to Stephen. "We can't do anything else?"

"Theft by the fae of human property is illegal—under the same rule that prevents their stealing children—but it's the proof that's the hard part. The word of a vampire's servant gained during trespass doesn't count. In the meantime Carmen's working on negotiating the book's safe return. The La Doyts might come back before we expect them to. All this could still work out."

"Dad . . ."

"Yes?"

Words burst out of Stephen. "You are *way* too calm. This is a disaster!"

"I'm handling this the best way I know how." His dad frowned at him. "We're expected downstairs now. You've got to face some music, and I have to get back to the kitchen." His dad paused. "I can make you breakfast down there."

"I'm not hungry." Which was almost true. He could eat later. There was zero chance that Ivan would let the adults get away with this minimalist plan. Hoping and quiet legwork weren't enough. "I need to see Ivan and Sofia."

"They're probably downstairs waiting for us. Carmen said she has your phone."

Stephen gave a short nod, and, after his dad gathered up his papers, they crossed the green to the elevator. His dad hit the button, and it took a few moments for the car to arrive.

When the little bell went *bing,* the doors flew open faster than Stephen had ever seen them move.

"Stephen! Thank the stars—not that I've ever seen the stars except for glimpses above the roof, mind you, because I am stuck here with my four walls, my top and my bottom, my cables and my electrical circuits, designed for movement and yet what kind of movement? Up and down, down and up, always. Never outside. Never where you can see the full, majestic sky." The elevator sighed. "Oh, I am so foolish! This is not about me. Step on board, Stephen! Let me look at you!"

Stephen's dad said, "After you," trying not to smile and failing.

"I'm fine now, Elevator," Stephen said as the doors closed and they descended, though a button hadn't been pushed. "I guess gateways don't agree with me."

"No!" said the elevator. "They most certainly do not. From what I have heard it was a harrowing adventure. And you were so brave! But you must be more careful with your choice of conveyances. I may only be able to take you up and down this hotel shaft, but Stephen, it is my solemn vow that no harm will come to you on my watch. Why, if you had but asked, I could have engaged the night clerk in conversation to be your distraction."

"Um." Stephen glanced at his dad. The "whole story" from Ivan and Sofia must have included everything they'd done.

"Though"—the elevator went on—"on second thought, that would have only freed you to go through the foul gateway, which could have *killed you*. Alas! What use would a conspirator trapped like me be anyway? Let us hope that Lady Carmen will save the day. Here we are." The doors opened, and Stephen's dad walked out.

As Stephen exited, the elevator called one last thing: "I am so happy you are well." And the doors closed.

No matter what, apparently he could count on the elevator's being in his corner. As long as they were still here.

Ahead in the lobby were two other people he could count on, Ivan and Sofia. They were dressed normally, Ivan in one of his dress shirts and tweed pants, wearing a plaid bow tie, and Sofia in a red dress with pink flowers sewn on the top. They stood very straight with their hands clasped in front of them, like the best-behaved kids in the world.

That was probably because of the other people with them in the otherwise deserted lobby. Carmen was there, and the woman Marina, in a collared shirt with the words *Medico/Trainer* embroidered on one side and a pair of shorts. She looked almost like a different person.

They were standing in front of the gateway from the night before. Now its vista was of a place with colorful trees and small people in work clothes rushing around them.

Carmen spotted Stephen and his dad first. "Free from sick bay just in time," she said, in a way that made Stephen certain the opposite was true.

"I was just asleep in my room," he said.

"Only because the Knight Medico here was able to stabilize you enough."

Stephen nodded to the woman. "Thank you," he said.

Marina narrowed her eyes at him. "You are welcome, but you come see me soon. I will make you stronger."

"Never mind that just now, Marina. I need a word with these three." Carmen raised an eyebrow at him, then at Sofia and Ivan. So that was where

Sofia got the gene for the single-eyebrow raise.

The healer shrugged a single shoulder and took off briskly across the lobby. "Last night," Stephen said, "she seemed, um . . ."

"It's a mermaid thing," Sofia told him. "When she's in her natural form, she enchants all who look upon her."

"She's a mermaid?" Stephen asked. He probably shouldn't have been surprised, but he was.

Carmen returned Stephen's phone to him with a hard look, then crossed her arms over her chest. "Listen up, all of you. The Manager is upset about your little trip last night. Oh, and he's not happy about how badly you frightened the night clerk either."

At this, Ivan's mouth dropped open.

Stephen was lost. Why on earth were they wasting time talking about this right now? When his dad was going to cook for a dragon's birthday without his extra-special culinary alchemy book? When he might lose this world forever?

"Your midnight shenanigans didn't just put you

in danger," Carmen said, "but others as well. Not to mention the hotel's reputation."

"What we found out was important," Stephen said, unable to take this any longer. "Why are we just standing here? We need to get the book back. Stop whatever those awful fae are up to."

"Ixnay on the fae-ay," Sofia said.

"Still not how pig Latin works." Stephen waited for the adults to answer him.

"We aren't just standing here," Carmen said.

Ivan put in: "She sent a communiqué to my parents. They should get it today."

"Yes, and the diplomacy here is delicate," Carmen said. "I've also sent a petition to Baroness Thyme to allow me to speak with her today."

"Yeah, well," Stephen said, "since the Manager's kicking us out for good if we don't find the book, it still seems like not enough."

Carmen and his dad both shot him quelling looks. The surprise on his friends' faces told him they hadn't known about that part yet.

"Now, listen, this organization hasn't kept the

peace for centuries by—" Carmen stopped and rolled her eyes. "Wait. What am I doing? You three are no longer involved in this. Not a word to anyone about any of it. Let us handle it. Understand?"

Stephen couldn't believe it. "No, I don't. It's not enough!"

"That *is* enough from you," his dad said.

"*None* of this is enough," Stephen said. "The fae aren't going to play nice."

Carmen stared at Stephen, then included Ivan and Sofia in the line of the fire of her gaze. "All three of you, back up to the Village. You're grounded for the rest of the day."

CHAPTER NINETEEN

Julio escorted them upstairs, staring straight ahead at the elevator doors, probably so that Sofia couldn't try to appeal to him on their behalf.

Though she made no move to. When Stephen looked at her, she shook her head. Meanwhile Ivan wore his distracted, deep-in-thought expression. How he was able to concentrate Stephen didn't understand, because the ride was the opposite of quiet. The whole way up to the roof, the elevator expressed its sympathies.

"Poor Stephen is just upset, and who could blame him? His family's very reputation hangs in the balance. And even one as old as I cannot remember the last millennial celebration for a dragon, but I have heard tell that the culinary alchemy required is tricky indeed. Of course I'll never see one, flambé and burn or no, stuck here as always . . ."

Stephen listened to this with one ear. The adults thought they were taking the right actions and following their fancy knight protocols, but waiting around for Ivan's parents to show up with proof or for the fae to decide to play nice didn't seem smart.

The elevator doors parted to reveal the gray-skinned housekeeping staff having a picnic in the grass. They were terrifying in their black-and-white uniforms, gnawing at giant turkey legs.

"Okay, jailbirds, straight to your cells," Julio said, his sword tapping his leg as he walked them to Stephen's cottage first. There he paused and called up to the gargoyles: "Do not let these three collude. Or escape," he said.

Sollie fluttered in the air above them. "You're the boss!" he chirped.

Were the gargoyles ever not cheerful? The rest of them flew into view around Sollie. Liz sang out, "Guess who gets to be croquet champion when Sofia's in trouble!"

Sofia scoffed. "Sure, when there's no competition!"

A laugh rang out from Julio, but he banished it just as quickly. "When you're grounded, there's no competitive taunting or any other kind of horsing around allowed."

"Neigh," Sofia said, in her best horse imitation. She clip-clopped her booted feet.

Julio clearly wanted to laugh. But he held it in somehow. He pointed at the door to Stephen's cottage and waited until he was inside.

Then Stephen heard a *plunk* and went over to the window to look out. Julio had the tip of his sword pressed against the door, while he said some incantation.

After Julio lowered the sword and strode away with Ivan and Sofia, Stephen tried the door.

It wouldn't budge an inch. He was magically trapped in the cottage.

Great.

He went to his room and took out the crime scene sketch from the other morning, to see if it had any new clues to offer. There were his dad and Sofia's mom and Trevor, the gateway painting of

Transylvania behind them. The gateways were still filled with slight motion.

He needed to do some research. He restashed the drawing and flopped down on his bed with the *Almanack*. He'd put it off long enough. He flipped to the lengthy entry about the fae.

Fae

The peoples collectively known as the fae, residing in the Realm of Faery, have a history stretching back to the earliest memories of humankind or even of dragonkind. Their natural magic is potent and somewhat mysterious, capable of expressing itself in a number of ways. Most typically, it is employed for glamours, passing between worlds, and bargaining for objects they desire. The importance of these is reflected in their history....

Stephen read on, a lot of very long words, making up very long sentences, making up paragraphs that went on for more than a page each. He decided to skip the rest of the history section for now. The next heading was "Politics." *Might be something useful there.* He skimmed through the closely lined pages:

The seemingly numberless Courts of Faery are practically impenetrable to most outsiders. Even the Knights Diplomatis have sometimes been known to throw up their hands in frustration when confronted with the tangled ways of the Fair Folk. The fae place great pride and importance on rank, lineage, and titles. Their seat on the Octagon has been occupied most recently by Princess Aria of the Primrose Court. However, she has been in self-exile and not present to attend meetings of the Octagon for more than ten years. As a result, the external clout of the fae with the other supernormal communities has declined.

Okay, thought Stephen, *my mother's being gone hasn't been good for them. They have complicated politics, they like titles, and they don't get along with anybody, not even other fae.*

He thought of that first night and the invitation they'd issued him. And then they'd sent Sarabel to follow him around; of that he was sure. Now they had the book back and had gone so far as to ally themselves with a vampire on the Octagon. The baroness wanted power. But what were they *really* up to? He was certain they didn't just plan to hang on to the book for safekeeping.

He flipped forward to a section titled "Customs and Mores" and then was about to skip it because it seemed to be mainly about clothes, but one last fact, at the end of a particularly lengthy paragraph, jumped out at him. It was the shortest sentence in the entry, by far: "The fae never lie." Right. Ivan and Sofia and even the baroness had said this was true. Now *that* might come in handy. And the baroness had said that Stephen *could* lie. Which he already knew, but it might come in useful for dealing with the fae.

The adults might be okay with their diplomatic

and aboveboard plans, hoping for the best. Stephen wasn't. He *had* created the opportunity for Lady Sarabel to steal the book. He had a duty to help get it back and save his dad's position.

If only he hadn't been trapped in the cottage, under Julio's spell.

Stephen got up and pushed aside the curtain to look out his window at the strange, overgrown garden. On one side it had tall, thick stalks, which he was developing a theory were beanstalks, and flowers that seemed to smile, and vines that crept and reached.

Huh, that's interesting. The garden did change depending on the time of day, but it had never had a path in it before. Someone had tramped down a path through the overgrowth, making a trail from the front yard to—

"Wait a second," he said.

He narrowed his eyes. Someone was tramping that path *right now*. An *invisible* someone! As he watched, more of the plants bent under footsteps that he couldn't see.

Could it be Lady Sarabel again? His heart pounded as he flung his window open and demanded, "Who's out there?"

"I told you that invisibility spray doesn't work all that great." The answering voice was Sofia's.

Ivan sighed, and the two of them slowly materialized. "It doesn't matter that Stephen detected us," Ivan said, spraying them both down with a cloud from another of his magic perfume bottles. "What matters is that we made it out of your house and across the Village without being seen by anyone who might tattle on us."

"Hello, Ivan! Hello, Sofia!"

The voice came from above, and the three of them looked up. Sollie, the gargoyle, slowly flapped his wings as he spiraled in for a landing. He was heavily burdened with a barely balanced stack of packages.

Sollie added, "And hello, Stephen! Can't stay to chat, this is the busiest day we'll have all year! The birthday deliveries have started coming in!"

Liz fluttered up to join him, also carrying a tall

stack of parcels. "They're supposed to be *grounded*," she said with a grimace.

"Oh, right!" Sollie chirruped. "You're supposed to be grounded," he told them, as if they'd forgotten. He hovered in the air with the teetering tower of presents.

"Oh, this is working out brilliantly." Sofia made a face, then called up to the gargoyles: "We just need to talk to Stephen. We're still in the Village. If you could forget you saw us, I'll make it worth your while."

Liz and Sollie dropped closer. "How's that?" Liz asked.

"I could, well, not be as good as usual at croquet tomorrow?" Sofia said.

"It's a deal!" Sollie called, and the two of them laughed and shot back in the other direction over the roof with their heavy loads.

"The sacrifices I make for the greater good," said Sofia dramatically.

Stephen leaned on the windowsill. "Since when can we become invisible?"

"Since the mid-seventeenth century," said Ivan,

"when Alexandra La Doyt formulated a potion that causes light rays to bend around anything it touches."

Stephen considered that. "But if it's a potion, that means you drink it."

Ivan looked flustered. "Well, yes, it turned her insides invisible. Eventually she modified it to an aerosol form."

Stephen glanced around, including up at the sky. Now that the gargoyles were gone, nobody else was in sight. "How did you get out of your house? I thought we were spelled in our cottages or something?"

"We are," Sofia said. "Or were. Dad always thinks that stupid door charm will work. He never remembers to do the windows, too."

Sofia reached in and pushed Stephen back out of the way, then climbed through the window. She turned to help Ivan do the same, then closed the window. She flopped down onto Stephen's bed, pushing the *Almanack* aside, and Ivan took a seat beside her, folding his hands tidily.

"I might have a plan," Stephen said.

"Do you think we should do another plan?" Sofia asked. "You didn't see yourself last night. You looked like you were dying. Cindermass *freaked* out. And . . . so did we."

Part of Stephen had wondered if the howling dragon and Marina healing him was a dream. "I'm fine now," he said. "Except that we still didn't get the book back."

Sofia said, "I just find it hard to believe you're ready to jump right back into trouble."

"Says the formerly invisible girl," Stephen countered.

Ivan cleared his throat. "Whatever your plan is, Sofia is correct: we must be more careful this time." Sofia smiled, pleased, and it was Stephen's turn to frown. "But Stephen is also correct that we can't stand by and wait. After all, that's why we came here."

"Also, I'm starving," Sofia said, "and I'll bet you have better snacks."

They followed her as she stalked into the kitchen

and started rummaging in the fridge without even asking.

"So, what's your plan?" Ivan asked him.

"We're going to go talk to the fae," Stephen said. "No waiting and hoping they allow us to talk to them—the baroness practically issued me an open invitation. And while we're there, I'm going to ask them questions that will make them reveal the truth. They can't lie."

Sofia and Ivan froze. Stephen was always skeptical when he came across that description in books, but they both went utterly still. Finally Sofia angled away from the fridge and said, "One does not simply walk onto the fourth floor and talk to the fae."

"We went to see the vampire," Stephen said. "And we *know* the fae are involved up to their green necks. There's no choice."

"He's not wrong," Ivan said to Sofia. Then he said to them both, "Sofia's not wrong either. Talking to the fae is dangerous. Especially for you."

Ivan was turning into quite the mediator, if not an especially helpful one.

"Not as dangerous as going to Transylvania," Stephen said.

"Probably way more dangerous," Sofia said, "given that we know they're fixated on your family and that you're, um—"

"Partly one of them?" Stephen asked. "I didn't forget. How could I, after last night? It doesn't matter. We have to go anyway. No, not anyway, *because* of that."

They were silent for a long moment, maybe waiting for him to change his mind. He wasn't going to.

Finally Sofia said, "This should be interesting."

"Let's just hope it's not so interesting we end up as a footnote in some handbook on fae etiquette," Ivan said.

Sofia closed the fridge door and blinked at them.

"What is it?" Stephen asked.

"There's no handbook, but . . . ," she said, skipping back up the hall toward Stephen's room. There was practically a lightbulb floating over her head.

Stephen shrugged at Ivan, and they went after her. They reached Stephen's room as she was clambering back out the window. Stephen let Ivan go through, then followed suit. He jumped down to the ground and scurried to catch up to them.

Sofia stalked up a narrow row of creeping and crawling plants in front of Ivan. A red-leaved tendril reached out and snaked around her wrist, and she slapped it away and continued on.

Stephen looked around to confirm that they were definitely alone out here. Everyone else in the Village must be either sleeping or working or—in the case of the gargoyles—accepting deliveries and also not paying attention to the three of them anymore.

As they tromped through the rich soil of the rectangular garden (undoubtedly another environmental trick of the Manager's), the same red-leaved plant tried to snarl around Stephen's arm.

Ivan turned and scolded the vine, "No, Lucy," and it waved once before lowering into harmlessness. When Stephen raised his eye-brows in question, Ivan explained: "Creeping crimson claw vine in general, Lucy in specific. She was one of your grandmother's favorites in the kitchen garden."

No wonder he didn't know what many of the plants were. Ambrosia's kitchen garden *would* have far more exotic things in it than the usual basil and oregano.

Finally they reached Sofia, kneeling in front of a patch of leafy green plants with soft pink blooms and hairy green pods. This wasn't among the more exotic offerings, but Stephen still didn't recognize it.

Sofia started talking as if she'd never stopped. "So we don't have a handbook, but there *are* a number of known wards and charms that are useful against the fae. And you know Lady Nanette wasn't on good terms with the Court of Thorns, so she kept a nice supply of common milkweed."

Feeling her way up the green plant, she plucked off a strand with leaves and a pod, then another.

"I remember a fae wedding we hosted here once, and all the non-fae guests and order members wore necklaces made out of milkweed. Ivan and I will do the same! It apparently keeps you from being tricked or kidnapped away to the revels."

Stephen was still trying to wrap his head around the word *kidnapped* when Sofia's face fell.

"Those necklaces were made of *dried* milkweed," she said. "This won't work."

"Will something that small matter?" Stephen asked, but he was already remembering how small substitutions had completely changed the effects of the *Librum* recipes he'd made. "I'm assuming you said you and Ivan because I can't wear it?"

Not being entirely human seemed to create constant problems and rarely solve them.

She nodded. "And for all we know, a fresh milkweed necklace makes us particularly susceptible to the fae's charms."

Ivan stepped closer to Sofia. "Sofia, hold out the milkweed."

She did, suspiciously. "Why?"

Stephen wasn't surprised when Ivan removed yet another small spray bottle from his pocket.

"How big can your pockets be?" he asked.

"As big as they need to be to hold the essential tools of the detective trade," Ivan said. "Our clothes are custom made by St. Vincent von Claire, tailor to the sleuth stars."

Sleuth stars? "Right, of course."

Sofia waved her hand around in the air. The milkweed sashayed in the breeze. Ivan began to spray it, and almost immediately—

"It's dying!" Sofia said.

"No," Ivan said, continuing. "It's drying. This is called *desiccato*. It removes the moisture from plants, instantly drying and aging them."

"Just out of curiosity, why would you have that in your special pockets?" Stephen asked.

Ivan didn't even pause. "To be prepared."

Sofia switched stalks, happily waving the dry, dead-looking milkweed around before she set it beside her on the ground.

"Has any La Doyt, in the history of La Doyt

crime solving, ever needed to use it before?" Stephen asked.

"Er, no," Ivan said. "Until now. La Doyts play the long game."

Maybe Ivan's parents *would* come back from Faery with his mother.

Sofia held up a few more strands of milkweed in Ivan's mist of decay.

Stephen reached out to pitch in, but the second he touched the milkweed his fingertips burned. "Ouch!"

"Told you," Sofia said. She began weaving the dried strands together. "Now, listen up, both of you. The fae have been interacting with humans since before recorded history. There are very specific protocols for dealing with them, which we must follow exactly. These count for you, too, Stephen."

"They seem mostly like greenish humans in funny outfits." He recalled again Sarabel's smirking and the baroness's constant amusement at him. "*Mean* greenish humans in funny outfits."

"They're much more than that," said Ivan,

pausing at his spraying. "In a way they're the most dangerous supernormals of all. They can slip right out of the world into an alternate reality that they rule absolutely. And they can take humans with them under certain circumstances, even today, if the humans aren't being careful."

"Like by wearing dried milkweed necklaces," Sofia put in.

"What do the fae call the 'alternate reality'?" Stephen asked.

"Faery," said Ivan.

"Clever," said Stephen. That had been in the entry in the *Almanack*, just put differently.

"They *are* clever," cut in Sofia. "You have to remember that. They'll always try to outsmart whoever they're talking to, so you have to pay very close attention. They like to bend the rules." She didn't have to say, "like you." It was implied. "Never say 'yes' when a fae asks you a question. They can't lie, but there's no way to be absolutely sure they won't twist the answer around into something opposite or dangerous. Never eat or drink anything they offer you. And always, *always* be superpolite."

"Polite?" asked Stephen. "They're trying to ruin my family."

"Trust me," said Sofia. "The baroness has already tried to get you to become her ward. You have to be careful *and* polite."

Fair enough. He did trust Sofia. And what she'd said gelled with his impressions about "fairies" from the stories he'd read and movies he'd seen.

Sofia accepted the rest of the dried milkweed and wove it quickly into one more necklace.

So far being half fae had zero to recommend it other than a cool bonus illustration skill.

"Hang this around your neck," she said, extending a milkweed circle to Ivan and putting on her own. The necklaces looked like sad wreaths made out of twisted dried weeds. "Put it *under* your shirt collar. This isn't like with the vamps and the crosses. If they see it, they might take it as an insult. But as long as it isn't literally visible, we should be okay."

There was a dusty smell rising from the necklaces that made Stephen's nose itch. Ivan loosened his bow tie, so he could follow the instructions.

Sofia tucked hers under the fabric of her dress. It made a lump, but the weeds didn't show through any other way.

Ivan had gotten the milkweed strung around his neck and was rebuttoning his shirt. It turned out he actually knew how to do the bow tie without a mirror. That was impressive.

"Now"—Sofia went on (unimpressed, but she'd probably seen Ivan knot up a tie before)—"the fae have, well, diplomatic immunity, essentially, for most minor infractions and so on while they're in our world. That's why it's been so hard to get evidence enough to accuse them. When they stay at the hotel, whatever floor they're on is treated as if it were part of Faery itself."

"Like how an embassy is the territory of whatever country it represents," Stephen said.

"If you say so," Sofia agreed.

Stephen had almost forgotten that he probably knew a whole lot more about the regular world than they did.

"Some even say that it has a pass-through so they can get back and forth without leaving," Sofia said.

"If that's true, they could have easy access to the book without keeping it here at the hotel," Stephen said.

"In theory, at least." Ivan finished with his bow tie, and it was as perfect as if he'd never removed it. "How are we going to get down to the fourth floor without being spotted?"

Stephen had already thought ahead to this part. His dad's restaurant back in Chicago had a dumbwaiter that ran from the old basement storeroom up to the kitchen. He'd mastered riding it alone, after discovering that he could jump out and scare the kitchen staff when his dad sent them on errands downstairs. "Didn't you mention there's an old system of dumbwaiters, no longer used? It's how we were going to escape Cindermass's lair, if I remember."

Sofia favored him with a beaming smile. "Yes, and there is one in the currently closed Ambrosia. Which isn't so far for us to sneak to, at all."

Ivan was already reaching into his miracle pocket, but Sofia said, "We shouldn't need to be invisible again."

Ivan was obviously disappointed. "You think you can ask your questions politely?" he asked Stephen. "Should we practice them?"

"I know what I want to ask," Stephen said. "And I promise to do what you said."

"Good," Sofia said.

CHAPTER TWENTY

A little while later they sneaked around the side of the cottage and peered across the deserted green. The gargoyles must have been busy bringing packages and parcels into the hotel because even they weren't in sight.

"Let's make a run for it!" Sofia said.

She was already bolting across the grass. Stephen sped up enough to catch her, and they reached the nearly hidden door to the stairs at the same time. In silent agreement they waited for Ivan.

Who was prepared for everything except running fast.

And then they went as quietly as possible down the short flight of stairs to the restaurant. Ambrosia was dark and empty, since it was the lull between lunch and dinner service.

"Dumbwaiters are this way," Sofia said, heading around the sign and through the space.

What a grand restaurant this must be when not packed with shouting, disappointed customers. Now that it was empty, Stephen could appreciate how luxurious it was, every table well appointed, roomy but also intimate. It was, he realized, the restaurant his dad always described as his ultimate dream.

This was where he'd always wanted to cook.

And no one was going to take that away from him, not if Stephen could help it.

They reached the back, where a smaller gateway showed a glazed brick wall that must be in the kitchen. It sat across from what Stephen instantly recognized as a shuttered dumbwaiter. Ivan and Sofia paused in front of the closed-up door, hesitantly, as if they didn't know what to do. Stephen stepped right up and hit the left-most button at the bottom.

There was a click as the catch that had locked

the door in place released, and he pushed the door up to reveal a flat shelf that would fit them all if they stood close.

"All aboard," Stephen said with a flourish.

Sofia made a fake stirrup with her hands, and Ivan climbed in first. She accepted his hand and leaped up to join him. She said, "But how will we close it and press the button?"

There was another button beside the first, to activate the dumbwaiter, and a dial with numbers that must correspond to the floors of the hotel. Stephen thumbed the setting to four. Once they were done on the fourth floor, the dumbwaiter would automatically bring them back here.

"Got it covered," he said.

He picked up a fork off the nearest vacant table, jumped up to join them, and let Sofia and Ivan guide him into place on the metal platform. There was room enough for him to crouch and pull down the door from the inside. He stopped to stick the tines of the fork out at the bottom and angled them. . . . Almost there . . . Almost . . .

The button depressed, he pulled the fork back into the cramped space above the platform, and down they went.

Slowly. Oh, *so* slowly.

It was dark, and the long-out-of-use pulleys creaked and protested.

After what seemed like an age, in which a million dragons must have had a million birthdays, the dumbwaiter shuddered to a halt.

"When in doubt, let me do the talking. And remember, *don't say yes* to anything," Sofia said.

"Got it," said Stephen.

He worked the fork under the edge of the dumbwaiter door to press the button that would open it.

He thought the fourth floor might look greenish . . . or enchanted . . . or otherworldly in some way. He was ready for almost anything.

But it turned out that he *wasn't* expecting the fourth floor to look exactly like a normal, if fancy, hotel floor. It boasted lush carpet, striped wallpaper, and doors with numbers on them every twelve feet or so. No indoor forests, no magical mists or bloodcurdlingly dim lighting, not even a croquet set. He would have been vaguely disappointed, if it hadn't been even more ominous that nothing on this floor looked ominous.

"Which room do we knock at?" he asked.

"It won't matter," Sofia said.

When Stephen started toward the closest door, she grabbed his arm and said, "Wait."

She hesitated and then walked halfway up the hall, where there was—unexpectedly—a sign that said VENDING. She pushed the button on what seemed to be a normal ice machine and gathered up three cubes of ice.

"Gifts are always important in dicey diplomatic situations," she said.

She handed off one cube to Stephen—so cold it froze his palm—and one to Ivan, keeping the third for herself. Only then did she walk over to the last door on the floor and, instead of knocking, dip into a deep curtsy and say, "Most serene and exalted Baroness, we come bearing gifts of crystal from the mortal realm."

Ivan was bowing and holding his ice cube out in front of him, palm up. So Stephen hastily did the same thing. He noted that the ice wasn't melting. His ears began to heat just as the door swung open.

Baroness Thyme didn't answer Sofia's greeting. It was the knight, Celidyl, in a pair of tight pants and leather boots to his knees, with a poufy shirt that laced in the front. His sword hung at his side. He tilted his head at an angle that made him seem extremely skeptical of whatever had brought them to visit.

"Stephen Lawson, you are welcome here," Celidyl said, casting a cool gaze over Ivan and Sofia.

Stephen looked to Sofia for a cue. She straightened and held her ice cube up higher. Ivan kept holding his ice cube out, too, so Stephen did likewise.

"Knight of the Evening Lands," Sofia said, "all three of us have come to visit with Baroness Thyme and inquire as to recent events."

"Ah, enter then," the knight said. He added, "And inquire, if you dare."

The taunt in the words was directed at Stephen, not the others. He was the one, after all, whom the fae had decided to set up. Lady Sarabel had smirked about it right to his face.

The fae knight extended his hand, and Stephen dropped his ice cube into it.

Should we have come here? Stephen thought, but it felt too late to turn back. He stepped across the threshold and turned to make sure the knight didn't shut the door on Ivan and Sofia.

As Sofia followed, the fae lazily reached down and collected her ice cube. Then, as he swept up Ivan's, his hand moved so fast that it blurred in the air.

Behind his glasses Ivan blinked. "I did not realize such speed was a gift of the fae," he said.

Lord Celidyl smiled and drew his sword. He whipped it through the air as Ivan shrank against the wall. "Lots of practice," he said.

Sofia shifted so that she was between the knight and Ivan. The knight slowly replaced his blade in its sheath.

Stephen definitely did *not* want to visit any alternate reality they called home—as an invited guest or otherwise. "We're here to see the baroness," Stephen managed to say.

"She and Lady Sarabel wait within," the knight said, leading them forward.

The suite was wide enough for Stephen, Ivan, and Sofia to walk side by side, and so they did. The inside of the hotel room was . . . the inside of a hotel room. Well, maybe too grand to be called a room. It was a suite. Fancier than any one he'd ever been in, with heavy drapes pulled back from a line of tall windows that revealed the city beyond, and dark wooden furniture bearing velvet cushions. Large oil paintings lined the walls: landscapes of trees and capering figures.

Movement to one side caught Stephen's eye. Hanging on the wall was a light-filled landscape, with clouds scudding across a blue sky within the frame. A stag leaped across the painting and into the woods.

"That is one of your mother's paintings."

Baroness Thyme's voice sounded as if it were speaking right against his ear.

Between one moment and the next, the two fae ladies appeared. The suite opened up, revealing a vast expanse. And in its center, dead ahead, were three chairs with high backs and curved arms.

Baroness Thyme sat in the middle minithrone. Her skin was pale green, but her cheeks were rosy, her shiny black hair piled on her head. The skirts of her dress had enough fabric for three, bulging out on either side of her. Her red lips curved into a smile of greeting, but her eyes were like the ice cubes Celidyl had taken from their palms, hard and cold.

On Baroness Thyme's right side was Lady Sarabel. She had on the same kind of satin dress as the baroness, but hers was feathered and cut shorter. When she grinned, her teeth were as pointed as a shark's.

Her teeth hadn't been pointy before. Stephen took this as confirmation that glamours were definitely her thing.

Celidyl eased into the unoccupied seat, his hand remaining on the pommel of his sword. "They've come to visit with you and make inquiries, Baroness," he said.

"Would you like to know about your mother, Stephen?" the baroness asked. "Is that why you have come?"

He *did* want to know about her, but not from the baroness. "I—"

"Come closer," she said, almost smiling. "I can barely hear you. After all, we don't bite."

Lady Sarabel laughed. "Speaking of bites, may we offer you some refreshment?" she asked. She lifted her hand, and there was a bell in it, so that she could ring for servants if they said the word.

"No," Ivan said, low and shaky.

Sofia spoke up. "Your offer is generous and most kind. But we would not want to *impose* on your hospitality in such a way. We value the rules of hospitality greatly. We wished only to . . ." She paused to swallow.

Stephen's heart beat in a much quicker rhythm than normal.

Baroness Thyme watched him as if she could hear it.

Sofia finished: "We wished only to visit and inquire about recent events."

Baroness Thyme folded her pale green hands in her lap. "Recent events," she repeated. "You are no doubt speaking of the loss of the *Librum de Coquina*. We received a request from the Diplomatis to discuss the very same thing."

Her eyes returned to Stephen. There was a hungry look to her, as always.

"But we were hoping to hear from you instead, dear Stephen, our lost son. And now here you are."

The room grew frigid. Stephen shivered.

"Family matters should be handled with family," Baroness Thyme went on.

Beside her, Lady Sarabel snorted. She subsided when the baroness glanced her way again.

"Are you trying to say that *we're* family?" Stephen recalled what his dad had said that first night at the hotel. "My dad said we're distant relations at best."

"Distance makes the heart grow fonder, they

say," the baroness said. "Your mother must be very fond indeed of you by now."

A low blow, but the baroness was forgetting that Stephen had never known his mother. He'd known his father his entire life.

She'd reminded Stephen why he was here: to save his father's job and their family legacy.

I can't fail him.

Sofia began to speak, choosing her words slowly. "Baroness, we wished only to—to—" She bit her lip.

Stephen could guess from her expression that she didn't know what to say next.

"Human child," the baroness said, "has your mother taught you no better? Be direct. What you want to know is if we are aware of the location of the Lawson family's prized possession. So, just ask."

Sofia's mouth dropped open. She was clearly still struggling for words.

"Wait a moment . . . ," Ivan said but trailed off when Lord Celidyl put his hand on the pommel of his sword.

"Wait." Stephen jumped in. "You know why we're

here. Someone in this room took my dad's book and pretended to be me." Uh-oh. That part wasn't polite. "Anyway, I've come here to ask for it back."

"Young cousin," Baroness Thyme said, and it was impossible to look away from her, "it's very important to you that the *Librum* is found, isn't it? We had even heard that your father's position is in jeopardy again because of its absence."

Stephen remembered Sofia's warning about answering any questions with yes. "Where is the book?" he asked.

Simple, straightforward, what they'd come for.

The baroness stood, and both Lord Celidyl and Lady Sarabel smiled.

"Oh, no," Stephen heard Ivan say under his breath.

Sofia said, under hers, "Courage."

"Unwarranted accusations," said the baroness, focusing intently on Stephen. "You imply that we have stolen the book." She turned to look at Ivan. "Unwelcome investigations. Not only are you here, but your parents are blundering around the Evening

Lands." Then, to Sofia: "Unauthorized negotiations. You come here mouthing words of diplomacy cloaking conspiracy theories. I count these as insults from all three of you. The Court of Thorns has the right to demand satisfaction for these insults. And we do."

Stephen turned to Sofia for guidance, but her eyes were closed, her expression shuttered.

"What does that mean?" he asked.

The baroness's red lips stretched into a wide smile. Then: "It means you will be given a chance to prove your allegations in a suitable time frame or we will claim reparations to restore our honor."

"You've twisted everything around," Stephen protested.

"It is what they do," said Ivan quietly.

The baroness sat back down. "We leave after the celebration tomorrow night, so you will have until then to recover the book—from the somewhere *we* have hidden it, if your claims are correct. Because we are kin, I will share with you one small confidence, a promise. . . ."

She exchanged a grin with Lady Sarabel.

"You *will* see the book soon, even if no Lawson ever holds it again. You will see it, and all the supernormal luminaries gathered for this weekend's august occasion along with you. There will be many on hand to witness your family's comeuppance."

Stephen tried to wrap his mind around what she was saying. "You mean the book will be at Cindermass's party? If we see it, then we'll get it back. And we will prove it was you who took it."

"We shall see," the baroness said. "We gave you the opportunity to come with us willingly, young Stephen, and you declined. So when you *fail* to recover the *Librum de Coquina* and prove your allegations, then, Stephen Lawson, Ivanos La Doyt, and Sofia Gutierrez, our reparations shall be the three of you. You will like the Evening Lands. And as your guardian I shall like holding the fae seat on the Octagon."

"What?" Stephen's heart was pounding so hard. Maybe he hadn't heard correctly.

"We should take our leave," Sofia said. Her voice quivered.

"Yes," Ivan said. "We have an investigation to continue."

Sofia and Ivan backed toward the door, so Stephen did the same.

Somehow he knew it was because none of them wanted to turn their backs on the smiling, gloating fae.

CHAPTER
TWENTY-ONE

The thick carpet of the fourth-floor corridor swallowed the sound of their footsteps as they beat a hasty retreat to the dumbwaiter. Stephen waited to speak until they were far enough along the hall that it felt safe.

"So . . . is what she said right? Can they *do* that?"

Sofia stopped, pivoted to face him, and took in a deep breath, as if she were about to say something, a *lot* of somethings. Instead she just nodded and continued down the hallway. When she reached the dumbwaiter, she stabbed the button below it.

"Should we wait to discuss this?" Ivan asked.

Sofia said, "I don't think it matters anymore." Then she muttered, "Stupid diplomacy," and kicked the wall. It was a good thing she didn't have her sword on her.

Though Stephen agreed with the sentiment. The rules of diplomacy were letting those fae get away with all of this.

Ivan let out a sigh so deep he reminded Stephen of the elevator. "Yes, it's as bad as you think. We're now entered into an unbreakable deal with the Court of Thorns of the Realm of Faery. We have until tomorrow night to recover the book or—"

"We go live with *them*." *And my dad goes back to Chicago.* Stephen's skin felt cold all over.

Ivan nodded. "Servants to them, most likely."

"Guys," Stephen said, and Sofia turned to face him and Ivan, "I'm so sorry I made you come with me. There has to be some way it can just be me—"

"No," Sofia said. "We're in this together. We all gave insult."

"They deserved it," Stephen said.

Sofia almost smiled. "Unfortunately that doesn't matter."

Stephen turned to Ivan. "Why do you think she

said we'd see the book again at the party?"

Ivan wore a look of profound frustration, which for him meant a deep crease between his eyebrows. "I do not know, but it can't be good for us. My parents often say that true mysteries tend to grow more and more complicated until—at last—they are resolved."

Stephen was developing a healthy respect for the field of hotel detection. It was fast becoming their only hope.

"That said," Ivan continued, keeping his voice down, "the baroness wouldn't have told us that if she thought we could win. The fae don't play fair. We still don't know what they plan to do with the book; bringing it to the party openly would be admitting they had a hand in its theft."

"Well, we'll have to figure it out later," Sofia said. "I just remembered that time passes differently in Faery. We need to get back upstairs as fast as we can."

"But we weren't—" Stephen started to protest but then remembered what she'd said before about the fourth floor's being an extension of Faery, like an embassy.

Bracing her palms on the metal ledge inside the dumbwaiter, she leaped up into it and held down a hand for Ivan. He climbed in next to her and lowered a hand to help Stephen.

Stephen's mind raced as he repeated his trick with the fork from before, and the dumbwaiter started to rise. In the close, dark space he asked, "Can your mom help?"

"Maybe," Sofia said. "We'll have to tell our parents."

"Lady Carmen will try to save us if she can," said Ivan. "But diplomacy takes time and is very constrained by protocols. If we don't get the book back, we'll probably spend years serving tea in the Court of Thorns if we're lucky, and acting as Lord Celidyl's squires in the fae tournaments if we're not."

"If that happens . . . ," Stephen said. "The Manager says if Dad doesn't have the book back after the party, he's out for good. When he was in exile, he wasn't allowed to have any contact with this world. I'd never see him again."

The dumbwaiter rose creakily as that silently sank in. It jerked to a halt, and at last Ivan spoke. "Our best hope is to recover the book. Which we intended to do all along."

Stephen crouched and released the catch to open the door.

Ambrosia was nearly as dark as the inside of the dumbwaiter had been before he'd unlatched it. They climbed out.

"The possibility of indentured servitude to the fae will only sharpen my powers of deduction," Ivan said. "I will solve this."

"Not tonight," Sofia said.

"Tonight? We still have most of the day left." Stephen paused. He'd only just realized that though Ambrosia had been closed and deserted when they came down that afternoon, it hadn't been nearly this dark.

That meant it was dark now because there was no light outside to sneak in. But they had been with the faeries for only a little while. A half hour, tops.

"Time passes differently in Faery." Stephen repeated Sofia's words from downstairs. "It's night now."

Sofia pulled her phone out and squinted at it. "After midnight."

"This will be bad," Ivan said. "We'll have to regroup tomorrow. I mean, in the morning."

With that, they marched out of the restaurant. "Is there any chance our parents don't know we got out?" Stephen asked.

The elevator's doors slid open. "Thank the heavens and the stars! There you are! Where have you been? I couldn't hear your voices anywhere. Everyone's been trying to find you. You'd better get up to the Village right now."

"We're headed there," Stephen told the babbling elevator without getting in. It didn't make sense to ride up one floor.

"You'd better be! Good night, and good luck!" The doors closed again.

"It really does love you," Sofia marveled.

"And I guess that answers my question about

whether our parents noticed we were gone," Stephen said.

Nodding, Sofia walked over to the stairwell, and they trudged up, pausing at the top.

The door was propped open, and Sollie's voice sang out: "Here they are! Safe and sound as house gremlins!"

The Gutierrezes and Stephen's dad were waiting on the green. The parents looked terrified, worried, frazzled, and then—in an instant—furious: the full rainbow of parental emotion.

"Mom," Sofia said, "sorry we scared you. We went to see the fae."

Stephen added "shock" to the list of parental emotions. Sofia's mom's eyes settled on him for a second, then migrated back to her daughter.

"Explain," Carmen said.

Stephen's ears weren't burning anymore. No. They were roaring. He didn't take in a word Sofia said as she relayed the result of their visit to the fourth floor. The shocked gasps from their parents hit like blows.

His dad, when Stephen finally had the courage to look at him, wore the saddest expression he'd ever seen.

Sofia finally finished, and there was a long pause.

"Stephen," Carmen said, and he flinched back to attention at his name, "I hate to say this, but Ivan's and Sofia's . . . adventures were minor before you came. You have put them in real danger. Again."

"Mom," Sofia protested, "he didn't make us do anything."

Carmen ignored her daughter. "They aren't half fae like you. They won't have your advantages in the Realm of Faery."

Advantages? The words hit like a slap. This was his fault. The fae *were* fixated on him and his family, and he *had* dragged Ivan and Sofia into it. That they'd come willingly hardly mattered.

His dad stepped up then. "They're not gone yet. There's still time."

The words were a plea, and Carmen answered them with a nod. "We'll do all we can to prevent it. For now, everyone, try to get some rest. I'll go call off the search party in the hotel and have a talk with the Manager."

Julio put his hand on Sofia's shoulder, and they started across the green toward their cottage, Ivan with them. Carmen left, and Stephen was alone with his father.

He could still barely look at his dad. He had his Cubs cap on and his chef's jacket.

"You must have lost party prep time because of me," Stephen said, knowing it was a dumb thing to say.

"I nearly lost my mind because of you." His dad took off his cap and held it by his side, then put it back on. "I . . . don't know what to say. I have to pray we get out of this. I can't lose you, too." The words were choked. His dad swallowed and then said, in something like his normal way, "I should get back to the kitchen. We have a lot still to do for tomorrow. I expect you to stay in for the rest of the night."

Stephen would have felt better if he'd gotten a real punishment. If his dad had yelled at him.

"I'll be good, I promise. I'll follow all the rules," Stephen said.

Unspoken between them was the question of whether it was too late to matter. Stephen took off toward the cottage, and his dad went in the opposite direction.

The next morning dawned bright and sunny. It felt wrong somehow. And when Stephen emerged from the cottage, he found the rooftop under siege—by presents.

Boxes, crates, and bundles were everywhere. Sollie and Liz flew into view, struggling to lower an oversize barrel that jerked this way and that, nearly tearing itself out of their hands. Loud screeching noises came from inside it. And when it slipped from the grasp of the two gargoyles a couple of feet from Stephen, the noises grew louder as it crashed to the ground.

Art flapped over to it carrying a clipboard and checked the label. He scribbled something on his papers, then paused beside Stephen. "Hi there, Stephen! Everybody who waited to the last minute has sent their gifts at once!"

The gigantic barrel rocked back and forth for a minute and appeared certain to tip over. The screeches from inside picked up volume.

"Are there monkeys in that barrel?" Stephen asked.

Chuck swooped down to land on top of it. He hammered on it with his fists and yelled, "Yes, there are!" Then: "Stop that, you monkeys!"

The rocking stopped, and the screeching quieted.

Art fluttered up into the air, pausing to call back: "And rumor has it the kitchen makes all this look like it's perfectly under control!"

That was the last thing he wanted to hear.

"Chuck, have you seen Ivan and Sofia yet?"

If they're even allowed to talk to me anymore.

The remaining gargoyle pointed toward the gazebo. Two familiar forms and a lot of stuff were packed inside it.

Stephen walked over and stopped at the gazebo's edge, not wanting to intrude unless they invited him. Maybe they'd rethought being friends with him after what had happened with the fae. He wouldn't blame them.

Inside the covered area, Ivan's tableau of investigation was impressive. There was a tripod with a whiteboard, covered in carefully drawn lines and tiny, neat handwriting. Names and dates were written into the boxes, some circled, some with arrows pointing from one to the other.

Sofia held a yellow legal pad and a pencil. Another pad and pencil lay on the ground.

"Stephen!" she said, spotting him. Her voice sounded welcoming.

"It's about time you showed up," Ivan said, pushing his glasses up on his nose. He glanced at the loud scene behind Stephen. "We don't have time for monkey business. I brought you a notebook."

Stephen picked up the notebook and pencil, and Sofia scooted over on the bench inside the gazebo to make room for him. Ivan was scribbling on the whiteboard, so Stephen idly sketched a small black cat. He blinked when it slunk along the green line on the yellow page and stopped at the edge. It didn't move again.

"Wow, you're getting good at that." Sofia nudged him and flashed him the contents of her legal pad so far. She'd drawn a pointy thing—wait, it was a sword—with flowers around it. Then she'd written: "We're doomed."

"Sorry about the doomed part," Stephen said.

"Oh, I was just doodling," she said. "We're not mad at you."

When they turned back to Ivan, he was looking at the two of them.

"Of course we're not," Ivan said. "But there's no time to waste talking about it. As should be clear from this chart, we have all the elements from the course of our investigation to consider. Perhaps we can figure out what the fae have planned regarding the book. The bottom traces the timeline, starting with the first incident, when Sarabel masqueraded as you, snatched the *Librum*, and put it through the gate to Transylvania."

Stephen squinted at the chart. It was hard to follow despite the explanation, with its crazy lines backing and forthing among a surplus of arrows and circles.

"The next significant incident was the revelation that the fae had then approached the Octagon's undead representative, Count von Morgenstierne." Ivan waved at the board.

"I don't think that first thing was actually first," Stephen said.

Ivan waved for him to continue.

"Their inviting me to come to Faery with them was first. That's what I think," he said.

"True," Ivan said, and violently scribbled on his chart. "Though I don't know what to make of that. And Trevor's proximity to the theft was just happenstance; the bigfoots took no offense." He drew a line through Trevor's name.

"Bigfeet," Sofia muttered under her breath.

"I'm ignoring that," Ivan said.

"You just didn't!" Sollie called out from beside them as he looped down and tossed another package, this one wrapped in red–and-white-striped paper, onto the green. He made a small circle around the gazebo and said to Stephen, "They will never agree on what to call them. And the bigfoot people will never tell which is right! See what I did there? Bigfoot people? I don't take a side, so I can't be wrong. Ha!"

"I'm not wrong," Ivan and Sofia said at the exact same time.

Ivan shook his head. "Where was I? Oh, right, relevant parties and incidents. This is all of them. Which is why we are stymied, no closer to figuring out what the fae have planned." Ivan dropped his pencil to the ground, and raked his hands through his hair. He tugged on the ends. "My toughest case yet, and I'm choking. The Lawson family's reputation will be ruined forever, and we're all going to go live in Faery to boot." He gave a funny-sounding laugh.

"Ivan?" Sofia said cautiously. "Maybe it'll work out all right. Somehow."

"No," he said. "It won't. I laid out all the evidence. I looked at all the clues. We know who is behind this. But we don't know how to prove it or how to get the *Librum* back." Ivan sank to his knees on the wood planks of the gazebo. "To be a failure, so early in my career . . . I apologize to both of you. I must be the worst detective in La Doyt family history."

"Don't say that," Stephen said. "You're a great detective."

Ivan said nothing.

Stephen was grateful they weren't mad at him—especially after what Sofia's mom had said the night before. But he still felt awful. The way his dad's voice had broken the night before had haunted Stephen all night . . . when he wasn't dreaming of the baroness's cold, gloating smile.

"Is your mother trying to get us out of this?" he asked Sofia.

"Yes, but . . ." Sofia put down her pencil and pad and tightened her ponytail. "They're delaying, as expected. *We* gave insult to the fae, so *we* have to see their terms fulfilled. One way or the other. Since that involves the book, my parents told us to do what we can to get it back while they work on a compromise. And I wouldn't bank on one."

"There was a missive this morning from the order's inn in Faery that said my parents will be returning soon," Ivan said.

Stephen's hopes rose until Ivan clarified. "But it included nothing about their success or lack thereof. It would be too dangerous to send such a message and risk interception."

Would his mother be with the La Doyts when they came back? And would it even matter if the three of them failed at recovering the book?

Liz shouted, "Look out!" as she and Sollie inadvertently went off course and into the gazebo with a huge square package that careened from their grip—and crashed into Ivan's complicated chart. The whole thing fell apart, the tripod flying into several pieces, the lines on the chart smearing into an even worse state of chaos.

Stephen and Sofia leaped up and attempted to put the tripod back in place.

But Ivan began to laugh. Loudly and maniacally.

"Ivanos, I'm so so so sorry!" Liz said, her wings flapping slowly. Beside her the fearsome folds of Sollie's face were schooled into an apologetic grimace.

"No, no!" Ivan said. "Don't be sorry." Through his laughter, Stephen could barely make out what he was saying. "I just remembered something! The case of the magnificent deception!"

"I don't know what that is," Stephen said.

"Me neither," added Sofia.

Ivan held his palm out to Sollie. "Without your blunder, Sollie and Liz, I'd never have remembered!"

Sollie tentatively high-fived him with one clawed hand. "Great?"

"Ivan," Sofia interrupted.

"Yes?" he said.

"Are you going to explain to us?"

The gargoyle motioned to his companion, and they hefted the mislaid package to take it away.

Ivan waited until they were gone before explaining. "The case of the magnificent deception was one of my ancestor Francis La Doyt's most famous cases. It was 1860s Paris, and a rare dragon egg belonging to the order went missing—a dragon egg, it must be a sign!—from the safe at the Hôtel Gabriel. After being stymied by an investigation that led to the culprit but with no usable proof—just like us!—he decided to stage an auction for none other than the dragon egg in question."

"But you said it was missing?" Stephen said, interested.

"Exactly. He knew the culprit wouldn't be able to resist showing up to gloat or see who was pretending to have it. So all the suspects were invited as bidders, and through observation during the fake auction, he was able to identify the actual thief."

An idea tickled the back of Stephen's mind at the

story. For some reason, an image of the flying books in the library came to him, followed by the cat he'd sketched, strolling across the page.

"How does this help us?" Sofia asked.

Ivan put down the pencil. "Think about it."

"He's right," Stephen said. "They want to watch their plan unfold tonight. That much seems clear. And if we get proof they stole the book, then your mother can get all this fixed, right? Baroness Thyme told us the book will be at the party. Everyone will be inside the ballroom to watch it play out—whatever it is they've got in mind. So *we* should fake up a gift, another book, call it the *Librum*, and give it to Cindermass as a present. See how they react to that. By pretending *we* have the book, in front of everyone, we just might be able to shock the fae into admitting that they do."

Ivan and Sofia stared at him. "You could be a criminal mastermind," Ivan said, nodding thoughtfully. "If we weren't friends, I mean. It's not a bad plan."

"Don't we risk Cindermass's getting mad and . . ."

Sofia asked, waving her hands around in a convincing imitation of flame.

"It's true that draconic law requires a fair valuation of gifts, and the dragon will be expected to judge them. But we're choosing between a peevish Cindermass or risking a lifetime in Faery," Ivan said. "I say we take that chance."

"I'll wrap a book for us to take," Stephen said. He already had one in mind—and something else he wanted to try his hand at. Maybe Cindermass would even be willing to help them out.

The three of them looked at one another, excitement palpable in the air. They had a plan. Sure, it might fail, but it might not.

"Okay." Sofia shrugged. "But what do we do *until* the party then? It's not for hours and hours."

Ivan gathered up his supplies. "Chores. Watch television. Read a book."

"We're just a day away from possibly shipping off to Faery for the rest of our lives—and who knows how long those will last over there—and you think we should *read a book*?" she asked.

Ivan ignored her question. "We'll meet at sunset on the ballroom level, eight o'clock sharp. Stephen, bring the bait."

Ivan began gathering his materials, and Sofia stooped to help. Over her shoulder, she said, "Stephen, you up for croquet?"

"Sorry . . . But I need to pay a trip to the kitchen."

Sofia gave him a sympathetic look.

Ivan said, "Good luck down there. It sounds like it's a madhouse."

CHAPTER TWENTY-TWO

The heat that met Stephen on his way into the kitchen was intense, and so was the shouting. The rumors weren't exaggerated. It really *was* chaos.

A thick blanket of smoke obscured the ceiling, and strange line cooks were darting past one another. What seemed to be a million pans and bowls and tureens—and yes, that was a cauldron— sat on every possible surface, steaming and bubbling and gurgling. The competing smells battled in his nose. The kitchen was a war zone.

"Dad?" he called into the melee.

"*Papa*, your enfant terrible is here!" shouted Tomas. He held a large flat pan in which various glassy, spiny things sizzled.

His dad emerged from the smoke.

Stephen had expected his dad to look over-whelmed, to be experiencing déjà vu of the night-mare scene in the dining room at Ambrosia. But he was back in his element, by all appearances, book or no book. He leaned over and dipped a spoon into Tomas's pan, tasted it, and nodded with approval.

"Finally," his dad said, reaching him. He put a hand on Stephen's arm and steered him back into the relative quiet of the hall. He stopped them just past the threshold, though, where he could still keep one eye on the kitchen. "I was about to take a break and come look for you."

Stephen didn't need to ask why his dad would do that with the kitchen in such a frenzy.

"Everything looks like it's going all right down here," Stephen said.

His dad's skin was red from the heat that filled the kitchen. And Stephen was sweating, too, liter-ally and figuratively.

"I realized when I got back down here last night that if this is the last time I ever cook for super-normal society, I want it to be the best birthday bash a dragon has ever had. The kitchen staff rallied. Lots of chefs sent us recipes from their family books. Even Tomas is coming through," his dad said. "I also knew that if I threw myself into cooking, it might keep me from doing something stupid that would just make things worse with the fae. Carmen told me to focus on this, and then the Manager might change his mind about exiling me. That way I'd be here, to help get you guys back if the worst happens."

"We came up with a plan," Stephen said, "to maybe trick them tonight."

His dad's eyebrows came up. "Really?"

"We're going to pretend we have the book and see what they do." If the feast went as well as the prep seemed to be, that would be another point that might work in their favor. At least part of what the fae wanted was to humiliate the Lawsons, obviously.

"Huh." His dad shook his head. "I should tell you no, but Carmen said at this point nothing can hurt. I'm hoping the La Doyts come through, but I believe in you, buddy. If I can pull off this"—he paused and looked back into the kitchen—"then maybe you can pull one over on the snooty baroness. I meant what I said last night. I can't even imagine losing you."

A silence stretched between them. Stephen couldn't imagine it, either. He and his dad were each other's constants. Even when Stephen had been (more) overwhelmed by the revelation that all this existed and that his dad had kept it secret from him, he'd never doubted that his dad loved him.

But he still wasn't happy to have been kept in the dark for so long.

"So"—Stephen swallowed—"if we make it through this, I want to know more about our family. And about my mom."

His dad said, "I think that would be good."

No reason not to start now. He was curious about something. "One question I've been meaning to ask: Do you know what happened with Baroness Thyme and Chef Nana? Why they didn't like each other?"

His dad's hand tightened a fraction on Stephen's arm. "Your grandmother got in a battle of wills with a fae. I realized after that first night that it was the baroness. I knew she looked familiar. It happened when I was just a boy. Apparently it wasn't the first time, just the worst."

"What happened?"

They each took another step into the hallway. It was cooler out here, the din more distant: some trick of the architecture.

"Baroness Thyme didn't like some of her court's being too admiring of Chef Nana's work in the kitchen. So she sent back a dish. And, well, *no one* had ever sent back one of Mom's plates. She was a perfectionist and a much better cook than I am— especially of supernormal specialties. No way she was going to let it just pass."

So far this sounded like an average rude diner story. "What could she do about it?"

"She sent out dish after dish to the entire table with her compliments. And some of these were incredibly rare. Your grandmother created one recipe specially for the occasion—Lark's Tear Soup." He tapped the side of his head. "That one I know by heart. Anyway, her companions couldn't resist tasting them. And they were in rapture. Completely showed up the baroness."

"Wait. All this is because she cooked them good food?" Stephen really didn't understand this world.

"Because she injured her pride. Baroness Thyme took it as an insult."

"Oh." The fae sure could overreact.

"I just hope Chef Nana would be proud of what I serve tonight . . . and not too mad at me for screwing up and losing the book."

"You?" Stephen said before he could stop himself. "I think you mean me. I'm the one who let the book get snatched from under my nose, who almost got myself killed going to Transylvania, who had the bright idea to go see the fae."

His dad gave him a concerned look. "I'm glad you're willing to take the consequences of your actions, Stephen, but you may be being a little too hard on yourself. All this was new to you. All these rules—it takes time to learn them."

"Time I hope we have."

His dad pulled him into a hug. "Me too. Be careful tonight. Okay?"

"I promise," he said.

"I'd better head back to the stovetop," his dad said. "That Lark's Tear Soup recipe is delicate. Getting the larks to cry is the trickiest part. Oh, and I also wanted to tell you I had your suit cleaned and pressed for tonight. It's in your closet."

"The party's a big deal, isn't it?" He knew it was, but not *how* big. Cindermass could be prone to exaggeration.

His dad's lips quirked into a smile. "Huge. Nobody's had to cook for a dragon's birthday since before I was born, and nobody's had to do it in America since Thomas Jefferson was president."

Stephen asked, "There were dragons in America back then?"

"There was at least one. One of our ancestors was chief culinary alchemist on the meal, and it's still talked about in the supernormal community. I just hope mine measures up." A strange expression crossed his dad's face. "I'll see you at the party, okay?"

Tomas shouted, "Chef, if you 'ave a minute, your soup, it eez on the boil!"

Stephen's dad sighed and took a step away, then came back and leaned in so no one would overhear. "Tomas is a great cook, but it turns out he's never even been to France. Wants people to think he's classically trained. He grew up in Chinatown in San Francisco; he knows a lot about fireworks." He chucked Stephen's shoulder. "Don't be late tonight."

While Stephen made his way up the stairs, he went back over the plan for the evening.

He was going to a party full of monsters, where he and his new friends—because Ivan and Sofia *were* his friends, and he was theirs—would have to outsmart the fae who'd managed to drag him and his dad into this elaborate mess.

His dad would never forgive himself for not doing more if they didn't beat the fae at their own game. So they would just have to win.

Stephen emerged into the bustling lobby and hooked a right to get to the stairs that led to Cindermass's lair, which he expected to be pitch-black, as usual. Instead he was met by the soft glow of ambient light from below.

He began his torchless descent.

Cindermass had a soft spot for him because of Chef Nana and his drawings. If there was any way he could convince the dragon to help them out tonight, it was worth a shot. Cindermass was obsessed with valuable things, and the *Librum* was extremely valuable. He might even have some tips on dealing with the fae.

The light grew brighter and the air warmer as Stephen walked down the steps. It was how he imagined it might feel to approach an isolated star in the night sky. At the bottom Stephen paused before the wide-open double doors. A loud harmonious humming had joined the light.

When he entered, Cindermass's lair was ablaze with more torches than he would have thought could fit—did the fire marshal ever inspect the hotel?—though Cindermass himself was probably a fire hazard anyway.

The dragon was the source of the loud, rhythmic humming. He was getting dressed. A variety of giant bejeweled armored breastplates lay on the floor in front of him, and smoke rolled from his nostrils as he reached a talon to *ping* one of the options and then another.

The dragon picked up one of the breastplates and held it against his scaly red chest, his head tilting from side to side to get a view in a large reflective urn he was using as a mirror.

"Hmm," the dragon said, unaware of Stephen's presence.

Stephen figured it was more of a risk if the dragon caught him and assumed he was spying. "Cindermass, excuse me," he said. "Is now a bad time?"

"Just considering the paucity of suitable wardrobe options available to me." Cindermass unceremoniously dropped the breastplate onto the ground. As he turned, he dislodged some coins from a stray heap behind him, but he didn't bother with them.

He beckoned Stephen in with a long claw. "My boy, it is so good to see you looking like yourself. Much more so than the other evening, I should say." Cindermass stopped where he was. "If you've come to look at my art collection again, I suppose I can accommodate you, although it is a very busy day. . . ." He let the silence stretch out meaningfully.

Stephen rushed forward. "Happy birthday!"

He wondered if he should burst into the song, but the dragon's mouth opened in a wide, fiery grin. "You've heard! We only celebrate every five hundred years. I hear the festivities will be the grandest in this age. I barely remember the last party, though I do remember the song."

He hummed a few bars of that same harmony again. Good thing Stephen hadn't tried plain old "Happy Birthday" on him.

"When one's life spans such a long time, and one is so isolated, the special occasions *do* become even more special. Just so long as there are no *surprises*. Surprises cause trouble. I shudder to think of causing another London— Though they did call it the 'Great Fire.'"

The dragon finished with a guilty expression, lumbering back to make more room for Stephen.

"Even a good surprise?" Stephen asked, thinking about their plan.

After a moment's consideration, the dragon said, "Good surprises are all right."

"I keep surprising myself lately," Stephen said. "And everyone else. And I think not in a good way. In the London way."

Cindermass immediately showed concern. "Tell

me what burden weighs upon you. That business with the *Librum de Coquina* still? I did happen to overhear a little of your meeting with Baroness Thyme and her party, and it did not seem to go well." He blew a stream of fire on a teapot he had on a stove that was ludicrously small compared with his bulk and waved Stephen farther in to sit. "You need tea."

Stephen eased down beside the row of finery on the floor. He was pretty sure the breastplate closest to him was set with real emeralds and rubies and diamonds. The gems glittered in the torchlight.

"Tell me everything," Cindermass said as he set a teacup on a saucer.

"Sounds like you know. We have to get the book back tonight or else."

Cindermass was surprisingly easy to talk to. He placed the tea in front of Stephen. "It is never wise to involve oneself in the fae's trickery"—he paused—"even if one is part fae. You are nothing like them, Stephen, if you're worried. Lady Nanette would have told you the same thing."

Stephen sipped the tea. The oolong tasted smoky. "Do you—" He hesitated.

"Ask me anything," Cindermass said. "It is an honor to inspire the trust of such an artist."

Stephen asked, "Do you really think she'd feel that way?"

Cindermass closed his liquid gold eyes, then opened them. "Yes, I do. She was always so proud of you. Nothing could have changed that."

It made him feel better. As if maybe what his dad had said that first night here were true: he was still himself, and being half fae didn't change that. Courage rose up, and he asked what he'd truly come to visit Cindermass to ask: "Do you think maybe you could—"

"What is it? I will do anything within my power."

He looked sincere.

"The fae said the book will surface at your party tonight. Do you think, if you get the chance, you can help us out? Me and Ivan and Sofia?"

Cindermass blinked at him. One nostril lit.

"I will of course do whatever is within my power."

He exhaled smoke. "However, I must warn you that there is a great deal of ceremony to be employed tonight, and I am bound by the rules of all my kind. This is the one time in which I do not add to my hoard by appropriation but through gifts. A dragon is forbidden from paying for items, you know, and is also forbidden from *giving away* gifts. It's why building my art collection was so difficult. The loot flows *to* the dragon, so I couldn't pay commissions to the artists."

"I see," Stephen said, surprised that knowing these rules actually seemed helpful. They might even be able to use them to their advantage during the plan. "Thanks, Cindermass. See you later at the party."

"I cannot wait," the dragon said, and set to humming once more.

Stephen had a busy afternoon. He had an ancient dragon's birthday party to prepare for and the real possibility—scratch that, *probability*—that he was about to move to another dimension and take up his new job fetching and carrying for dangerous Baroness Thyme, devious Lady Sarabel, and deadly Lord Celidyl.

He got a reference photograph of the Empire State Building and studied it. Then he labored over several large pieces of parchment paper for a solid two hours, experimenting. None of the results were right for what he wanted. Every drawing either possessed a twitch of motion like his first sketch of Cindermass, or the image moved but then stalled out, like the cat he'd drawn earlier to the edge of the paper.

When he was about to give up, he stopped and remembered the way that the elements in the painting of his mother's in the fae's hotel suite had moved together seamlessly, almost as if they had been alive. He thought of what Ivan had said about his having the fae gift to make a drawing live on the page. The times it happened before, he hadn't been trying.

A gift wasn't exactly the same as a talent or a skill, was it? What if it was more like a superpower in one of his comic books?

Maybe he shouldn't be straining to use his gift. Maybe he should just envision what he wanted to draw and let it flow through him.

He needed to embrace the gift as part of himself.

And so then, finally, he pictured Cindermass on the page in majestic movement. His colored pencil flew across the thick paper, stopping only when he needed to switch to a new color. He worked to capture the image in his head in as much detail as he could with red and green and orange and black, shading and fine-tuning, until it was pleasing to his eye, until the rendering of the dragon *moved* around the building the way he wanted it to.

Afterward he prepared the decoy *Librum*, wrapping his grandmother's *Almanack* carefully in the paper so that the side he'd drawn on was hidden.

He took a bath and put on his suit. And when the time came, he went to meet his fate.

CHAPTER TWENTY-THREE

The elevator doors parted within moments of Stephen's pushing the button.

"Stephen, at last," said the elevator. "I've been waiting forever to take you to the third floor!"

"You're supposed to be taking *us* to the third floor," said one of the crammed-in passengers, a tall woman, with a voice like bells and skin like the bark of a willow tree.

"Is this the *roof*?" asked a dwarf, his beard braided and woven with gems that matched the colors of his military uniform. "I don't think we're supposed to be up here."

"The third floor is where the library is, isn't it?" Stephen asked, hesitating. The elevator car was full of various . . . beings . . . in dressy clothes.

"Not when the ballroom's needed, and tonight it will be as grand as it ever has been," the elevator said. "Get on. I'll take you right away so you can bask in its grandeur . . . for the both of us."

"Whoooo are yooooou?" asked a looming figure in the middle of the elevator, in a slow, booming voice. "Are yooooou the reeeeason for our delaaaaay?"

"Maybe I'll just wait," said Stephen.

"No!" said the elevator. "I won't allow it!"

Mumbling under her breath, the willow tree lady stepped back amid the people of various shapes and sizes, making room for Stephen to squeeze in.

He almost slipped on a puddle of something thick and sticky on the floor. Stephen threw his hands out automatically and caught himself just in time on the shell of the snail man beside him.

The snail man? Stephen took a step back.

Wedged beside him was a snail the size of a pony. Except that where the neck and head should have been, there was the chest, arms, and head of a stocky man wearing a tuxedo. Horns stuck up from his bald head, and eyes the size and color of boiled eggs stared at Stephen, who hastily looked at his feet to avoid eye contact.

Oozy snail stuff was pooled on the tile floor.

"Do be careful," said the elevator. "I'm afraid some of this evening's guests have the most dreadful manners, not to mention personal hygiene."

"Iiii caaan heeeear yoooou, yoooou knooow," said the snail man.

The elevator started down, and Stephen noticed that a skinny figure wrapped in voluminous robes jumped up in the air as it did so. The elevator sighed, almost drowning out the sound of the unexpected clattering noise the robed figure made when it landed. Stephen looked closer and saw that the hands and feet of the figure were skeletal.

Undead, he thought. *Always with the jumping.*

"You have to pay very close attention at the party so you can tell me every detail," said the elevator. "I so wish I could attend. I've never been to a dragon's birthday party. Or to anybody's birthday party. Or to any kind of a party at all."

"Theeere's a siiiign that saaaays we're not sup-poooossed to talk to the elevatooooor," said the snail man.

Stephen ignored him.

"I'll do that, Elevator," he said. "I'll tell you all about it tomorrow."

The willow tree lady smirked and spoke softly: "As if he's still going to be here tomorrow."

Word of the ill-starred deal with the fae must have gotten out.

The elevator came to a jarring stop. The dial indicated they were between the sixth and fifth floors. *Uh-oh.*

"You take that back," said the elevator. "Stephen is a very accomplished and brilliant young man, and he'll figure out a way to best those wretched fae at their own game."

The willow lady and every other supernormal in the small space stared at Stephen. "Lady Nanette Lawson's grandson and an *elevator* are friends?" asked the lady.

Stephen waited for the elevator to say something,

but there was only silence. He looked the woman straight in the eye and said, "We sure are."

The elevator started back down toward the third floor, and this time the skeleton didn't jump.

When they reached their destination, the doors opened onto a scene out of a storybook. The third floor had, as promised, entirely changed from the last time Stephen had visited it. Gone were the winding hallways, replaced by a spacious foyer, chandeliers dripping with crystals above it.

A grand receiving line was populated with the most bizarre creatures imaginable. The dwarf and the willow lady and the skeleton and the others filed out. Stephen squeezed up to the side so that even the snail man glided past, leaving him alone on the elevator.

"Thanks for saying that about my getting out of all this," he said. "I hope you're right."

"I hope I am, too," said the elevator, its voice full of worry. It added, "Thank *you* for saying that we're friends."

"We *are* friends," said Stephen, realizing that it

was the truth. He thought of Sofia and Ivan and Cindermass and the gargoyles. "I've made more friends here in the last few days than I ever had back in Chicago." He hesitated and then stepped out into the oddly glamorous scene. "If this doesn't work out, I'm going to miss it here."

The elevator's doors were closing, but its parting words were clear and fierce: "Then don't go. Stay."

I'll try my best. Stephen entered the throng of supernormals milling around and waiting to be admitted into the ballroom. *For Ivan and Sofia. For my dad* . . .

It was going to be some night, no matter what happened.

"The most honorable dryad Linwyra! Keeper of the oak Roatencohn and mistress of Central Park!"

Stephen didn't recognize the person calling out names from a scroll, but he was one of Julio's guards. Julio stood beside him wearing a coat made of shimmery red cloth with big gold buttons down the front. A sash crossed his broad chest, and his sword was belted around his waist.

The willow lady from the elevator nodded regally at Julio before going through an arched entrance hung with crystals, the passageway into the candle-light and conversation in the ballroom proper.

Ivan and Sofia appeared through the crowd.

Ivan was wearing a tuxedo that looked as if it had come from an old movie—an old movie about detectives. Undoubtedly it had been made by the master tailor, with hidden extra pockets. Sofia was wearing a long, glittery dress the blue of a night sky and had her curly hair piled up on top of her head. She was still wearing her scuffed-up boots, though.

"I see you brought the gift," Ivan said. He eyed the book-size parcel Stephen carried.

Stephen half expected Ivan to pull out a spray bottle that would reveal its contents. He wasn't entirely confident he'd made the right call with either the choice of book or the wrapping, so he was evasive. "I did."

"The paper is a little plain but good," Ivan said. "The game is afoot."

"A bigfoot," Stephen said, trying to make a joke.

He nodded over to the entry, where the announcer was about to call out the names of the next people in line.

It was Trevor and a large bigfoot in a flowing red gown. Stephen assumed she was Trevor's mother. Trevor saw them looking and waved. A tie was knotted at his throat, the length of it probably enough for escaping through a high window. Trevor gave Stephen a nod, which Stephen hoped meant he was forgiven for the hot sauce debacle and everything that had come after.

"Roams over Rivers and Mountains, high lady of the Octagon on behalf of the furred folk"—and here the guard segued into bigfoot language with its clickings and special emphases—"and her son and heir, Treks Ever Upward over Adversity to the High Summits."

His mother looped her arm through Trevor's and guided them inside the ballroom.

Stephen's fingers tightened on the book. "So, how does this work? Tonight, I mean."

"We should get in line," said Sofia.

They did, and she continued. "The meal will be served first, and assuming your dad survives that, Mom said, the presentation of gifts to Cindermass takes place during the feasting and party . . . which will go on for hours."

"Cindermass must inspect each gift, and it has to meet with his approval." Ivan peered at them over his glasses, then at the simple parcel in Stephen's hands again. "We should be first in line for that, give our gift at the very beginning."

"No reason to wait," Stephen said.

Stephen was gambling that the dragon would see enough meaning in the gesture to accept the wrapped decoy, the simple supernormal almanac found in every hotel room in the building, without getting angry. And the card he'd made called it the *Librum*, so that should get a reaction from the fae.

The wrapping might *not* meet with Cindermass's approval—then again, the dragon might not even have cause to examine it closely. Stephen didn't believe he was any sort of great artist yet. He didn't know if he ever would be.

The line advanced.

A pair of centaurs called Lord and Lady Quinas clip-clopped into the ballroom, and Stephen spotted the gargoyles flying in with a few last gifts. They were each wearing a wreath of bright red flowers, and their wings fluttered a little less energetically than normal. Probably exhausted from their day's receiving work. He also noticed a human-looking man in a nice suit chatting with a man who wore a tuxedo jacket and had the legs and horns of a goat. The human man's face was vaguely familiar.

"Who's that talking to the faun?" he asked Sofia.

She glanced over. "The mayor of New York City."

It took some time for them to work their way up to the front. Just as it was their turn to enter, it occurred to Stephen that he was about to be "announced" in the same way as the other guests. He had no idea what to expect.

Julio gave them a serious look as the guard consulted the scroll. "You three . . . I just can't bear to think about it."

"Dad," Sofia said in a commanding tone, "you

can't cry when you're on duty. You know we have a plan."

Julio's eyebrows rose, and Stephen lifted the parcel. It really didn't look like much.

"And my parents could arrive at any moment," Ivan said. Julio did look somewhat comforted at that reminder.

"Stephen, scion of the Lawsons!" shouted the guard at the door. "Son of the Hotel New Harmonia's knight of culinary alchemy, Sir Michael Truman Lawson, and grandson of Lady Nanette Lawson."

Sofia shoved Stephen, and he went forward into the ballroom. For once no one had pointed out he was half fae. They'd announced him as he thought of himself: Stephen, of the Lawson family.

The ballroom was beyond grand. As he entered the chandelier-lit, wood-lined room, a number of people in the sizable crowd turned to get a look at him, including, creepily nearby, the vampire count and his three zombie attendants.

Count von Morgenstierne was dressed in a tuxedo, with his usual cape. The zombies wore their usual ripped attire—except that they all had single red roses pinned to their ragged collars. The count gave a slight bow, a mocking one, to Stephen.

Stephen returned the favor, bending completely at the waist with a flourish he intended to be sarcastic.

When he straightened, the vampire was smiling, showing off his fangs.

Laugh now. You chose the wrong team, Count.

Sofia and Ivan must have been announced— and Stephen had missed it—during this exchange because they appeared in front of him.

Ivan said, "We should all keep an eye out for anything unusual."

Sofia said dryly, "You mean, like Stephen and Count von af's bowing contest."

"I won," Stephen said.

Sofia patted his arm. "Of course you did."

Brave faces or not, Stephen knew the others were nervous, too. Sofia was fidgety, and Ivan turned away from the count, only to glance back over his shoulder twice to make sure he and his zombies weren't coming toward him.

A lion with bat's wings and the tail of a snake moseyed past the three of them.

Stephen raised his eyebrows. "How am I supposed to tell what's 'unusual' at a dragon's birthday party?" he asked Ivan.

"We should just stick together," Sofia said.

He didn't miss that when she moved, it was in the opposite direction from the zombies. That also brought them deeper into the ballroom crowd. Stephen nearly collided with someone holding a glass of something green and fizzy.

"Sorr—" He didn't finish apologizing. He *wasn't* sorry.

The drink holder was Lord Celidyl, standing in a group with Lady Sarabel and Baroness Thyme.

"Ah, if it isn't our future companions," said the baroness. Her eyes were as hard as ever, cold as chips of ice. She had on a ball gown even more extravagant than her usual, designed to look like the overlapping petals of a deep red flower.

"I hope you are enjoying the party," Lady Sarabel

said, "since it will be the last you attend as guests. You do not seem to be making much progress in recovering what you've lost."

The three fae stared at Stephen's parcel as if it were emitting some foul odor. He wished people would stop doing that.

Ivan opened his mouth to reply, but Stephen spoke first. "The night's not close to over yet. Everything's going just as *we* planned."

"We feel the same way," Lady Sarabel said.

"Excuse us, Baroness Thyme," Sofia said. She grabbed Stephen and Ivan by the arms and guided them firmly away. "Don't let her get to you. We don't want to give away our surprise. She's just trying to distract us."

Ivan pushed his glasses up his nose. "Of course she is. We have a plan, and a good one. I wouldn't have thrown my support behind it otherwise."

A hand clapped down on Stephen's shoulder, and there was Marina. She was stunning, wearing a dress made of glimmering green scales. "I hope you're feeling better, Stephen," she said. "I still

haven't seen you or your father in the activities center voluntarily."

"Sorry," he said. "Thanks again for healing me."

Or whatever she'd done to fix him. He had little
memory of that part of the evening, after they'd
gone through the gate.

She peered closely at him, her eyes green as seawater. Breathtaking. "I sense no remaining effects.
What *does* cause an ill effect is avoiding health and
fitness activities. And—"

"Look at the time!" Ivan said, pulling at Stephen's
arm. "We'd better get a good place for dinner."

"Right!" Sofia chimed in. "Stephen wants to see
his dad!"

"Fitting right in with these two," Marina
grumbled, but she let them slip away into the
crowd.

Sofia led them over to the far wall, where a
wavy velvet curtain concealed either another wall
or an exit, with a long banquet table in front of it.
The announcement of guests had tapered off, and
from the press of people, it certainly seemed that

everyone in supernormaldom was crammed into the ballroom.

The next voice that rang out was Sofia's mother's, using a microphone. "And now the moment you've all been waiting for, prepare to greet our birthday boy himself—" Carmen paused.

If Stephen wasn't wrong, she was exhausted and putting on a show of energy.

Exhausted because her daughter was in danger of being taken to the realm of Faery. Because of Stephen.

It wouldn't happen. It couldn't. He smoothed the wrapping paper on his gift.

Carmen resumed her introduction. "The terror of Manhattan and the New World, third richest supernormal in history, please welcome Cindermass of the Mighty Redwing Clutch!"

The ballroom broke into applause and, for those without hands or flippers or some means of clapping, into stomps and cheers.

Who knew how they'd got Cindermass out of the basement? Stephen was positive, witnessing the dragon's size in full light for the first time ever, that there was no way he'd have fitted through those double doors or up the steps.

Cindermass wore one of the shiny golden breast-plates from before, stuck all over with jewels.

The dragon was toothily grinning with an "all this for me?" bashful aspect . . . bashful until he emitted two showy flares of fire from the end of his nostrils that blazed out over the heads of the audi-ence. Over the heads of all of them, that is, except for a giant who had to duck to avoid getting singed.

The crowd parted to make way, and Cindermass preened as he paraded to the far side of the room, close to where Stephen, Ivan, and Sofia were.

In addition to the long table in front of the curtain, the side of the room nearest them was where the presents had been set up. The gargoyle Art hovered on a platform beside the arrayed parcels and packages and statues hung with bows.

When Cindermass finished his parade through the ballroom, everyone turned toward the vel-vet curtains. Stephen's father stuck his head out through a break in the middle and did a slow scan of the crowd. When their eyes met, his dad mopped his brow in exaggerated worry and then disappeared back behind the velvet.

The curtains slowly parted to reveal the entire kitchen staff. They marched out in two rows, holding a huge serving platter on their shoulders like the bearers of a palanquin carrying some ancient emperor. Instead of an emperor, the platter bore a feast.

A feast unlike anything Stephen had ever seen.

"Take one and pass it on," came an urgent whisper to his left.

It was Marina, and she was handing over a sheaf of papers. He did as he was told. Soon everyone in the room held a sheet: the gargoyles, the centaurs, the mayor of New York, and even, he saw, the eyeless night clerk. Sofia had positioned herself so that she would block Ivan's view of the ghoul.

Aside from the night clerk, the people around them were alternately reading what was on the paper and staring at the platter. The kitchen staff, directed by Stephen's dad, set the feast down on the long table in front of Cindermass. The rustling of paper stopped as soon as his dad spoke.

"Cindermass of the Mighty Redwing Clutch!" his dad said, his voice shaky as it carried throughout the hushed ballroom. "I bring you food. I bring you drink. I bring it in celebration of your thousandth birthday. But the feast is not complete!"

Stephen was clutching both the book and the sheet of paper Marina had handed him so hard his knuckles hurt. *Please let Dad pull this off.*

Cindermass's features fell into a frown, and Stephen's breath caught in his throat. Then the dragon grinned broadly, toothily. "Oh, yes, I remember this part." The dragon cleared his throat. Then: "Whatever can complete this feast?"

"The dishes are prepared, but they are not fully cooked. They must be exposed to dragon fire!" said his dad.

"I remember this part, too," said Cindermass, and inhaled deeply. The people in the crowd closest to him leaned back as far as possible, and then fire erupted from the dragon's throat, spreading precisely out over the laden platter.

There were roasts and puddings, huge bowls of vegetables and noodles, things Stephen almost recognized and things he wasn't even sure were food. The fire danced over the table. The flames flickered blue in some places, and white in others, and all the colors fire can be in between.

Cindermass's breath was somehow varying its temperature over each dish, no doubt cooking them all to perfection. Well, the occasional bowl and pot overflowed in ways that didn't seem intentional, but overall, his dad's meal might make the dragon's grade.

Stephen gasped when a stream of yellow sparks shot up from the center of the tray and Cindermass stopped breathing fire. He was sure this was disaster.

Cindermass only watched as the stream was joined by another of red sparks, followed by one of orange. The dragon sat back on his haunches and said, "This is new! I've never seen this!"

The sparks wove together in streams, growing

up and out, filling the room with light and noise. Gradually the magical fireworks began to coalesce into a shape—the shape of a fiery dragon—flying around the room. The dragon hovered in front of Cindermass and breathed a stream of sparks over him that flowed over his head and talons, outlining him in gold.

The sparkling dragon flew up to the ceiling, and the sound it made changed to music, a catchy melody that repeated itself once and then again. Sofia's mom stepped into the center of the room, holding one of the papers, and began waving her hand back and forth like a conductor.

Stephen consulted the paper in his hand and, with the others massed in the ballroom, began to sing.

"Who's the terror of New York?
Cindermass! Cindermass!
Who has the biggest shiny hoard?
Cindermass! Cindermass!

Who's elegant and handsome, too?
Who loves all treasures old and new?
Cindermass!
Cindermass, the dragon!"

Cindermass's face hovered over his dad's shoulder; the dragon was reading the lyrics as everyone sang. His wings and haunches flexed in time. He picked his taloned feet up, one by one, each in turn.

Stephen laughed in relief and said, "He's dancing! He's happy with the food!"

"Catastrophe one, averted," Ivan said.

The ballroom erupted into cheers, and his dad took a half bow before disappearing back behind the curtains. He'd be headed to the kitchen, in case there was cleanup or desserts to oversee.

Cindermass, however, took wing. He flew over the crowd, then landed gently—like a bus-size butterfly—on the dais, where Art would present his gifts.

Some of the other guests gravitated toward the food, and some to watch the gift receiving begin.

It was time. They had to present the fake book now in order to find the real one.

But when Stephen, Ivan, and Sofia walked toward the dais to present their gift, someone else had beaten them to it.

"Looks like someone wanted to be first in line," Art said. Sitting on the stage was a velvet cushion with an object that looked ominously book shaped on top of it. Art plucked a note off the package. He frowned.

"Well, what is it?" Cindermass asked. "What's the first gift?"

Stephen heard Lady Sarabel's high-pitched laugh. Lady Sarabel, who could glamour herself to be unseen by anyone, who could have slipped this "gift" onto the stage.

Would they dare?

Art did not look happy, but he answered the dragon. "A delivery sent by Anonymous . . . 'For Cindermass, a gift befitting such an occasion . . .'"

Cindermass said, "And the gift?"

Chuck flew the pillow over to Cindermass.

Stephen suspected what the gargoyle would say. His heart seemed to stop beating anyway while he waited for confirmation.

Art sighed and finished reading the note, ". . . a gift befitting such an occasion—the *Librum de Coquina*, famed book of the Lawson family."

CHAPTER TWENTY-FOUR

For a long moment the entire crowd was silent. Then Baroness Thyme spoke from near the stage: "What an unexpectedly delightful present."

Her words were like the first rock falling in an avalanche because suddenly everyone was talking, shouting, and, in a few cases, *roaring*.

"Is this as bad as I think?" Stephen shouted the question to Ivan and Sofia, though he was pretty sure he knew the answer.

As one, his friends nodded their heads: yes.

"What is this infamy?" Cindermass exploded, sparks flying in every direction.

The babble of conversations and pronouncements came to a halt. Stephen's ears rang.

"Oh, Great Dragon, please," said Art, and

Stephen didn't hear the rest because Ivan was whispering rapidly in his ear.

"He's reminding him that dragons are bound by the rules of hospitality not to injure messengers," said Ivan.

And then Sofia was whispering in his other ear: "And he's also going to invoke the Draconian Privileges of Property."

"What does *that* mean?" asked Stephen.

"It means that not only can Cindermass *not* refuse an obviously valuable gift like the *Librum* but that he's beholden by law and tradition to add it to his hoard," Sofia said. "Cindermass is now the owner of the *Librum*."

Still, there had to be a bright side, right? Cindermass was greedy, but . . . "Can't he give the book back to my dad now?" asked Stephen.

"Dragons never give anything away," said Ivan. "They can't. It's against their nature. The only times dragons ever willingly part with their treasures is when they're traded for something of even greater value. An impossibility here."

An impossibility. Everything he and his dad owned, all put together, probably wasn't equal to the value of the *Librum de Coquina*.

Cindermass roared, "I will not accept this *treachery*!"

The crowd parted, shrinking back, as Baroness Thyme stepped nearer still to the stage. "Great Dragon," she said, "you cannot mean to refuse this gift?"

The dragon's eyes glowed, but the baroness did not move. Lord Celidyl and Lady Sarabel appeared behind her, none of them giving any sign of fear.

She's so confident, Stephen thought.

"Was it you who did this?" Cindermass demanded.

"I regret that we cannot take credit for it," said Baroness Thyme. "We brought rare metals from the Realm of Faery for our own gift tonight."

Cindermass growled.

She's lying. No, wait. Stephen realized she'd just worded her statement very carefully. They couldn't take *credit* for it.

The baroness continued. "Whoever *anonymously* gave this to you plainly understood its tremendous value, as I'm sure you do. Luckily one of your kind cannot refuse such a gift, even with a lack of provenance. I had heard rumors that the book had been stolen or"—she paused and found Stephen with her gaze—"lost by the Lawson son. But now it belongs to you."

Smoke coiled from Cindermass's nostrils. Stephen held his breath, waiting to see if the dragon had a counterargument.

At last he turned his head to Art and said simply, sadly, "Please present the next gift."

Stephen checked to see how Ivan and Sofia were reacting.

Ivan was wiping a lens of his glasses. And Sofia was steaming almost as much as Cindermass, scowling in the fae's direction. Neither looked hopeful.

He wasn't going to let his friends down. He still had Cindermass's present in his hands, in his careful wrapping. And he had an idea.

As he stepped forward, Sofia protested, "Don't! It's too dangerous."

"I've got this," he told them, pocketing the card that had falsely identified the book as the *Librum*. "You two stay here."

Their plan was going to have to change to avert the big catastrophe and thwart the fae.

Stephen had nothing to lose at this point. That meant he had to try to make all these rules work in his favor. For once.

He made his way to the front of the crowd and stood before the dais, waiting.

It didn't take long for Cindermass to notice Stephen. The look that passed over the dragon's features could only be described as one of deep sadness.

"Hey, Art," said Stephen to the gargoyle, "I want to present my gift now."

The crowd murmured. Lady Sarabel's giggle rang out again, from off to Stephen's side.

Cindermass breathed a gout of flame at the ceiling and shouted, "Silence!"

Sarabel—and everyone else—shushed.

Art breezed over to Stephen. "I'm supposed to announce what it is," he said.

Stephen whispered into the gargoyle's pointed gray ear.

"Are you sure?" Art asked.

"Yes," Stephen said.

Art flew back to his place on the stage, cleared his throat, and said, "A gift from Stephen, scion of the Lawsons!" He hesitated, then said, "A, er, well, he says it's a copy of *An Almanack of the Mores and Ways of Supernormal Kind*."

Several people whispered to one another. The noise abruptly cut off when Cindermass arched one scaled eyebrow. "Surely it is a first edition?" asked the dragon. "One signed by the editors and illustrators perhaps?"

Stephen began to carefully unwrap the package. "Nope," he said. "It's just the one from our cottage up in the Village."

A low rumble grew deep in Cindermass's chest.

"Stephen," he whispered, even though his

whisper carried across the whole ballroom, "I am bound by draconic law to judge the gifts given to me fairly. I am"—he choked, and Stephen realized that Cindermass was about to cry—"I am bound to judge the gift givers harshly if it is not of suitable value."

Stephen swallowed. This next part was tricky.

He held up the book, keeping the wrapping paper in his other hand. "This copy is pretty much the same as the one you'll find in every room of this hotel. And in every other supernormal hotel in the world, as far as I know."

Stephen gazed out over the crowd. Everyone was watching him. The snail man from the elevator stretched his head high so he could see over the crowd. Count von Morgenstierne's fangs were bared. Baroness Thyme wore a frown of concern—probably afraid that Cindermass might roast Stephen before he could become her ward.

Well, he wasn't giving up yet.

"But *this* copy, Cindermass"—Stephen went on—"is special. Because it once belonged to my grandmother Lady Nanette Lawson, your dear friend. And she inscribed it to me. Would you like to know part of what she wrote?"

Cindermass looked at Stephen. He looked at the book. His golden eyes glistened.

"Very much," Cindermass said.

Stephen's own eyes were a little watery as he opened the front cover and read the line that seemed most applicable to this occasion. "Remember,'" he said, "'our characters are determined by our actions.'"

The glistening in the dragon's eyes turned into tears. A gallon of salty water dropped onto the stage as each tear fell.

"I loved your grandmother," said Cindermass.

"I loved her, too," said Stephen.

"Sentiments," said Cindermass. "Sentiments have great value. I gladly accept this wonderful gift. But Stephen, while I would love nothing more than to be guided by my own sentiments, I cannot give you the other book. I cannot give you the *Librum de Coquina*. Dragonkind would strip me of all property. And a dragon without a hoard cannot live."

"Oh, that's all right," said Stephen, and he idly waved the parchment paper he'd used for the wrapping. "I'm glad you liked the present. And that you liked Dad's feast. I'm glad you're having a happy birthday."

Another tear dripped down the end of Cindermass's nose. "But it's *not* a happy birthday because those cursed fae . . . and . . ." Cindermass trailed off. He shifted his head to the side, trying to get a better look at the paper in Stephen's hands. "Those cursed fae . . . ," he said again.

Then his head snaked out and loomed right in front of Stephen. He closely examined the wrapping paper.

"I say, what is that?" he asked.

"This?" Stephen said, and held up the paper so everyone in the crowd could see it.

The image depicted a fearsome red dragon winging around the Empire State Building. The dragon was flying, actually flying, in motion around the building, the drawing moving just as Stephen had wanted it to. Alive.

Because when Cindermass had said that Stephen was like him, not like the bad fae, it had given him the courage to try something his human half would never be able to. He had made a living portrait of Cindermass, something the dragon had said he'd wanted for many years.

"This is a drawing of you in flight above the Empire State Building," Stephen said, for those who couldn't see (or in case the building was unfamiliar to the dragon). "Do you like it?"

"It's—it's *magnificent!*" said Cindermass. "It's the best of your drawings yet! It's *masterful!*"

"I'm glad you like it, Cindermass," he said. "Too bad I already gave you my present."

Cindermass looked at the drawing. That rumbling was growing in his chest again.

"But . . . ," said Stephen, as if he were deep in thought.

"But *what*?" asked Cindermass.

"I don't know much about the draconic rules and regulations," said Stephen, "beyond knowing that you can't give me the book and that you've already accepted my gift. But—"

"But *what*?" Cindermass demanded once more.

"But I was wondering," said Stephen, "if there's anything in the rules about *trades*."

Cindermass blinked, confused for a second. Then thoughtful. Then excited.

"No!" he roared. Stephen and everyone else within a dozen yards had to take a step back. "No!

Trading is not proscribed! As long as the value ratio is in balance! You've already given me a gift! So trading is indeed possible!"

Stephen held up the drawing again. "So I'll give you this drawing, and you give me something valuable in exchange. Something that you value less than the drawing, but that I value more."

Cindermass banked rapidly, his tail lashing out and accidentally knocking over one of the count's zombies who'd gotten too close to the stage—probably accidentally. When the dragon turned back, he held the *Librum de Coquina* in his talons.

"What about something like this?" he asked.

"Yes," said Stephen. "Exactly like that."

"Stephen Lawson, grandson of the great and good Lady Nanette," said Cindermass, "I offer up this book in trade for the fine living portrait you bear. I've always wanted one."

Stephen accepted the *Librum* and handed over the drawing, careful to avoid placing it where one of Cindermass's claws would tear it.

"Thanks, Cindermass," he said, the old leather

book that was so precious to his dad in his hands. "You're the best."

Cindermass sniffed back another tear. "Yes," he said. "Yes, I really am."

Stephen faced the crowd once more. He found the trio of fae. They'd backed away from the stage, which seemed smart.

But to his surprise, the baroness was smiling again.

Count von Morgenstierne approached the fae. Stephen clutched the book tightly and walked right over to them. His ears burned as he got closer.

Ivan and Sofia met him just as he reached the fae. They beamed at Stephen.

His dad swept up to them, wild-eyed. "Stephen!" he said. "You are going to give me a heart attack. That was dangerous and risky and . . ."

Stephen braced.

"Brilliant!" his dad said, folding him into a hug. "You did it!"

Stephen hugged his dad, even though the fat, extremely valuable book was squished between them. He pulled back and pressed their family legacy into his dad's hands.

"Here you go, Dad. I'm just glad I was able to get it back."

His dad shook his head. "I am, too. I'm even more glad that you're not going to be carted off to Faery."

"Oh, I'm afraid that's where you're wrong," Baroness Thyme said. "Get ready, children. It's time for us to leave."

Stephen's dad sputtered. "What . . ."

Sofia raised a hand. "We didn't prove they took it. We got the book back, but we didn't prove our allegations."

"Everyone knows it was them!" Stephen said.

"That may not matter," Ivan said, turning pale.

Stephen's dad searched the room. "Where's Carmen?"

"Make way!" The ballroom quieted. Even Cindermass blinked toward the entrance when the announcer shouted. "Make way for Princess Aria of the Primrose Court of the Realm of Faery, fae delegate to the Octagon, first of her name!"

Stephen's dad grabbed his hand.

The woman who glided into the ballroom was glamorous, her skin a pale robin's egg blue rather than green. She had pointy ears and long blond hair, and she wore a regal gown and a tiara with jewels that caught the chandelier light. She looked . . . a bit like Stephen.

"Mom and Dad!" Ivan said.

A few steps behind her were Ivan's parents. Ivan's dad had on a fancy tux, no doubt filled with secret pockets, and his mom was in a slinky ball gown, also no doubt with hidden pockets. They sported matching black-framed glasses.

Wearing a relieved smile, Carmen was rushing the group toward them.

"Ow!" Lady Sarabel exclaimed.

Sofia's boot rested on the hem of Lady Sarabel's dress. "You're not going anywhere," Sofia said.

Stephen whirled back toward his mother. As she, Carmen, and the La Doyts approached, her eyes skated across the crowd and paused for a second on him. They were warm until they landed on the three other fae.

"Why, Princess Aria," Baroness Thyme said breathlessly, sinking into a curtsy, "in seclusion no more. It's been so long."

"Your delegation from the Court of Thorns will be departing for the Evening Lands within the hour," said Princess Aria briskly, "*after* you give me your truthful statement on your activities of the past week, including your theft of the *Librum*. Carmen has filled me in on what you've been up to, Baroness. I see from the presence of the book in Sir Michael's arms that my son outwitted you. Made to look ridiculous by a Lawson yet again, though you've never needed any help on that count."

"Princess, I—We—" The baroness couldn't seem to finish a sentence.

"I will be reclaiming my seat on the Octagon immediately," Princess Aria continued. "My first act is to forbid the Court of Thorns all access to the mortal world for the time being." She directed her next words to the vampire. "Sorry to disappoint you as well, Count von Giertsen af Morgenstierne, but you won't be gaining a fae ally or bathing in a midnight sun garden anytime soon either." She lifted her voice so the assembly could hear her next words: "I apologize for any offense or disruption the fae have caused at your festivities, my dear Cindermass."

Cindermass inclined his head, smiling toothily. "It is good to see you again, Princess. You won't believe how talented your son is. The drawing he made of me is the new centerpiece of my collection!"

Stephen's cheeks burned. This glamorous creature was *his mother*.

"I can't wait to see." She sounded as if she meant it. She paused, and then said, "Now, on with the celebration!"

She turned to Stephen and his father. "I must take care of seeing these three off." She paused and dipped her chin almost bashfully to both of them. "But we will all talk soon. I promise."

"That sounds nice," his dad said, still holding Stephen's hand.

Stephen appreciated that. He might have fallen over otherwise. "Yes, it does," he said.

"It will be good to get to know you," she said to Stephen, and she waved for the fae to follow her. The baroness was seething, but she went along without protest.

Stephen couldn't resist lifting his hand and giving them a sarcastic salute.

Julio hustled over to greet the La Doyts, who were busy hugging Ivan and Sofia. Carmen went with the fae party and Stephen's mother. Several others from the hotel gathered around, chattering and laughing.

Stephen watched until his mother's blond hair and tiara disappeared out the ballroom door.

"I can't believe it," Stephen said to no one in particular.

"Now, this . . . ," Cindermass thundered, as Art prepared to announce another present, "*this* is a party!"

CHAPTER
TWENTY-FIVE

Stephen and his dad both slept in the next morning. After the week they'd had and the festivities and excitement of *Stephen's mother*'s showing up the night before, his dad trusted Tomas Goatface to oversee breakfast service at the newly reopened Ambrosia.

Stephen was already up when his dad appeared at the door to his room with some toast and scrambled eggs. "We'd better eat something before we go," his dad said.

His mother had sent word the night before that she had to spend the day at an emergency meeting of the Octagon, called in honor of her return. His dad had proposed a field trip out of the hotel to pass the time so neither of them would obsess about it.

His dad paused when he saw what Stephen had

in his hands: his sketchbook. He had it open to another page of living drawings, this one of the two of them out on the green. They were picnicking among their new friends.

"I think I'm getting better," Stephen said. "I just have to think about what I'm drawing and imagine it moving while I'm drawing it. Do you think . . . will my, um, mom maybe teach me how to do this better?"

His dad came the rest of the way over. He set the plate down on the night table and lowered himself onto the edge of the bed beside Stephen.

"I bet she will. Being half fae isn't going to be all bad," his dad said. "The reason I haven't told you much about being half fae is that I don't really know what to expect either. But *this* is pretty cool. And your drawing of Cindermass. Well . . ."

"Imagine if he hadn't liked it."

His dad laughed. "No. I'd rather not do that. I realized something else, though, about the book."

"What's that?"

"That it would be a great loss if it were truly gone, and I would grieve for it. But also that eventually I'd have had to pick myself up and move on, start over, and do the best I could with what I *do* have," his dad said, "the most important thing: you."

"Me, too," Stephen said, "I mean, about starting over . . . But I think I'm okay with all this new stuff now."

Stephen put down his sketchpad and pointed at the nightstand. "There was a new *Almanack* in there last night when we got back. I checked."

"The Manager must have been watching over everything." His dad smiled, and this one was sad. "I miss your grandmother."

"Me, too. It was kind of like she was there last night, though. To help save the day."

"Yes, it was," his dad said. "I didn't know she'd left you her *Almanack*. And I'm sure no matter what I tell you not to do going forward, you and your new friends will be on to the next mystery before long. Now eat up, we don't want to be late for the game."

Their next mystery? Excitement coursed through Stephen at the very idea.

※　※　※

The elevator was all too pleased to see them. "Oh, happy day," the elevator said. "Hail the conquering hero."

And music that Stephen recognized from the Superman movie began to play.

His dad cracked up.

The elevator kept up a steady stream of conversation, taking them down to the lobby without waiting for the press of a button. "I did not even mind transporting hairy, heavy Trevor downstairs a little while ago. Just thinking of how wonderful your big moment must have been. The entire supernormal world talks of nothing else. Oh, if only I could have been there. If only I could ever be there . . ." A heavy sigh interrupted the excited chattering.

Stephen said, "Well . . . what if I made a drawing of last night? I don't know if I can capture everything, but I'm getting better at making the pictures move."

The elevator, for the first time ever, was stunned into silence.

"That would be the nicest thing anyone has ever done for me." They stopped on the lobby level, and the elevator added, "Now, get out fast, I don't want any of those monkeys in here!"

Stephen and his dad looked at each other and shrugged. His dad said, "Ready, set—"

"Go!" Stephen shouted.

The elevator doors slid open, and they jumped out into the chaos of the lobby.

"Over there!" Carmen yelled, and two of the gargoyles flew past hefting large butterfly nets. They were chasing a trio of tiny brown monkeys. In fact there were tiny brown monkeys capering and climbing all over the lobby.

When, the night before, Cindermass had opened the barrel, it turned out to be a gift from the concierge of the supernormal hotel in Mumbai, an old rival of Sofia's mother's. A dozen monkeys had come scrambling out, going in every direction, climbing all over Cindermass, eating the banquet food, and making nuisances of themselves.

They'd quickly found their way to the forest in the lobby and were jeering at the gargoyles, who apparently were going to have to work with Carmen to train them to live in the hotel; Cindermass couldn't return them. Draconic law had its drawbacks.

Sofia, Ivan, and Trevor stood by the entrance, watching the spectacle.

"Let's get going, kids," said Stephen's dad, "before we're roped into the monkey rodeo."

Trevor led the way, barely containing his happiness at going to a baseball game, with the added bonus of having friends along. His mother knew someone who worked for the Mets and had managed to get the extra tickets at the last minute—and according to Trevor, they were for excellent seats indeed. Stephen's dad had volunteered to go along as chaperone, even though he still wore his Chicago Cubs cap. Trevor wore a Mets cap, a Mets T-shirt, and a pair of enormous jeans.

Julio had already hailed them a taxi—a van that they just managed to squeeze into. They drove across the island of Manhattan, chattering about the beautiful weather and the baseball game. The taxi let them off at a pier, and from there they took a water taxi across the East River to the baseball stadium. Stephen had yet another view of the skyscrapers.

Chicago had wonderful skyscrapers, but New York had the most famous ones.

At the ballpark they followed the ushers' instructions to seats right above first base. "This is a great place to watch the game!" said Trevor.

They sat in a row, and Stephen's dad got hot dogs and peanuts and sodas for everyone except Trevor, who had packed a snack of leaves. Ivan and Sofia admitted that they'd never been to a baseball game before, and Stephen and Trevor told them stories about other games they had been to. Stephen had been to both ballparks in Chicago, and Trevor had been to more than twenty different stadiums.

"It is said to be the thinking person's professional sport," said Ivan, paging through the program he'd bought on the way in. "Do you know how to keep score, Trevor?"

Trevor hunched over the program with Ivan as the game began, marking off strikes and balls, walks and hits. Sofia proved to be an excellent whistler, and she cheered whenever anything exciting happened on the field. A foul ball came fairly close to them once, but it was too far for any of them except Trevor to catch it. He shied away from it.

"People would have difficulty believing a human boy jumped eight feet in the air to catch the ball," he said. "Plus, I'm still working on my speed."

At the bottom of the second inning Stephen saw a figure clambering up out of the Mets dugout and understood why Trevor was such a fan of the Mets even though he lived on the opposite side of the country, in Oregon. And he supposed he could guess now who Roams's friend who worked for the team was, too.

A bigfoot wearing an even larger version of the team's uniform than Trevor's warmed up, swinging an enormous bat.

Stephen pointed him out to the others, and Trevor stood up, clapping with excitement.

"It is Sees Farther Runs Faster Lives Mightily!" said Trevor. "The greatest bigfoot baseball player ever!"

Stephen glanced over at Ivan, who just said, "Five that I know of. They tend to go in more for football. And professional bicycling, oddly."

Stephen's dad had excused himself a few minutes

before and now reappeared with more snacks and a pennant. "Well, look who's up to bat," he said, grinning.

The Phillies pitcher threw a hard, fast strike that looked to Stephen as if it were somewhere well below the bigfoot player's knees, but he supposed for those who saw him as human it had been right down the middle. He wondered if the commissioner of baseball knew there were supernormals playing in the league.

There was a loud crack, and the ball sped up and away from home plate. Sees Farther Runs Faster Whatever had hit the ball hard, and it was still rising when it crossed the outfield wall. Before he started around the bases, he waved to Trevor with a big grin.

"A home run!" cried Trevor.

The ball kept rising higher and higher, disappearing completely out of the ballpark. The crowd was on its feet, cheering. Stephen turned to slap his dad a high five.

And that's when he noticed that his dad was wearing a brand-new New York Mets cap instead of his Cubs cap.

His dad leaned down and shouted over the noise of the crowd, "I got you one, too!" He pulled a cap out of a bag at his feet and handed it to Stephen. Stephen saw his dad's old Cubs cap still in the bag. His dad noticed him looking at it.

"Or you can wear the Chicago cap if you'd like that one instead."

Stephen bent and picked up the Cubs cap. The Mets cap was in his other hand. Somehow it felt significant, as if this were about more than just baseball teams. Goofy as it sounded, it felt as if they represented his past and his future, his human side and his fae side.

"I think I'll keep them both," he said.

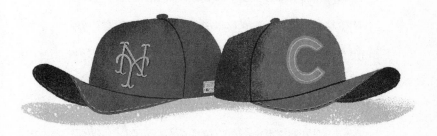

THE END. FOR NOW.

RECIPE FOR LARK'S TEAR SOUP

INGREDIENTS

1 bottle's worth of tears, lark

Shavings of leprechauns' gold (or, if unavailable, salt quarried from caves inhabited by dwarfs)

INSTRUCTIONS

A flock of larks is not called a flock, but an exaltation. *First, you must find the nearest exaltation of larks friendly to our kind. Australia and New Zealand are the best sites, but there is a secret long-lived exaltation in New Jersey. Then you must find the most melancholy poem you know, one that makes you nearly cry when you read it. Take the poem to visit the larks, and read it to them. They will repeat it back to you, crying. (This should work. If all else fails, however, you will need to sing country-and-western songs. In a pinch Patsy Cline will always work, but the larks may seem depressed for years afterward.) Collect the larks' tears in a crystal bottle to prevent the introduction of impurities.*

Cook at low temperature for twenty-one hours and three minutes exactly, and read the same poem to the tureen that you previously read to the larks, each hour on the hour. If the soup is missing a little something, try more Patsy Cline.

Remove the larks' tears from the heat, and season them with shavings of gold from a leprechaun (Note: never attempt the use of poetry to obtain these) or dwarven rock salt.

HISTORICAL NOTES

Recipe created by Lady Nanette Lawson and served to the fae folk at the Hotel New Harmonia. It is suggested that one never prepare this dish for the fae unless insult is intended.